Several minutes passed and I was suddenly aware of my own fear. Something was wrong. It was silent, and the silence was terrifying. I whirled around. He was leaning in the doorway, his thumb hooked in his belt. He looked menacing as he stood there, casually blocking the door. I stepped back, and the boards creaked. The water behind me slapped loudly against the wood.

"Two more steps back," he said quietly, "and you would be in the water. It would carry you out to sea. No one would ever know what had happened to you."

I stood on the edge of the platform, my knees weak. He put his hands on my shoulders. His fingers gripped my flesh.

"Or someone could push you," he said. "Just one little shove and you would be gone. You could never swim in those skirts, not in this water. It would be so easy." His voice was beautifully modulated; it seemed to caress the air. "So very easy...."

Other Ace Books by Edwina Marlow:

WHEN EMMALYNN REMEMBERS

Falconridge
EDWINA MARLOW

ace books
A Division of Charter Communications Inc.
A GROSSET & DUNLAP COMPANY
360 Park Avenue South
New York, New York 10010

FALCONRIDGE

Copyright © 1969 by T.E. Huff

All rights reserved. No part of this book may be reproduced in any form or by any means, except for the inclusion of brief quotations in a review, without permission in writing from the publisher.

All characters in this book are fictitious. Any resemblance to actual persons, living or dead, is purely coincidental.

An ACE Book

Printed in U.S.A.

I

IT HAD BEEN RAINING all day. It was a steady, pelting rain that drummed on the roof and splashed noisily on the pavements. Standing at the windows, I could look down at the school courtyard, enclosed by a high stone wall. The trees were dark green, barely visible through the rain, and the drive was a sodden gray mass. Across the street, the church was like a tall sandstone mountain, incredibly ugly. As I stood there, the bells tolled. The sound had an eerie quality heard through the pounding noise of the rain.

An atmosphere of tension had been building up in Mrs. Siddons' School for Young Ladies all day. The young ladies were ordinarily well behaved, perfectly bred in every respect. Life within the confines of the school was usually placid, content, smoothly ordered. Mrs. Siddons believed in organization. Her young ladies were much too busy to misbehave, but today rain had made the ordinary activities impossible—no archery, no lawn tennis, no trips to the museum with sketch books.

There had been a quarrel at breakfast. One of the girls refused to eat and was promptly sent to spend the day in the infirmary. During the morning, when I was conducting French lessons with the younger girls, they had paid no attention to passages from Moliere. They had whispered, passed notes, made faces at one another. All the while the rain pounded, streaking the leaden windows of the classroom. It had been hard for me to concentrate, too, and I had not scolded the girls. I, too, felt the atmosphere that hung over the school.

Something was going to happen. I had known it. I had sensed it all day and when the summons from Mrs. Siddons came it had been no surprise. I knew what she was going to tell me. There were no more funds. Mr. Burton, who had been my mother's lawyer, had written me a letter earlier in the month. The money was all gone. There were only a few pieces of jewelry left, and they were of no real value. Did I wish to sell them?

I had written Mr. Burton a polite letter, thanking him for his kindness and requesting that the jewelry be kept in its box at the bank. I was helping out at the school, I informed him, and would manage nicely. Then I went to my room and cried. I knew it would be the last time I could afford to cry, and I unleashed all the pent up emotions that had tormented me since my mother's death. When I was finished, when the last tear had dried on my cheek, I sat for a long time in the darkness of the room, wondering what I should do.

I had been at Mrs. Siddons' for four years. Before that there had been a number of other schools, and before that a long line of governesses. My mother had been a ravishingly lovely woman, full of vitality and zest for life. She had not wanted to be bothered by a daughter. She was always on her way to someplace exciting, usually with an attractive man beside her, and what little affection I got was hastily given between engagements. She was a frivolous creature, radiant, and I remembered her silvery laughter and her flushed cheeks. No one dreamed she had consumption until the end. Even then she had retained her zest.

"Lauren, my dear," she told me that last day, "smile, darling. I do want to see you smiling."

I tried, but my lips trembled.

"You must smile, dear," she said. "And you must enjoy. Life is not very pleasant—unless you fight it. I have fought it, ever since your father died. You don't remember him, do you? He was a lot like you, so serious, so resourceful. You have all his best qualities. And I hope you have a few of mine, too. I haven't been a good mother, have I? But I have provided—" She coughed violently and clasped the lace handkerchief to her lips.

The doctor came into the room and nodded to me. I started to leave, but mother seized my hand.

"There is plenty—all those stocks. You can finish at Mrs. Siddons' and then find some nice husband. Be wise in your choice. Be careful. It is very important—" Her eyes sparkled like blue sapphires, her blonde hair clung in damp ringlets about her head, and it seemed to me that she had never been lovelier. "You will manage, Lauren. You're so much like your father in that respect. You'll not make a mess of things as I did and Helena. . . ."

"Helena?" I said.

"My sister. You don't remember her. Dear Helena—and that ghastly old mansion. . . ."

Those were her last words to me. The doctor ordered me out of the room. My mother died that night. I went through the funeral in a trance and for weeks afterwards, back at school, I could not believe that she was gone. Then Mr. Burton began to correspond with me. The stocks were mere paper, valueless, and there was barely enough to keep me in school for another year. Now a year had passed, and the money was gone. I stood at the windows watching the rain and holding Mrs. Siddons' note in my hand.

Clarissa came down the hall, looking for me. She was frowning, her light blue eyes filled with concern. Clarissa and I had been friends for four years, ever since we both arrived at Mrs. Siddons'. We shared a room, and I did not know how I could have managed without her gaiety and her undeviating companionship. We were like sisters, and what problems one had the other shared without question.

"Siddons is waiting," Clarissa said. "She sent me to look for you. She's in a dandy mood, too. All smiles and gentle tones. When she's like that you know not to cross her."

"I suppose I had better go," I said, my voice low.

"You look so downcast. Have you been crying?"

"You know I don't cry," I replied, stiffening my shoulders.

"I know—it's a pity. Lauren, what will you say to her?"

"I don't know. I am at her mercy."

"Surely she won't throw you out."

"She could."

"Oh, Lauren. . . ."

"I am merely facing the truth. I must."

"Term ends in two weeks. You'll surely stay till then. Then we can make plans. . . ."

"I must hurry, Clarissa. She hates to be kept waiting."

"I'll be in our room. Oh, Lauren—do be nice to her. Don't show your temper, and—don't be so proud. You know how the old hag loves to put people in their place. Don't give her a chance to humiliate you. She can be terrifying."

"No one terrifies me," I said.

I walked down the hall, inwardly bracing myself. I was afraid, but I was determined not to show it. I had learned long ago not to reveal any of my emotions. They made one vulnerable, I thought, and I kept mine closely sheltered. I was certainly not going to give Mrs. Siddons the satisfaction of seeing how I felt.

There was a long mirror in the hall next to her office, and I stopped to arrange my hair before I went in. My face was drawn, too serious, and I looked very pale in the dim light. I patted my cheeks to give them some color. My hair fell in rich auburn curls about my shoulders, and I pushed it back, examining the reflection. I was not at all like my mother. She was all cream and pink and gold, whereas I took after my father. There had been a portrait of him once, and I remembered the enormous brown eyes with their long curling lashes, the fine arched brows and firm pink lips. He had been a dashing, handsome fellow, and I was glad I was like him. I had color and character, if not my mother's ethereal beauty.

I knocked quietly on the office door. After a moment I heard a calm voice bidding me come in. Mrs. Siddons sat behind her desk, a smile on her lips. She was playing the benevolent lady today, I noted, and I was on guard.

"Good afternoon, Miss Moore," she said.

I nodded, my lips tight.

"This rain," she remarked, "it's terrible. And the fog. Sometimes London is unbearable. I often long for the country, the open air." She made small talk for a few moments, her shrewd eyes narrowing. I was reminded of a cat toying with a mouse. Mrs. Siddons was enjoying this. She had me at her mercy, and it gave her a great deal of pleasure.

She was a large woman with two huge coils of red hair braided on top of her head. The vigorous color of her hair seemed to drain her face of color, giving her complexion a dead white look. This she augmented unwisely with too much rice powder. Her black eyes were lined with pencil, the heavy lids shadowed with blue, and her thick lips were painted blood red. She would not allow any of the girls to use cosmetics, and her own bizarre application of them made us happy to comply with her rule. I had never liked the woman, and as I watched her now prolonging the thrust, I felt complete loathing.

"The term is almost over," she said.

"Yes," I replied.

"Have you any plans for the Easter vacation?"

I shook my head, waiting.

Mrs. Siddons smiled. It was the smirking smile she ordinarily saved for parents of the girls. There was a silver paper knife on her desk and she picked it up, playing with it. I stood in front of the desk with my hands behind my back, my chin high. Outside the rain still poured. The window behind her desk was streaked with gray rivulets.

"You could stay on here," she suggested. "There

is a great deal of work to be done while the girls are away. Inventory to be taken, cleaning to be done, supplies to be laid in." She looked up, her black eyes glittering. "I should be glad for you to help, my dear."

"You wish to employ me?" I asked.

"In a manner of speaking."

"I don't think I would be interested, Mrs. Siddons."

She put the paper knife down and folded her hands on the desk. Her nails were painted a bright red, and they looked like claws, I thought. All the girls despised her, were intimidated by her cold manner, yet she ran a perfect school, one of the best in London, with only the most select pupils.

"I may as well be blunt, Lauren," she said. "You are not in any position to refuse my offer. Mr. Burton has written me a long letter. It was most specific about financial conditions. Your tuition is paid for until the end of this term, and after that there will be no more money."

"I am aware of that, Mrs. Siddons."

"And what do you intend to do about it?"

"That is my concern."

"Don't be snippy, Miss Moore. It doesn't become you. Let me continue. Mr. Burton also sent a letter to your aunt in Cornwall, explaining your situation. There has been no reply from her."

Mother had mentioned her sister Helena. The woman was a stranger to me. She had not come to the funeral, had not sent a wreath or a card. She might just as well not exist as far as I was concerned. I knew nothing whatsoever about her and did not care to. There were no other relatives. I was alone. Mrs. Siddons knew this, and she felt it gave her more power over me.

"Let's be realistic," she said. "You are eighteen years old, and you have no one to turn to. You've been at this school for four years, Lauren, and you have been an asset, if I may say so. The girls adore you, particularly the younger ones. You helped conduct the French classes during Mademoiselle Delong's illness and that was appreciated. I would be glad to have you take over completely in that department, as well as in embroidery and deportment, as I doubt that the Mademoiselle will be returning. Her health—or so she claims."

I made no reply. I stared at the window behind her desk, watching the rain streak the gray glass.

"This in return for room and board, with a few pounds for spending. I think this arrangement would be splendid for both of us. Of course, a few changes would have to be made. You could not continue to share a room with Miss Neville, but there is a fine room in the attic annex, small but nice enough I should think."

"Thank you, Mrs. Siddons, but—no."

"You refuse?"

"That's right, Mrs. Siddons."

"You ridiculous girl—what shall you do?"

"I will manage."

She did not say anything for a few moments. I could hear the ticking of the clock over the mantle and the monotonous sound of the rain. My face felt flushed, and I was trembling inside, but I held my composure. I was not going to let this woman know how her suggestion affected me.

"You are a foolish girl," she said, finally, "very foolish. I will tell you now that I had a great many reservations about accepting your application to this school. Your mother was not exactly my kind of person, you know—not the proper background, to say nothing of her appearance. But I was persuaded—she had influential friends. That kind always does."

I could see that she was trying to make me angry. I braced myself. I would not let her get the best of me in this way. I listened to her words objectively, as though she were talking about the weather.

Mrs. Siddons stood up. She was a formidable figure in her dark black taffeta. She pointed a finger at me.

"And you—you stand here like a duchess, head high, as if you were too good to work on the staff here."

"Perhaps I am, Mrs. Siddons," I replied quietly.

"Who are you, may I ask? Nobody. Penniless. The daughter of a Captain in the regiment and a woman no one ever heard of. Don't be so grand, Miss Moore. I have offered my help. It shall not be offered again. That I can assure you."

"Very well, Mrs. Siddons."

"You have no one else to turn to, no one to help you. I don't think I need go into detail about the fate of young girls alone in London. The newspapers are full of stories. Even Queen Victoria has expressed her concern about the sordid traffic that exists in this city."

"Are you trying to frighten me, Mrs. Siddons?"

"I am trying to make you see things sensibly."

"Are you quite finished?"

"Not quite. The best you could do would be work in one of those foul sweatshops. Even that would be preferable to anything else that might happen. You're a stubborn girl, much too willful.

Only a miracle will save you—"

"Then I shall wait for that miracle," I said.

I turned and left the office without waiting for her to dismiss me. It was an unthinkable thing for one of the girls to do, and I heard her gasp as I closed the door. She was not accustomed to being crossed, and it gave me satisfaction to know that I had had the last word. I was not by nature rude, but Mrs. Siddons brought out the worst in me. She ruled the girls with an iron hand, crisp, cold and condescending with them, only to simper with fawning humility when their parents came to visit. I could not abide hypocrisy, and Mrs. Siddons was a glowing example of that.

She had succeeded in her purpose, though. Her words had brought home the desperation of my situation, and the sheer folly of my refusal. It would be humiliating to work here in the school I had known for four years as a student, to be relegated to a shabby room in the attic, yet it would mean security. As it was, in two weeks I would literally be on the streets and at the mercy of the world.

I could find work of some kind, I told myself. Surely I could. There were any number of things I could do well, yet most of the jobs were given to men. A woman's place was in the home according to our Queen, and there was very little employment a woman could take and remain respectable. I thought of the sweatshops Mrs. Siddons had mentioned. I remembered reading about them in one of Mr. Dickens' novels, and I shuddered. As for the other thing she had mentioned, I tried not to think of it.

Clarissa was in our room, curled up on the sofa in front of the window. Her yellow skirts were spread about her like the petals of a buttercup, and her light blonde hair was caught up with a blue ribbon, the curls spilling down her shoulders in a shiny cascade. She was a lovely girl with delicate features which belied her robust health and saucy temperament. Her pranks had caused many a headache at school, and her liveliness made her a favorite with the other girls.

"Was it awful, Lauren?" she asked.

"Very."

"Oh, dear. I was afraid it would be. Is she going to let you stay?"

"She wants me to work here. She wants me to take a room in the attic. Mademoiselle Delong probably won't be back, and Mrs. Siddons wants me to take over her duties."

"How outrageous!" Clarissa cried. "You refused?"

"Of course."

"The old dragon—what nerve. What shall we do?"

"I don't know. My tuition is paid until the end of the term. Then I must leave. I'll find something. . . ."

"You will go to Paris with me. My parents are dragging me off to the continent for the Easter holidays. They'll be delighted to take you, too. We'll go to all those dreadful museums and art galleries and it will give us time to think of some permanent solution."

"I wouldn't accept charity from Mrs. Siddons, Clarissa. I certainly won't accept it from you."

"Bosh! You know my father is fantastically rich. He will do anything I say. But we won't argue about it now—you look so tired, Lauren. You are quite pale. Look—I've stolen some cakes from the pantry. Cook will be furious when she finds out. I do wish we could manage tea, too. If you will light the spirit lamp we'll boil some water. See, I stole a bag of tea as well. Now, get out the cups. We'll have a party, Lauren. There is no reason to be depressed. It's just this awful rain. . . ."

II

THE GIRLS WERE making excited preparations for the Easter holidays and the school was a hive of activity. Shrill, elated voices rang up and down the corridors. Packages arrived and were opened amid squeals of laughter. Clarissa's parents sent her a gorgeous new bonnet. She threw aside layers of pink tissue paper and lifted out the creation of blue straw, trimmed in white and yellow daisies. As she tried it on in front of the mirror, a flush of excitement colored her cheeks and her blue eyes sparkled. It was reassuring to see her so happy. For Clarissa my problem was already over. I would go with her to Paris, and after that her parents would see to it that I got some employment, even if it were as her own paid companion. I wished it were that simple for me.

"You're absurd, Lauren," she told me. "Making such a tragedy about all this! It will be such fun—we'll be together. One more term in this dreadful place and then I'll be out. We'll go to the country—my parents have such a gorgeous place. We'll fascinate all the men. You'll dazzle a rich young squire."

Nothing would damper her high spirits, and I

tried not to let my own depression become infectious. I continued teaching the French classes and supervising exercises for the younger girls. I avoided Mrs. Siddons. When I passed her in the hall two days after our interview, she smiled sweetly and nodded her head, as though she knew that I would capitulate and meet her terms. Mademoiselle Delong had sent word that she definitely wouldn't be back, and Mrs. Siddons had made no other arrangements for a teacher to replace her.

I was in the garden one afternoon, two days before school was to close. It was late, and the sun had begun to sink, leaving the sky stained with a pale yellow glow. Inside the school I could hear all the sounds of activity, but here it was calm, the tall stone walls closing out most of the sounds of London. Occasionally a carriage would rumble over the cobbles outside, and the bells of the church across the way would toll mournfully. I held a novel in my lap, but I made no effort to read. I stared at the espaliered apricot trees that grew along the wall without seeing them.

Clarissa had written to her parents against my will, explaining things to them. Her father had replied immediately that he would be glad to have me go to Paris with them, and her mother had written a note saying that she was delighted that Clarissa would have a companion as France could be very dull for a young woman without someone her own age to share it with. I had met the Nevilles once. Her father was a large, blustering gentlemen with red cheeks and side whiskers, devoted to riding the hounds and hunting. Her mother was a pale, weary-looking creature with none of her daughter's vivacity, spending most of her time giving tea to the Vicar and managing the country estate. They were an affable pair, charming in their own way, and completely controlled by their lively daughter. I could accept their charity and put an end to my immediate worries, as Clarissa was determined that I do, but I wondered how that would work out.

Clarissa was the best friend I had ever had, but the relationship would undoubtedly change if I became her paid companion. Although she would not be demanding, I would be at her beck and call. I would have to train myself to be docile and submissive to suit my position, and that would be hard. My nature would rebel. The dear friendship would terminate. No, I could not let myself accept Clarissa's offer. I was prepared to be a paid companion. I was prepared to become a governess. I was prepared to swallow all my pride, but not at the expense of my dear friend.

As I sat in the garden musing, Mary, one of the maids, came rushing out. Her cap was perched haphazardly over her tangled copper curls, and her freckled face was alive with excitement. She waved a blue envelope in her hand.

"A special delivery letter, Miss Lauren," she cried. "For you! The boy just brought it."

I stood up, the novel dropping to the ground. Who could be sending me a letter? I took the envelope from Mary's hand and waited until she was gone before examining it. It was addressed to me in wild, erratic handwriting, the purple ink standing out against the heavy blue paper. It was postmarked from Cornwall. My hands trembled as I slit the envelope, taking out a sheet of paper that smelled of violets.

I read the letter through twice, unable to fully comprehend what it meant for me.

My Dear Child,

How preposterous of Louise to die without telling me. She always was an abominably independent creature, even as a young girl. I was so shocked when I received a letter from this Mr. Burton, whoever he is. He told me all about your plight, and I was outraged, simply outraged, not to have known anything about it before. What can Louise have been thinking of, not letting me know she was ill.

My dear, you don't know me. I saw you once, when you were a very little girl. Louise brought you along when she visited me in London. That was shortly after your father died—what a lovely man he was, so dashing in his uniform. Things had not been well between your mother and me for years, and the visit did little to clear up the misunderstanding. You know these old family feuds—so tiresome, really. But she's gone now, my baby sister. Bless her sweet soul.

You will come to Falconridge immediately. It will be wonderful to have some new blood here after such a long time. It's rather drafty and dull, but you'll bring a whiff of fresh air, I'm sure. Perhaps I can make up for the hard feelings Louise and I had by taking care of her little girl. It will be a most welcome task.

Your Uncle Charles will come to the school to pick you up when the term is over. He's pleased to have some excuse to get to London. I must say this is an unexpected turn of events for all of us, but one which gives an old woman much excitement.

Love,
Helena Lloyd

I folded the letter and put it carefully back into its envelope. The sun was almost gone now, and dark green shadows crept across the path. A sparrow perched on the wall, scolding me loudly. Lamps were being turned on inside the school, and I knew Clarissa would soon be looking for me. Slipping the letter into the pocket of my apron, I wondered what kind of a person my aunt was. I wondered what had caused bad blood between her and my mother, and I wondered about Falconridge, too—and what might be waiting for me there.

Clarissa had mixed emotions about the letter. She was pleased that I had someplace to go and disappointed that I would not accompany her to Paris. We were in our room, doing the final packing. My uncle would arrive the next morning, as well as Clarissa's parents, and we were both sad as it would probably be a long time before we would see each other again. The room was a nest of boxes, tissue paper, clothes, and books, all strewn in every direction, littering every piece of furniture. The school was strangely silent, a mood of melancholy prevailing within the old walls. Clarissa sat on the floor, her long blonde curls hiding her face as she arranged bits of jewelry in a jewel box.

"I still don't feel right about it," she said. "They

are strangers to you—even if they are relations. Why didn't your mother ever mention them? I don't like it at all."

"It's a solution to all my problems," I said.

"I suppose so. But—Cornwall is so far away. And whoever heard of a house called Falconridge? It sounds dreadfully dreary, Lauren. Do you really have to go?"

"I must, Clarissa," I said, wishing she would stop.

I had my own apprehensions about it. I would be a stranger, among strangers, in a part of the country alien to me. There was a mysterious air about the whole thing. How I longed to stay at this school, even after Mrs. Siddons had been so odious. At least it was familiar, and there were people I knew, however hateful some of them might be. I folded my dresses neatly, determined to keep busy, to keep from thinking too much about what was soon to happen.

"Life is so strange," Clarissa said. "You find people and then you lose them. We won't lose each other, though, will we, Lauren? We've been like sisters. So much has happened."

I nodded, putting the dresses in a small trunk.

"You will probably meet some terribly exciting man. It could happen, you know. You will sweep him off his feet with your good looks. I have seen the way men look at you when we walk down the street. They turn and stare."

"They were turning to stare at you," I protested.

"No. I'm pretty—I know that—but you're—you've got something. You have—destiny in your face. It's written there, plainly, for all to see."

"What a ridiculous way to talk, Clarissa. You've been reading too many novels."

"Have you ever been in love, Lauren?"

"Of course not."

"Neither have I. Isn't that sad?"

"Not at all. I'm sure it would be quite unpleasant."

"Perhaps it is. And then again. . . ."

"You're talking nonsense," I snapped.

"We'll find out. I think it's terribly romantic, really, you going off to an old house in Cornwall. The men there are supposed to be tall and very good looking, with sun-bronzed skin and dark hair, very devilish. Perhaps you'll meet one, Lauren."

"I'm sure I wouldn't care to."

Clarissa stood up, holding a pendant in her hand. It was a bright red drop of ruby, suspended on a thin silver chain. She dangled it on her fingers, watching the stone swing to and fro. Then she clasped it firmly in her palm.

"I am giving this to you," she said.

"But you can't. How absurd. That's a real ruby. Your father gave it to you."

"He'll get me another," Clarissa said firmly. "I want you to have it. I want you to wear it, so that you will remember me when you are surrounded by all those devilishly good looking Cornish men. Here, take it, Lauren. It's a farewell present."

She slipped the pendant over my head and fastened it behind my neck. The cold hard stone dropped beneath the collar of my dress and rested on my bosom. Clarissa sat down on the bed beside me, and I took her hand. I squeezed her fingers tightly, afraid to say anything. All the sadness of the past weeks welled up in me, and I closed my eyes.

"If you ever need me," she said, "you know you can call on me. I am so worried, Lauren. If only we knew something about these people. I can't help but think it strange...." Her voice faded away, and we sat in silence for several moments.

I opened my eyes and looked into the mirror across the room. I saw two young women, one very blonde and pretty, her head resting forlornly on the shoulder of the other whose dark eyes stared so seriously. We made an attractive picture—Clarissa dressed in soft pink, my own dress dark tan, all the colors blurred slightly in the foggy gray glass. The bells of the church tolled again, and the sound was indescribably sad. I felt so close to this girl, the only person in the world with whom I could feel secure. In a few hours I would be leaving her. I would be leaving everything I knew. I stiffened my shoulders and gave Clarissa a gentle shove, trying to smile.

I could not afford to lose courage now. I would need every bit of it in the days to come.

The sun was bright the next morning, sparkling on the cobbles and making bright pools of yellow on the sidewalks in front of the school. Pigeons scattered about the bell tower of the church, cooing loudly, fluttering silvery blue wings. Stacks of luggage almost blocked the way in front of the school, and the girls waited eagerly as carriages drove up and stopped. There were squeals of delight, arms were flung about parents, and carriages drove away with wheels rumbling over the stones. Clarissa wore her new bonnet and a blue dress trimmed with white lace. She carried a white lace parasol, twirling it by its ivory handle. She was very excited, her cheeks very pink, her blue eyes sparkling. We had said our goodbyes the night before and resolved to let no shadow fall over the actual moment of parting. We stood there together, waving to girls who were leaving. My own gaiety was forced, and I sensed that Clarissa, too, was putting on a front for my benefit.

"I do hope your uncle arrives before my parents," she exclaimed. "I so want to meet him. I wonder if he will be tall and distinguished. His name certainly is—Charles Lloyd, so distinguished sounding. He must be terribly wealthy to have an estate in Cornwall, don't you think?"

"Falconridge is merely a house," I replied.

"But it must be awfully large to have a name— probably an estate. I think it's exciting. You must write me all about it. . . ." She continued to babble, filling the minutes with words, as neither of us wanted to lapse into silence.

"Perhaps I'll come to visit you," she said. "I'll be out of school in June. Just think—no more Mrs. Siddons'. It'll be wonderful. Maybe my parents will let me come for a long visit. And you can come see me. I would love that so. . . ."

We both looked up at the old clock on the bell tower. It was almost eleven. The pyramid of luggage had been greatly diminished, and only a few girls stood waiting, impatiently now. Clarissa tightened her white gloves, pulling them closer to her wrists. She gnawed her lower lip and tried to smile.

"Are you still wearing the pendant?"

"Naturally."

"I'm so happy you'll have it."

"I'll treasure it, Clarissa."

The dreaded silence came. Another carriage pulled up, and the last girl clambered inside while a servant strapped her bags to the roof. The carriage drove off, the horses stomping briskly on the cobbles. The only luggage left was Clarissa's smart set of dark blue leather and my own battered brown trunk with its tarnished brass tacks. The pigeons whirled in the air above us, looking for food. The school behind us was empty now, except for servants. Mrs. Siddons had left early in the morning to catch a train that would take her to visit her sister in the country.

"I don't know what Father can be thinking," Clarissa said. "He knew I would be waiting at ten."

"They'll be here. You must be patient, Clarissa."

"And your uncle...."

"It's early. And—my aunt just said today. She didn't say what time. He probably doesn't know to be here in the morning. Don't worry."

"Oh, dear. Lauren...."

"Here comes a carriage," I said hastily.

"It's them!" she cried. "See—Mother's waving her handkerchief!"

The Nevilles got out of the carriage and embraced their daughter. I stood back in the shadows of the wall, trying to look away but unable to do so. Mrs. Neville wore a dress of pale gray linen with a coral brooch. She smiled tearfully as her husband growled and whirled Clarissa in his arms. Here was a kind of love that I had never known, shining clear in the faces of all three of them. Mr. Neville set his daughter back on her feet and patted her shoulder. The coachman began to fasten her luggage on top of the carriage.

Clarissa talked quietly with her father and mother, and I could tell that she was explaining to them why I would not be going along. Mr. Neville looked at me curiously, a solemn expression on his flushed face. I smiled, nodding my head. Mrs. Neville came and took me by the hand.

"We're so sorry, my dear," she said. "We were so looking forward to having you along. You would have been such company for Clarissa."

"Yes, the more pretty young ladies the better I like it," her husband added in his gruff voice.

"I'm sorry, too," I said politely. "It was so nice of you to have considered taking me—but I'm sure this is better. My uncle should be here any time now...."

"We'll wait until he comes," Mr. Neville said, adjusting his vivid green ascot. His side whiskers were bushy, and his dark brown eyes were very solemn.

"There's no need for that," I protested. "I don't want to keep you here. You'll be going to lunch...."

"If you really think it's all right...." Mrs. Neville said timidly.

"Nonsense," her husband snorted. "We can't leave the child here all alone."

I looked at Clarissa. Her eyes were shining, and I could feel the tears welling in my own. I smiled, my lips trembling at the corners. I nodded my head, and she took her father by the hand, leading him to the carriage. They all three climbed inside, Mr. Neville protesting quietly to his wife. The coachman climbed upon his seat and took the reins. The horses, sleek chestnuts with glossy fur, stamped and snorted. I felt a great surge of sadness, but I was still smiling as the carriage began to move slowly down the street.

Clarissa leaned out of the window, waving to me. She called something out, but I could not hear the words. I lifted my hand and waved to her, and then the carriage was gone. My own shabby trunk stood alone on the sidewalk now, looking even more pitiful. I sat down on it, spreading my dark green skirts out.

I watched the pigeons. I watched the hands of the clock move slowly around the old stone face. Two women dressed in black went into the tiny shop next to the church, coming out soon with candles. Then they went into the church, moving slowly through the dark, yawning arch. An old man with a bag of apples shuffled past, his shoulders hunched, looking sad and defeated. The church bell tolled. Several carriages passed but none of them stopped.

Little Mary, the maid, came outside, wiping her reddened hands on her apron. There was a look of concern in her large brown eyes, and her lips were turned down at the corners. She was hardly more than a child, barely thirteen, yet she had been working at the school ever since I had been there.

"Your people haven't come, Miss Lauren?" she asked.

"Not yet, Mary."

"Well, you can't just sit out here like this. Come inside, and I will give you a cup of tea."

"It's all right, Mary. I'll wait here."

"No, Ma'am. You come inside right now. You look peaked. It won't do you a bit of good, sitting here in this sun. Come along now."

She stood with her hands on her hips and spoke sharply with the voice of authority. She was a comical sight with her golden brown freckles and her tangled copper curls, her face very stern. I felt very weak, as if all the life had been drained out of me, and I hadn't the energy to argue. I stood up, looking at the clock. It was after twelve.

"My trunk—" I said feebly.

"I'll see that it's brought inside."

"But—my uncle will be here."

"Of course he will," she said firmly. "He's been delayed. You come on in, Miss Lauren. It's better to wait inside."

The front hall was dark and shadowy, and there was an eerie feeling about the school now that all the girls were gone. It seemed much larger and more depressing. I sat down in a chair near the front door, where I could look out. Mary scurried away, and soon a man came to put my trunk on the front steps. I closed my eyes, trying not to think about Clarissa and the expression on her face as the carriage drove away.

I could hear the sounds of cleaning and smell the odors of lemon oil and wax. The crew of servants were working furiously, for Mrs. Siddons would be returning in four days to oversee the inventory, and she wanted the school in perfect order by that time. I could hear the banging of cupboard doors and the swish of mops, and wondered if I would soon be doing that kind of work.

It must have all been a joke, I thought, a cruel, malicious joke. Perhaps my aunt hadn't really written the letter; perhaps my uncle wasn't coming at all. I was stranded, with no place to go. I had never felt so desolate in all my life.

Mary came back with a cup of tea and some little cakes on a plate. I sipped the tea slowly and stared at the cakes without interest. My stomach fluttered nervously, but I could not eat. I set the cup and plate aside and listened to the noise of the servants at their work. I looked out at the street, my heart palpitating every time a carriage passed.

I thought about my mother. She had loved me in her way, but I had never really been a part of her life. Hers was a glamorous existence and she had moved in a bright, glittering swirl of activity. I was shut out, provided for nicely but shut out just the same. I remembered the luxury of earlier years, when I had had the finest clothes, and the best teachers. The quality gradually decreased, blue velvet smocks giving way to sensible cotton dresses, the vivacious French governesses giving way to brusque stern women to whom I was merely a charge. It had been a stroke of luck to be entered in Mrs. Siddons' school, but even here I had always felt a little out of place. The other girls were rich, and pampered, receiving a generous allowance, while I barely got enough for necessities. I had not ever resented it. I had merely accepted it as part of life.

It seemed that all my life had been gradually moving toward this day, this point in my life, this moment of desolation. One event after another paved the way, and now I sat here intolerably alone, waiting for the arrival of a man I had never seen, doubting that he would come at all. I closed my eyes, fighting self-pity, knowing it would defeat me if I let it take hold.

I must have fallen asleep, for my head nodded violently and I opened my eyes with a start. A carriage was stopping in front of the school and the noise of wheels grinding on the cobbles had awakened me. I stood up, my throat suddenly dry. The carriage door opened and a man got out, pulling on a pair of soft kid gloves. He looked up at the school and hesitated a moment. Then he began to walk briskly towards the door.

Charles Lloyd had arrived after all.

III

HE WAS A tall man, heavy set, with a thin, neck and powerful shoulders, and he carried himself with assurance and the suggestion of a swagger. He had dark blond hair, very thick and graying slightly at the temples. His dark brown eyes were almost black, the kind of eyes that could intimidate anyone, and his brows were thick, arched heavily over drooping lids. He had a Roman nose, large and distinguished, and his mouth was thick the lips turned down at one corner. He was a man born to command and one who accepted his right to rule without question.

"You are Lauren Moore?" he asked abruptly.

I nodded, frightened by his manner.

"I am Charles Lloyd. Is that your trunk?"

"Yes—Mr. Lloyd."

"Very well then. We will leave. I have reservations at the hotel. Is there anything you need to do first, anyone you need to speak to?"

"No."

"Come along then," he said brusquely. He had a rich powerful voice with a strong guttural quality. It was like the man, extremely masculine, extremely commanding.

I followed him meekly out to the carriage. He

was dressed elegantly in a dark gray tail coat and pants, with glossy black riding boots that came up almost to his knees. He wore a rich blue satin vest and an expensive gray ascot with a garnet stick pin. The clothes showed considerable taste and a certain fastidiousness.

Charles Lloyd took my hand to help me into the carriage. He looked directly into my eyes, his mouth tight. It was obvious that he did not relish this duty at all, and I was made painfully aware of my position. I was a poor relation, someone dependent on the charity of others, and I was really not related to this man at all. He had married my mother's sister, so there were no blood ties, only those of law.

"How old are you?" he asked.

"Eighteen."

"You look older."

"Is that a compliment?"

"It was a statement of fact."

He stood impatiently while the coachman got my trunk. Mary came out of the school, shading her eyes with her hand, peering at the carriage. I waved at her, and she nodded her head happily, relieved that someone had finally come for me. Charles Lloyd climbed into the carriage and we were on our way. He stared at me, quite openly, not trying to hide it. I had never met anyone so rude.

"Is there something wrong with me?" I asked.

"You are like your mother. The coloring is completely different, of course, but the features are the same."

"Did you know her, Mr. Lloyd?"

"At one time—briefly."

He leaned forward, his hands on his knees, rocking his body easily with the movement of the carriage. The cobbles were rough, and we were joggled unpleasantly. Charles Lloyd smelled strongly of leather and of perspiration and some strong male lotion. He still stared at me, but he seemed to be preoccupied with something, and I sensed that he was not really seeing me now.

"I am sorry about this," I said.

"What are you talking about?"

"I am sorry to be a bother to you."

"You are my wife's niece. There was nothing else to do."

"I hope I won't have to impose on you for long."

"Oh?" he said, arching a brow.

"I trust I'll be able to find some kind of employment."

"Don't prattle," he said sternly. "It's a most unpleasant quality in young women. They feel called upon to fill every moment with words."

I sat back, firmly put down. My cheeks were burning with humiliation, and I looked out the window, wishing that I could be anywhere in the world besides in this carriage with this insufferable man. It was not going to be pleasant, I thought.

"I suppose you'll want lunch?" he asked.

"No, thank you. I had something at school."

"Fine. Then we'll go directly to our rooms."

"Are we leaving for Cornwall tonight?"

"I have business in the city tomorrow. We'll leave after that."

"Very well," I said.

The hotel was not one of the elite, but it was elegant nevertheless. Charles Lloyd gripped my elbow and ushered me across a wide sweep of dark red carpet and up a curving staircase with mahogany banisters. He took a key and opened a door on the second floor, showing me into my room. It was very pleasant, with dark gray carpets and green velvet drapes at the windows. The furniture was heavy fumed oak, a green velvet spread on the bed, and there was a pitcher and bowl of white porcelain adorned with tiny pink roses.

"It's very nice," I said.

He ignored my comment. "I will see to your trunk. I have an appointment at two. I will call on you when I get back."

He left, closing the door behind him. I was incredibly weary, and my head ached. I stood at the mirror, rubbing my temples with my fingertips. A manservant brought my trunk and I took a coin out of my purse to tip him with. I wondered what kind of appointment Charles Lloyd had. He was probably a man of affairs. He certainly seemed to know London well. I supposed it had something to do with Falconridge.

I rested fitfully for a while, trying to compose my thoughts. I was sitting at the mirror, brushing my hair, when Charles Lloyd returned. He still had that preoccupied look. He stood with his hands on his hips, his head held a little to one side, a frown creasing his brow.

"Is that your best dress?" he asked.

I was still wearing my dark green taffeta.

"Yes," I replied.

"You have nothing more—stylish?"

"I haven't much need for stylish frocks."

He stood there examining me, pressing his lips tightly together. "It won't do," he said after a while. "We'll have to buy you something more fitting. We're going to the Burmese tonight. There may be people I know there. Come along, we'll go to the shops."

"I can't let you buy me a dress," I protested.

Charles Lloyd smiled grimly. "You have no voice in the matter," he said. "You will do as I say. If you will remember that, it will save us a lot of time and trouble in the future. Now hurry up, the afternoon is half over already."

We went to a very expensive fashion salon. A woman in black silk met us at the door and seated us in elegant gilt chairs before a tiny stage. I marvelled at the lush gold carpets, the cream colored satin draperies, the exquisite crystal chandelier. Charles Lloyd sat back, entirely at ease. I wondered if he had been here before and, if so, upon what occasion. He had come here directly, without making any inquiries.

"What do you wish to see?" the woman in black asked. She was middle aged, with enormous brown eyes and silver gray hair arranged in coils on top of her head. She spoke in a cultured voice, her manner patronizing. My uncle lounged in the chair, not at all intimidated.

"Something grand," he told her.

"For this young lady?"

He nodded. The woman examined me carefully, pursing her lips as if trying to visualize a dress that would suit me. Then she clapped her hands and a servant appeared. They talked quietly for a few moments, pausing to glance at me. Then the servant left, and in a few minutes a woman walked across the stage, wearing a lovely gown, pink and girlish.

"It's the very latest thing," the woman in black assured my uncle.

"The color is wrong," he said, "and the dress isn't sophisticated."

"I think it's beautiful," I remarked.

He ignored me. "Something else," he said.

The model came out four different times, but none of the dresses had the right flair to suit Charles Lloyd. I thought them all lovely, but he made it clear that I had nothing to say about the matter. Finally, he chose a dress of honey colored satin, lavishly trimmed with black fox fur about the bodice and hem. He nodded his approval.

"It's a little grown up for the young lady," the woman informed him.

"I think not. We'll take it. Is there a matching cloak?"

"Yes. When would you like it delivered?"

"Now."

"But—I'm sorry. It will take two weeks at least to make it up for the young lady. This is only a model. We never sell—"

My uncle smiled. He became very charming, telling the woman that we would be in London for only two days and that I had set my heart on a gown from this establishment. The model wearing the dress was about my size. A few quick alterations—I saw the woman melt under the power of his charm, and I realized that Charles Lloyd had quite a way with women. He could do anything he wished with them merely by exercising his powerful magnetism. I wondered if he had always been faithful to my Aunt Helena. He must be over fifty, but even I could see he still had a quality that would prove irresistible to most women.

We left the shop an hour later with the dress and cloak in a long flat box. I wondered why he had gone to all the trouble and expense to buy the dress for me. It was certainly not out of consideration for me. My uncle was a vain man, I had already noted that, and it would be part of his vanity to want the woman who accompanied him for an evening on the town to be as attractive as possible.

I was rather excited that evening, waiting for him in my hotel room. I had never worn such a lovely gown before. The thick honey colored satin and soft black fur heightened my coloring, and I felt truly beautiful for once. The gown was cut rather low to suit my taste, but it certainly showed off my shoulders to advantage. I had never gone to an expensive restaurant with a man before, and it was going to be a satisfying experience, even if the man was as detestable as Charles Lloyd.

When he came into the room, secretly I had to admire him. He might not be the escort a young woman would wish but he was certainly a handsome one. His black pumps were polished to a glossy sheen, his black trousers sleek, with black satin lapels on the elegant jacket. He wore a gleaming white shirt, a white silk tie, and there was a red carnation in his button hole. As he came in he swirled the folds of a black cloak with a heavy white silk lining about his enormous shoulders. With top hat and cane, he presented the perfect picture of an affluent aristocrat.

He was silent in the carriage. He had passed judgment on me back in the room, he eyes sweeping over me and showing their satisfaction. It was quite plain that I was an ornamental accessory for the evening, not a companion. Looking out the window and seeing the lights of the city burning mistily through swirls of fog, I was content to keep silent. I wondered what he was thinking about as he sat there, his arms folded on his chest. About the distastefulness of taking on the responsibility of a niece he had never seen until today? About the splendors of London after spending months in relative isolation on the coast of Cornwall? About the business he was attending to while he was here?

The restaurant was even more elegant than I had imagined it would be. We entered through a colonnade of white marble and stepped into a room that was all white and gold. The carpet was golden, the walls pale white, the heavy draperies a stiff gold cloth that glittered in the light from half a dozen chandeliers that dripped crystal pendants. Music was coming from a recess hidden behind tall green plants, and stunningly dressed people sat at tables laden with exquisite china and silver. There was the gentle hush of subdued voices, the pleasant tinkle of glass, the pop of corks and the fizzle of champagne being poured. Several heads turned as we entered, and I felt regal as I stood waiting while my uncle checked our cloaks.

A waiter showed us to a table and handed my uncle a wine list. I was far too impressed to speak, and I listened quietly as he chose an appropriate wine and ordered our meal. A man across the room nodded to my uncle, and after saying something to the woman he was with, he rose and came over to us.

"Ah, I see we meet again today, Mr. Lloyd. What a nice surprise. And who is this charming young woman?"

"My niece, Lauren Moore."

Charles Lloyd introduced me to the man, a Mr. Stephens, who managed an insurance firm he had been to that afternoon.

"Charming," Mr. Stephens said. "Is this how they grow them in Cornwall?"

"Miss Moore had been going to school in London. I am taking her back to Falconridge with me."

"I am sure Cornwall will be fortunate to gain what London must lose. A lovely young woman like your niece must grace any part of the country she is in."

"Thank you, Mr. Stephens," I said. I am afraid I blushed slightly. He gave me a little bow, quite pleased with himself.

"Has any decision been made on the policy?" Charles Lloyd asked. His voice casual, his manner relaxed, yet I could tell that the question was an important one to him.

"Ah—" Mr. Stephens said, spreading out his well groomed hands. "I think we can safely say so. Yes, we can say so. It's a big policy, and I must say there was some hesitation about it, but I am sure any man who is taking such a lovely young niece back to Cornwall with him must be planning on a long and active life."

"The policy is a precaution, merely a precaution," Charles Lloyd said. "Falconridge isn't what it used to be, and I want to make sure that Helena is provided for in the event. . . ."

"Of course, of course," Mr. Stephens interjected. "Well, Lloyd, I just wanted to pop over and meet the young lady. The paper will be ready for you to sign in the morning."

"Fine, Stephens. I'll be in your office at ten."

Mr. Stephens left, and my uncle sat with his chin resting on his fist. He looked very pleased with himself, as though he had just accomplished a business coup, and it suddenly dawned on me that meeting Mr. Stephens here had been no accident. Stephens must have mentioned that he was coming, and that had been when my uncle decided to come too. There had evidently been some doubt about the policy my uncle wanted to take out, and here in this conducive atmosphere, Stephens had decided to pass his approval on it. It was obvious, even to me, that he had decided to grant the policy only a few moments ago, while he was standing at our table.

That was the reason for the dress. That was the reason my uncle had brought me here. It had been carefully arranged. He must have known Mr. Stephens was susceptible to attractive young women. I was just a prop, and my uncle had had no scruples in using me as such. He was the kind of man who would stop at nothing to get his way.

"What kind of policy were you talking about?" I asked.

"Just life insurance," my uncle replied. "Nothing you need bother your pretty head about."

"Life insurance?"

"I am fifty-two years old," he said, "and in my prime, but one never knows—ah, here is the wine. Let me pour some for you, my dear. It is beautifully chilled."

He twirled the slender bottle around in its bucket of ice and took the gold foil off the top. He removed the cork expertly and poured the sparkling beverage into our glasses. I sipped it slowly, feeling the tiny bubbles tickling my nose. My uncle was smiling to himself, drumming his fingers gently on the edge of the table and drinking the wine with a great deal of savor.

I noticed the strange ring on his finger for the

first time. It was black onyx, carved in the shape of a falcon, set in silver, an old and very unusual piece of jewelry. I asked him about it.

"It's a family piece," he said, "an heirloom of sorts. It's been worn by the master of Falconridge each succeeding generation. It was made to order for the first master, the man who built the place three hundred years ago."

"Your son will wear it after you?"

He smiled tightly. "I have no son. The ring will be passed on to my nephew, Norman Wade."

"Norman Wade?"

"My sister's son. I suppose that would make him your cousin by marriage. He will inherit Falconridge after I die."

"Does he live there?"

"He has had lodgings over the carriage house ever since he came to us eight years ago, when both his parents died in a boating accident, but he hasn't made much use of them until recently. He was out of the country awhile, pursuing some highly improbable money making schemes in Europe and other parts of the world. He's back now, a rather surly fellow. I have turned most of the duties of running Falconridge over to him."

"He runs the estate for you?"

"Most of it. I find it a bore."

"You don't love Falconridge?"

He smiled that tight smile again, and I felt I was asking too many questions, but this was the only way I could get any information. I was probably going to spend a long time at Falconridge, and I wanted to learn all I could about the place and the people I would meet there.

"It's too large," he said, "too taxing. One whole

wing is closed off, and all the attic rooms. It's a grand old estate, or was once, but it's damp and drafty and takes far too much money to keep up. I would gladly sell the place, if anyone were fool enough to want to buy it."

"But it's been in the family for so long," I protested. "Surely you feel something for it."

My uncle shook his head, his eyelids drooping like hoods. "You will find me a very unsentimental person," he said. "Things like that are for weaklings, people who cling to the past because they have no present. I live at Falconridge out of necessity, not because of any deep sense of family ties."

"How does my aunt feel about the place?" I asked.

"Helena would gladly die for the place. It is her life."

He said this disparagingly, and I wondered what kind of relations the two of them had. I could not imagine my uncle attached to anything human or material. He was cold, calculating, and I doubted if he had the ability to love.

"And Norman Wade?" I asked.

"My nephew has all those sentiments you seem to think appropriate. He will attach himself to Falconridge like the captain of a ship that is slowly sinking, holding on to the helm until the last wave has gone over his head."

"You don't think that admirable?"

"I think it foolhardy," he replied brusquely.

The waiter brought our food. We had guinea hens stuffed with wild rice, the meat succulent and tasty. I ate slowly, looking around at the glamorous people and thinking about what Charles Lloyd had said. He was at least honest about his sentiments, or lack of them. I did not ask any more questions, and we ate in silence. I was not enjoying the meal. My uncle kept staring at me, his mouth curled in a wry smile. There were brandied cherries with our coffee, and after that we left. The wine had gone to my head a little, and I felt slightly dizzy as he helped me into my cloak.

Charles Lloyd left me at the door of my hotel room. He took some money out of his wallet and put it in my hand.

"This is for tomorrow morning," he said. "I will be gone and you can amuse yourself, do some shopping. I will pick you up here shortly before noon."

"I don't want your money," I said.

"Take it," he ordered.

"No, thank you."

Charles Lloyd gripped my wrist, twisting it a little.

"I should think you would have already learned not to argue with me, Lauren," he said, each word sharp and distinct. "You are in my charge, and you will do what I think best. You will take what I give you, and you will obey me without question. Is that clear?"

My cheeks flushed and my eyes flashed, and a quick retort rose to my lips, but I did not speak. His eyes were staring into mine, and he was smiling grimly. His fingers gripped my wrist like bands of steel. For a long moment we stood like that, defiance in my eyes and determination in his. Then I looked away, unable to stand the force of that cold stare.

"I seem to have no choice," I said.

"That's right, my dear. You have no choice."

He released me and walked away, leaving me there holding the wad of notes. I went into my room and locked the door, leaning against it and trying to still my pounding heart. All the dizziness of the wine was gone now. My head was very clear. I felt as though I had just been submerged in ice cold water. I walked across the room to the mirror and looked at myself. A lock of auburn hair had fallen across my forehead, and my eyes were very dark. I sat down, the heavy folds of honey colored satin making a loud rustling noise. I suddenly hated this dress, just as I hated the man who had given it to me. Charles Lloyd was a demon, but I must not be afraid of him. I must not let him have that power over me. If I was to endure at Falconridge, I must fight him in every possible way.

It seemed that I had been on the train forever. It was noisy and uncomfortable. I tried my best to concentrate on Mr. Thackery's novel, but I turned the pages listlessly, unable to keep interest in the characters. My uncle sat facing me, his arms folded across his chest. He seemed to be in a reflective mood, his lids lowered, his brow creased. We had exchanged hardly a dozen words since we got on the train yesterday afternoon. He was polite enough when it was necessary, but I might as well have been another piece of luggage as far as he was concerned.

A woman with three children sat across the aisle. She passed out apples and the children munched on them loudly. Her old face was lined, and she wore a soiled black dress. The youngest child began to cry. She took him in her arms, resting his small blond head on her shoulder and hummed a lullaby. Together, they presented a picture of pathos. I wanted to talk to the children and try to make the ride more pleasant for them, but I knew that Charles Lloyd would disapprove.

I sat back on the cracked green leather, putting the novel aside. Someone had opened a window up ahead, and a cold wind blew into the car with a cutting force, but the wind was better than the smell. I lifted my handkerchief to my nostrils. It was dampened with rose water. We could have had grander accommodations on a train that was leaving later this afternoon, but my uncle did not want to wait. His business successfully accomplished, he was eager to leave the city.

We were passing through Devon now. I saw ancient hedges of hazel, brown and bleak, and flat wastelands with towering gray granite heights called tors. This terrain alternated with lovely green meadows, neatly plowed fields and pleasant farm houses. It was a country of great contrasts, completely unlike anything I had ever seen before, and it made me feel all the more lost and lonely. The train rocked and rattled, and I stared through the dirt smeared window, watching the black clouds that were massing together. Soon it began to rain, and I could see nothing through the driving downpour. The rain outside made the inside of the car seem all the more depressing.

I felt Clarissa's pendant on my bosom. It seemed years ago since she had given it to me. I wondered how long it would be before I would see her bright, happy face again. I wondered if I would ever see her again. She belonged to a part of my life that was closed forever. The grim reality of the moment made those days seem a dream world. I picked up the novel again, determined not to indulge myself in such thoughts. I couldn't afford them.

"Restless?" my uncle asked.

I looked up, startled. This was the first time he had spoken in over an hour. He was looking at me with those brooding brown eyes that looked like impenetrable black pools. His brows were arched like raven wings, and his mouth was pressed tightly together.

"Not particularly," I replied.

He laughed. "You are determined, aren't you?"

"Determined?"

"Not to give me the satisfaction of knowing you are uncomfortable. You haven't uttered a single complaint, even when the cinder blew in your eye. You've got spunk."

"I try to make the best of things," I retorted coldly.

"And spirit, too. I like that. You don't whine. That is something I admire. We may get along better than you think. Most people are easily intimidated. They give way. Personally, I prefer a good fight."

"You enjoy imposing your will on others, don't you," I said.

"That's man's nature," Charles Lloyd replied.

"Not all men," I retorted. "There is kindness. . . ."

"There is weakness," he interrupted.

"You think that's what kindness is?"

He nodded. "The world is for the strong. The weak perish, or suffer silently in the backwash of life. That's something they didn't tell you at your fine school, young lady."

"How does my aunt feel about your philosophy?" I asked.

"Helena lives in a world of her own. She's blind to any other kind. She lives for her sudden enthusiasms, her teas and bazaars, her cocker spaniels, her tobacco and novels and noise, and her beloved, decrepit old Falconridge. She goes blithely through the day, untouched by the world around her."

"And you think that's bad?"

"Oh no, to the contrary. I admire Helena for her stamina. She is one of the strongest women I know. She has the kind of life she wants."

"And you?"

He frowned. The question did not please him.

"Strong people take what they want, make the kind of life they desire," I continued, paraphrasing his words. "And you are still living at a place you do not like, leading an existence that doesn't suit you, or so you have implied."

His eyes were cloudy, and I could see that I had touched the sore spot. "There are some things you are too young to understand," he said curtly. His tone made it clear that the conversation was over. I picked up the novel again, trying to read in the faint greenish light. Charles Lloyd stared out at the rain. He was vulnerable after all, I thought. I had scored a point. I wondered how he would take his revenge.

The rain had long since ceased as the train began to slow down for its stop in a small town in Devon. Everything was peaceful now, the sky pale blue and cloudless, the grass a vivid green, with lemon colored sunlight filtering through the boughs of massive oak trees. The town was serene, resting in its nest of farmland in a huddle of brown and gray buildings. I saw the towering bronze steeple of a church and the faded red buildings of the depot. The train chugged to a stop with much jerking and screeching, and I sighed with relief at the cessation of motion.

The mother across the aisle got up, gathering her things together. I watched as she took down a shabby carpetbag and packed away the things her children had scattered over the seats. Then she took the youngest child in her arms, gripped the arm of another child and proceeded down the aisle. This was evidently her final destination. I fancied that she must be a widow, coming to live off the kindness of relatives.

"There will be a thirty minute stop," my uncle said. "You may want to stretch a bit while we're waiting."

It was eleven o'clock, and this was the first stop since early in the morning. I gladly left my seat, eager to stretch my cramped legs. It was nice to leave the stuffy confines of the train and step out into the vivid sunshine on the platform. Men were unloading crates further on down, and most of the other passengers had alighted, too, brushing the dust off their clothes and taking great breaths of the fresh air. An old woman wearing a faded blue shawl was selling fresh eggs and vegetables, and a small girl in tattered clothes held up bunches of flowers, her large blue eyes pleading silently for someone to buy them.

I took a coin from my bag and purchased a bunch of daisies. They were white and gold, with dark brown centers. The little girl looked up with a weary smile on her dirt smeared face. She was very skinny, the basket of flowers on her arm almost dwarfing her.

Charles Lloyd stood behind me, his hands in his pockets. He had an indulgent expression on his face and I knew that my sympathy for the child amused him.

"When will we reach Falconridge?" I asked.

"Late this afternoon, if everything goes well."

"They are expecting us then?"

He nodded and began to stroll on down the platform. He held his head a little to one side, the dark blond hair ruffling in the breeze. Great puffs of steam spewed from the engine of the train, blowing bits of trash and paper over the platform. I watched my uncle sauntering along, taking long strides, disdainful of the other people around him. He was like a lord among peasants, too mighty even to notice them. Then he stopped and took his hands out of his pockets, bowing to a woman who stood beside the door of the station house. She nodded to him and pointed to the small brown suitcase beside her.

I had not noticed the woman before, and I studied her carefully now. I wondered who she could be and why my uncle had stopped to speak to her. She was in her late thirties, and very beautiful in a sad, resigned kind of way. Her long black hair had a dark blue sheen and fell in soft waves about her pale oval face. She had delicate features, thin nostrils, and pink lips turned down at the corners as though in defeat. Her brown eyes looked up pensively at my uncle, and I noticed that there were light mauve shadows about her eyelids. She looked like someone who had suffered a grave disappointment in life and found it hard to carry on. She wore a white silk dress printed with tiny lilac blossoms and minute jade green leaves, and she held a lilac parasol, protecting her face from the sun. She and my uncle exchanged a few words. She seemed to be protesting something. Then she smiled submissively as he picked up her suitcase and they came towards me.

"This is my niece, Lauren Moore," he said. "She is going to stay with us at Falconridge."

"I am sure that will be nice," the woman said. Her voice was silken and melodious, a lovely voice.

"This is Mrs. Graystone, Lauren. Lavinia and her husband are a part of Falconridge, so to speak. They live in the Dower House, and Andrew has charge of the fields and tenants. He also does odd jobs around the estate. Lavinia is also our local seamstress. She makes the dresses Helena wears."

"I am pleased to meet you," I said.

Lavinia Graystone smiled. It was a warm smile, her large brown eyes glowing, yet I felt that she was uncomfortable.

"I have been visiting my sister here in town," she said. "I was very surprised to see your uncle. I had no idea he had left Falconridge. He insisted on taking my bag and having me join you. I am on my way back, too. Will you be staying at Falconridge long?"

"She's been put out of her school in London," Charles Lloyd said before I could reply. "Both her parents are dead. She'll be staying with us indefinitely."

The woman sensed my discomfort at his abrupt manner of answering her. She gave him a brief glance and then turned her attention back to me. She smiled again and took my hand.

"I am sure it will be nice for you," she said. "It's a large place, and you'll find many things to do. Your aunt will be delighted with your company, I know."

"We'd better board the train," my uncle said. "They're getting ready to leave. Lavinia, you will join us, of course. I'll talk to the porter about your seat."

"Please don't go to any trouble. . . ." she began.

"Nonsense. You'll sit with us."

The three of us rode silently for a long while. The presence of Lavinia Graystone did nothing to improve my uncle's sullen mood. He looked out the window, brooding. Mrs. Graystone sat with her hands in her lap, very ill at ease, I thought. My uncle was her husband's employer, and I was sure the relationship could not be an overly friendly one. I felt she would much rather be in her own seat, away from the man, but she no doubt knew that he would not stand for any opposition. After a while, he went up to the front car so that he could smoke a cigar, and Lavinia let out a little sigh.

"You live at Falconridge?" I asked.

"The Dower House is about a mile away from the main house," she said. "You can see it over the tops of the trees if you are standing at one of the second floor windows. It was originally built so that young married couples could get away from the rest of the family for a while. It's small, but I find it very comfortable."

"How long has your husband worked for my uncle?"

"For three years now. Before that, we drifted about. Andrew took one job after another, never staying with one for long. He doesn't have a particularly easygoing disposition and it's hard for him to get along with the people he works for."

"And he gets along with my uncle?" I asked, surprised.

"Mr. Lloyd gives Andrew a free hand. All he is interested in is the money Andrew collects from the tenants—and that everything is run smoothly. He never interferes. We seldom see him."

"What about Norman Wade?"

Lavinia frowned. "Mr. Wade makes his presence felt very strongly. He and Andrew have many conferences. There's been a little disagreement, but your uncle has managed to work things out to the satisfaction of both men. I am afraid Mr. Wade has quite a temper...." She looked up, afraid that she had said too much. I was, after all, part of the family now, or I soon would be.

"Tell me about your school," she said, clearly anxious to change the subject. We talked about inconsequential things until my uncle came back, and then the silence settled again. There was only the sound of screeching wheels and rattling windows. I watched Lavinia Graystone, fascinated by her beautiful, tragic face.

Was she unhappy because of her husband? She had said they had drifted about before coming to Falconridge. That implied instability. Perhaps he was cruel to her. She had mentioned his disposition. He did not get along with people. Did he get along with her? I studied the sad eyes and the drooping mouth, and I wondered what secrets they held. I wondered too about Falconridge. The people there were a strange lot. I wondered if there was something about that place that caused them to be this way.

IV

THE SUN HAD NOT yet gone down as the carriage drove us towards Falconridge. It sank slowly, spreading gold and yellow banners of light that gradually melted against a darkening green hued sky. The air was different here. It was more bracing, laden with the tangy salt smell of the sea. I could sense the presence of that great body of water, just out of sight, a magnificent power that dominated this part of the country. We were driving through a wooded area, tall oak trees close on either side and spreading their heavy boughs over the road. Lavinia Graystone had remained at the station to wait for her husband but the carriage had been waiting for Charles Lloyd and me. I was tense with excitement, all the fatigue of the long train ride momentarily forgotten. My uncle seemed depressed, not at all eager to get to the house.

"How much farther is it?" I asked.

"Be patient. We'll be there soon enough."

"You're not glad?"

"Is one ever glad to meet his doom?"

"Doom?"

"A mere choice of words," he said.

I thought the remark an odd one, but I was far too excited to pay any special attention to it. My uncle was an enigma, but I was not going to let him spoil this for me.

We seemed to be going uphill, the road gradually slanting up. The oak trees began to thin out, and I could see patches of sky through their tall limbs. We passed through a gate, two large gray stone portals standing on either side, and the heavy iron gate swung back. The carriage swung around a curve, and I had my first glimpse of Falconridge, sprawling at the top of a hill, sharply outlined against the greenish sky.

It was a formidable place, massive in size and beautiful in a rough-hewn, rugged kind of way. It was two stories high, constructed entirely of huge gray stones with a dark green roof. There were many turrets, and many towers, with two huge wings that spread out over the hill. A circular drive of crushed shell led one up to the portico, four flat gray slabs of steps before it. The woods came up almost to the house on the left side, and to the right there were terraces and gardens, all of them untidy and ragged looking and desperately in need of work. I could see a corner of the carriage house, and my uncle told me that there was a courtyard in back. Falconridge perched on the edge of the hill like the bird of prey that gave it its name and behind the house the lawns stretched down to the edge of a cliff that fell sharply down to the rocks and waves below. I could hear the sound of the waves pounding on the rocks as we drove around the drive and up to the portico. The house would never be free of that sound, I thought. It was like the labored breathing of some gigantic monster who constantly watched over the place, waiting for an opportunity to claim it as its own.

"Well?" Charles Lloyd asked as he helped me out of the carriage.

"It's overpowering," I said, rather awed by the place.

"Yes, Falconridge is overpowering."

"And—and beautiful, too, in a strange kind of way. It doesn't look like a house at all. It looks like something out of a history book. It is hard to believe that people actually live here."

"Many dozens of people have lived here since it was built," he said, his voice dry. "And each one of them has left his mark on the place. You will find Falconridge full of the dead. The walls seem to have taken them in, absorbed them, and they watch you as you move along the corridors. It has a character all its own, this place. I hope you don't find it too strong for you."

"I'm sure I shall love it."

"I certainly hope so, my dear," he replied grimly.

He led me into a vast hall, dimly lit. I saw a great staircase at one end, leading up into a nest of shadows, and caught glimpses of faded tapestries on the walls and dark, heavy furniture. A woman in a severe black dress came to meet us. She was large, with big bones and fleshy features. Her iron gray hair was coiled tightly on top of her head, and her sullen black eyes stared at me as I stood there beside my uncle. The woman was sixty, at least, and a set of keys dangled from her belt. Charles Lloyd introduced her as Mrs. Victor, the housekeeper. She was a severe woman, tight lipped, harsh in manner, and I took an immediate dislike to her.

"Martha," Charles Lloyd said, "this is my niece.

We've just arrived."

"I heard the carriage," Martha Victor replied. She looked at me with those cold, flat eyes, as though I had no business being here. I could sense that this old woman was a tyrant with the other servants. I imagined that she ran the household with shrewd efficiency, countering no disobedience from the staff. I would merely be in the way, her eyes seemed to say.

"Where is my wife?" my uncle asked.

"In the front sitting room, with the spaniels," she replied, as though she disapproved.

"Has everything gone well since I've been away?"

"Everything has run smoothly, Sir."

"Then I can thank you for that, Martha," he said.

She smiled, a peculiarly girlish smile for that heavy face. I felt sure that she did not smile often, and when she did, I was certain it was only for Charles Lloyd. When she turned to him, her whole manner changed and I could discern a kind of slavish devotion to him in her eyes. She would do anything to please him, I thought, anything in the world.

"That was very kind of you to say," she replied primly.

"It's nice to have someone to depend on, Martha, and I can always depend on you."

He patted her shoulder, deliberately exercising his charm. Martha Victor held her head down, trying to hide her pleasure.

"Is my nephew with Helena?" he asked.

"No, Sir. Mr. Wade went to visit a friend in the next county. He will be gone for two days."

"Damn," Charles Lloyd said, frowning.

"Shall I see to dinner, Sir?"

"No—not just yet. I am going to go up to my room. Tell my wife I will be down later. That will give her a chance to see her niece for a while alone. See that the bags are brought in, will you, and take Miss Moore to the sitting room."

He left us alone. For a moment we stood there in the dark hall. I was extremely uneasy under the gaze of the housekeeper. Her lips were pressed tightly together with disapproval. She seemed to be sizing me up, and she quite clearly did not like what she saw. I wondered why she should be so cold towards me. Perhaps she thought I would make things more difficult for her. Perhaps she just didn't like people. I waited patiently, meeting her stare with level eyes. I was not going to let her bully me.

"Shall we go?" I said, my voice icy.

"This way, Miss Moore."

She led me down the hall and around a corner. She opened the door to one of the rooms and held it aside. I heard loud barking, and then three spaniels charged towards me, leaping and jumping at my feet. One was blonde, one brown, one brown and white, all three fat and glossy and beautifully groomed. I stood back, startled, but the dogs were not unfriendly. They merely wanted attention. I knelt down and stroked the ears of the blonde, and it responded by licking my palm, the other two clamoring for similar favors from me.

"They adore you already," a loud, rather scratchy woman said. "I think that's marvelous! They know instinctively about people, you know, much better than we do, of course. Come, my dear, let me really see you. I've been in a panic all afternoon, afraid something would happen and you wouldn't get here safely."

"Mr. Lloyd said he would be down later," Martha Victor said.

"Very well, Martha, You may go."

I stood up, brushing my skirts, and Martha Victor left, closing the door behind her. The dogs bounded at my feet, cavorting and carrying on with remarkable vigor. My aunt called to them, and they all three went scurrying across the room to leap on a sofa in a wriggling, glossy pile. I looked at my aunt, unable to speak. She held both of her arms out, smiling brilliantly. Her face was aglow with pleasure. I knew immediately that at least one person at Falconridge wanted me here.

"Lauren, dear. I am your Aunt Helena!"

"I—I don't know what to say...."

"Don't bother to say anything. We've ages of time for that. Let's just look at each other. Oh, dear, I hope I shan't cry. That would be so sloppy. Louise's little girl...."

"I'm so happy to be here," I said, my voice weak.

"I'm ecstatic! At long last...."

My Aunt Helena had been ten years older than my mother. That would make her fifty-six, four years her husband's senior. She had not held her age as well as he, but she was a stunning figure just the same. She was small and thin, with delicate bone structure, but there was nothing fragile about her. She seemed to be charged with energy, full of a startling vitality that showed in her quick movements, the toss of her head, her rapid, eloquent gestures. Her silver hair was piled carelessly on top of her head, caught up with a purple velvet ribbon, some of the curls spilling over her forehead. Her clear blue eyes were alert and intelligent, the lids shadowed with lilac, and her mouth was the mouth of a young girl, the lips pink and firm and slightly pouting. Her brow was lined with tiny wrinkles. She wore a royal purple dress and a starched white apron. A yellow paperbacked French novel and, strangely enough, a tack hammer stuck out of the pocket of her apron.

She saw me looking at the hammer and laughed.

"I've been tacking down the carpet in this room," she said. "It's come loose on one side. There's so much to do, really, and I hate to ask the servants! They're always so busy trying to keep the place in some kind of order, there's just never enough time to see to all the little things. Besides, I adore puttering. Yesterday I varnished the stair railing. Martha was horrified."

"She looks very efficient," I remarked.

"Martha? Oh, but she's such an old dragon! I stay out of her way whenever possible. She's been at Falconridge since the place was built, or at least for the past fifty-five years. I don't think she approves of me. She thinks I'm an intruder, although I've lived here ever since Charles and I got married. He is the only one who can do anything with her. She looked after him when he was a baby, although she was merely a child herself. She may be a grim old thing, but she runs the house with amazing skill. We couldn't do without her."

My aunt sat down, spreading her skirts over the sofa. One of the spaniels crawled into her lap, but she pushed him aside, scolding him gently. She reached into a wooden box on the table beside her and took out a cigarette, then fumbled into the pocket of her apron for a match to light it with. I watched with amazement as she lit the cigarette. I had never seen a woman smoke before. My aunt settled back on the sofa, filling the air around her with blue-gray plumes of smoke.

"Are you horrified? Most people are. It's a vice I picked up in Spain several years ago. The local parson is outraged. He thinks I am a regular Jezebel. But, pooh, life is too short to worry about what other people think." She blew another plume of smoke and laughed. Her laughter was a cackle, really, a rasping, amusing noise. "You must forgive me for rattling on, my dear. It's been so long since I've had anyone to talk to."

She looked up at me, and her mood seemed to change. She grew very quiet, and her eyes were sad. She took a final puff of the cigarette, then crushed it out in a tray. The blonde spaniel crept cautiously into her lap again and she stroked its long ears. She seemed to be lost in thought. For all her vitality and verve, I could sense that she was an extremely sensitive person, full of emotions she kept closely guarded.

"I was thinking of your mother," she said quietly. "Poor Louise. We were so close as girls. We worshiped each other. Then I married Charles and came here and she married your father, and—things were not the same."

"Was my mother ever at Falconridge?" I asked.

"Once, for two weeks, before she married. She was eighteen, and Charles and I had been married for ten years. It—it wasn't a happy time. Something happened, and—when Louise left we lost contact with each other. There were hard feelings

—I'm so sorry about it all, but life does that, makes barriers...."

I wondered what had happened at Falconridge so many years ago. My mother had never mentioned her sister Helena until her death bed, and I was certain that whatever happened at Falconridge had caused her to completely close her mind to the house and the people in it. My aunt must think this, too, I thought, and it was the reason for her sudden sadness.

"But you're here now," she said, smiling gently. "I'll make it all up to Louise. It's going to be so wonderful, Lauren. You're mine now. You must tell me all about yourself."

"I am afraid there is not much to tell. I've done nothing but go to school...."

"It must have been dreadful," she remarked.

"It was," I agreed.

"Have you had any young men?"

I shook my head. She arched an eyebrow.

"You've never had a young man dying of love for you?"

"No, Aunt...."

"Helena, my dear. You must call me Helena. But it's absurd! You are eighteen and have never had a lover. You don't take after us then, your mother and I. There were always dozens of gallants, far too many of them! It was such fun—but, I forgot, young ladies are not supposed to have fun nowadays. It's like smoking, strictly forbidden. I am dreadfully out of step with the times!"

She laughed again, her high spirits completely restored. I found her delightful in every way, and I loved her already. She took out another cigarette and lit it, holding the match for a moment as the flame burned down. I noticed that her nails were polished a dark pink, and there was an enormous diamond ring on one of the slim fingers. It flashed as she shook the match out.

"Was the train ride awful?" she asked.

"It wasn't too bad."

"I abhor them. That's one of the reasons I never leave here if I can avoid it. I've done all the gadding about I care to. I'm much too old to have my poor bones shook loose in a railway coach."

"We met a Mrs. Graystone in Devon. She had been visiting her sister and was coming back."

"Oh?" Helena said, looking up. "I didn't know that Lavinia had left."

"Yes, she was at the station when the train stopped."

"I didn't know she had a sister in Devon," Helena remarked. There was a look of puzzlement in her eyes.

"I understand she is the local seamstress," I said.

"She made this dress. She's quite wonderful. She had a shop of her own in Liverpool before she married. She makes gowns for all the ladies in these parts. We'll have to see about a new wardrobe for you, Lauren. Lavinia has dozens of bolts of the most exquisite material.

"Mrs. Graystone is a very attractive person," I said.

"Yes, Lavinia is attractive, poor thing. Her husband is such a sullen brute, one of those solemn, silent types, always brooding. He gives her a hard time, I'm afraid. Beats her. Once she had a perfectly wretched black eye, and she always looks as though she were going to burst into tears."

"Why doesn't she leave him?" I asked. "Surely

she could support herself with her sewing."

Helena cocked her head, smiling mysteriously. "That's something you wouldn't understand, not at your age. He is quite good looking in a rough, rugged sort of way, with those smouldering brown eyes and that large, lumbering build. Many women would take a lot from a man who looks like that."

"Life doesn't seem to have been very kind to Mrs. Graystone."

"It's not kind to anyone, my dear. Surely you know that already. It's a constant battle. It's how one goes into battle that counts. One can run away from it, one can stand and take the blows and whine about it, or one can have style. It is style, my dear, style that matters in life. One must learn to make the best of all circumstances, no matter how unpleasant they may be, and do it with style."

Aunt Helena stood up, her purple skirts rustling. She pushed a silver curl from her wrinkled brow and dropped the cigarette in a tray. She drew herself up, and there was something regal about her as she stood there, her eyes turned inward on some private thoughts. She certainly had style. She might be an eccentric old woman, outrageous in much of her behavior, outspoken and opinionated in speech, but she was an aristocrat to the tip of her toes.

"We had better change for dinner," she said. "It's getting late. I will show you your room. Come along, dears—Simon, Philip, Adele. Get off that sofa. Hurry up—behave yourself, Adele."

The dogs leaped off the sofa, their paws pattering on the parquet floor. The blonde, Adele, shook her fur, and the other two pranced about my aunt's skirts. She led the way down the hall. The light was almost gone now and the hall was filled with shadow. I could hear the sea pounding on the rocks far below, a constant background.

"Your room is upstairs," Helena said. "In the right wing. It is a little isolated from the others, but it's the best bedroom open."

"How many rooms are there at Falconridge?" I asked.

"Over a hundred," she replied. "We only use twenty or so. The left wing is entirely closed—everything covered with sheets and a generous layer of dust. I hope that someday we can open up all the rooms and restore the place. It's my one dream."

"You love this place, don't you?" I asked.

"It's a part of me. I've loved it since the first day I saw it. I belong to Falconridge."

"And does my uncle share your sentiments?" I inquired, already knowing the answer.

Helena laughed, a dry, crackling noise that sounded very loud in the empty hallway. "I don't think Charles loves anything," she replied. "Certainly not Falconridge. He would gladly watch it burn to the ground, but it's all we've got. No, Charles is the kind of man who needs constant change, constant excitement. He thrives on it. There's not much of that at Falconridge, and that's the tragedy, my dear. To each his own prison."

"It's very sad," I said.

"Not sad, merely ironic. We want that which we don't have, and since Charles has Falconridge, he wants something else."

She led me up the dark staircase. One of the servants began to light lamps and the flickering yellow light began to glow in pools, pushing back the shadows. I ran my hand along the varnished banister and followed my aunt, the dogs prancing along behind. We reached the second floor and turned right, going down one hall, turning, going down another. A servant carrying lamps passed us, making a curtsey to Helena.

"Finally," she said, pausing before a door. She opened it and led the way into the bedroom that had been assigned to me. I caught my breath. It was a beautiful room.

The walls were covered with an embossed ivory material, and the floor was laid with a thick gold carpet. The draperies were dark yellow, falling to the floor in heavy satin folds, the bedspread and canopy were of the same rich cloth. The furniture was white oak, delicately carved in simple design. A bowl of vivid blue gentians sat on a small white table, and there was a footstool covered in the same shade of blue. It was the loveliest room I had ever seen.

"I've just done it over," Helena said, leaning in the doorway. "It was so dark and dreadful with those massive mahogany pieces and the stuffy green velvet hangings. I thought a young girl would like something a bit lighter."

"I love it," I said, turning around to take in all the features of the room.

"I didn't know whether it would be ready or not. I made the draperies and bedspread myself as soon as I knew you were coming. Covered the stool, too."

"You shouldn't have gone to all that trouble, Aunt Helena."

"Helena, my dear, just Helena. Trouble? Nonsense. My only trouble has been that I haven't had anyone to do things for in such a long time. That's changed now that you're here. And old woman like me needs someone to fuss over. What is this? Are you crying...."

I shook my head, trying to hold back the tears that welled up in my eyes. Helena moved across the room and put her arms around me, holding me to her in a tight embrace. I had never felt so warm, so secure. She released me after a moment, standing back and smiling radiantly.

"You're tired, Angel, that's all. I see that they've already seen to your trunk. You freshen up and dress for dinner, and you'll feel much better. I'll send Lucy up to help you. She's to be your maid. Hurry up now. This is certainly no time for tears...."

V

I STOOD VERY QUIETLY in the room after my aunt left. I tried to compose myself. I had resolved never to cry again, yet the tears had come, and I was ashamed of them. I brushed them away from my lashes, scolding myself for the emotional indulgence. I had never known anyone like Helena Lloyd. I had never known that anyone could be so wonderful, so kind. It moved me deeply to know that I was wanted, that I would be a part in the life of someone else at last. I moved to the bowl of gentians, picking up one of the little blue flowers and holding it to my cheek. After all the unpleasantness at Mrs. Siddons', after my uncle's rudeness and the encounter with Martha Victor, my aunt's warmth was overwhelming. I was filled with a soft glow, surrounded by the beauty of the room, at home at last.

There was a timid tap at the door, and I opened it to see a small, wide eyed child with pale yellow hair and a thin, pug-nosed face. Her eyes were very blue, surrounded by long sooty lashes, and her mouth was bow shaped. There was a smudge of dirt on her cheek, and a perky white cap rested on her curly head. She bowed, lowering her lashes, and introduced herself as Lucy, my new maid.

"I've come to help you unpack, Ma'am," she said. Her voice was thin and reedy.

"Come in, Lucy. My, how small you are. How old are you?"

"Twelve, Ma'am. Almost thirteen."

"And how long have you been at Falconridge?"

"Since always. Cook's my ma. I was born here."

She went over to my trunk and began to unpack it, laying each dress carefully across the bed. Her hands shook a little, and I could tell she was frightened. She glanced at me out of the corners of her eyes. I smiled at her, sitting down on the edge of the bed, hoping to put her at ease.

"You mustn't be nervous, Lucy," I said. "I won't hurt you."

"It's not you I'm afraid of," she said, taking the last dress out. "It's Mrs. Victor. This is my first important job—seeing after you. I was in the pantry before, helping ma with supplies and things. Now I'm a lady's maid and I'm sure I'll do everything wrong. Mrs. Victor would love that. She hates me anyway, says I'm always getting into mischief. If I make any mistakes she'll send me back to the pantry."

"You're doing beautifully," I told her, "and you won't make any mistakes. Even if you do, I won't tell."

Lucy looked at me for a long moment as though doubting the truth of what I said. Her thin face was very serious, her eyes searching mine intently. I sensed that she hadn't known much kindness in her short life. She was hesitant, not knowing whether to take me at my word or not, and then she smiled.

The corners of her mouth turned up like a tiny rosebud opening, and contentment flooded her face.

"Gar," she said. "I didn't know what to expect. I didn't know I was goin' to have a princess for my lady."

"A princess?"

She nodded. "Like in all them stories my ma read to me. This is a big castle, like the ones in th' pictures, and you're the princess come to break the evil spell."

"But Falconridge doesn't have an evil spell," I said, laughing at her fantasy.

"Oh, yes, Ma'am, it does. It's got a spell and everyone is unhappy. You'll see for yourself."

"That's silly, Lucy."

She shook her head. "No, it's the truth. Honest it is."

"You've listened to too many stories."

"Maybe so. Anyway, you're here now to break the spell."

"Silly child," I said, amused at her foolish convictions.

I washed up while Lucy hung my clothes in the closet. She brushed each dress and smoothed it out before hanging it up. She put all my toilet articles on the dresser, the ivory handled brush set, the bottles of cologne and lilac water, the tiny box of rice powder that I never used. She hummed softly to herself, and I could tell that she was at ease with me now, ready to do anything I wanted.

I sat at the dressing table, brushing my hair. There were shadows about my brown eyes, and my cheeks looked a little drawn and pale. The trip had been very long and tiring, and my emotions had been through an upheaval. It all showed on my face. I took out the tiny pot of forbidden rouge Clarissa had given to me months ago and rubbed a little of the pink salve into my cheeks. That looked better, I thought. I parted my hair in the middle and let it fall in lustrous auburn waves on either side of my face. Lucy watched me, fascinated.

"What shall I wear to dinner?" I asked, wanting her to feel that she was taking part in my preparations.

She put a finger to her lips and held her head to one side, examining the dresses in the closet. Then she took out my old white taffeta overlaid with yellowing ivory lace. "This one," she said, holding it up for my inspection. The dress had once been beautiful. It was a bit shabby now, but then all of them were. I put it on, letting Lucy fasten it for me.

"There," she said. "Now you really do look like a princess."

The sleeves dropped off-the-shoulder, and the waist was very tight, as the dress was at least three years old. The lace had begun to yellow, but the effect was not at all bad. I wore Clarissa's ruby pendant, and the drop of glowing red against the white was pleasing. I whirled around for Lucy's inspection. The stiff skirts made a crackling noise, and she clapped with approval. The child's delight made me feel much better. I asked her directions for getting to the dining room and then left, resolving to be bright and cheerful for my aunt.

A window had been left open somewhere down the hall. I could feel a chilly breeze on my bare shoulders. I quickened my step, anxious to get downstairs. I went down the hall and turned at the corner. The breeze was much stronger here. It was actually cold, zephyrs of wind billowing down the hallway and causing the old tapestries to flap against the wall. It was an irritating sound, a little unnerving. There was only one lamp burning, far down the hall, and its yellow light flickered and spluttered, making dark shadows leap over the floor. As I hurried towards the light, a sudden gust of wind rattled a window violently and the light went out. I stopped, startled.

I stood very still. It was ridiculous, of course, to be alarmed but I felt a chill of apprehension. The hall was in total darkness and the tapestries beat against the wall with a steady rhythm. I fancied I could hear footsteps, but I knew it was my imagination. The house seemed to surround me, holding me in its dark center, and my heart beat rapidly. I could feel the damp walls all around me. I could smell mildew and moisture. I remembered what Lucy had said about an evil spell, and I had a moment of complete fear before I pulled myself together. I bit my lower lip and forced myself to move down the hall.

Some rays of moonlight filtered in from somewhere, spreading a silver sheen over everything but giving very little actual light. There were dense blue-black shadows on either side as I walked along, but I wouldn't let my imagination invest them with spirits. I seemed to have been going down the hall for a long time before I found the staircase. I was surprised that there was no lamp here. Surely there had been one when Aunt Helena and I came up.

Suddenly there was a loud crash behind me. I grasped the railing, trying not to scream. I realized then that the wind had knocked over a vase or something and it had crashed to the floor. Some servant would be severely reprimanded for leaving the windows open, I thought, moving on down the staircase. It seemed more narrow than it had earlier, and there was a musty smell about the carpet that was unpleasant. The railing gave a little as I leaned against it, and a stair creaked loudly. I knew then that I had missed a turn and was coming down the wrong stairway. The only thing to do was to go on down to the ground floor and try to find my way to the dining room from there.

I stopped at the foot of the stairs, all my senses alert. There was someone watching me. I was sure of it. I could feel the eyes on me. It was a physical sensation. I leaned against the railing, afraid to move. My eyes were gradually growing accustomed to the darkness and as they did I began to see large, moving blurs of white. The whole room was full of these objects, and I heard a rustling noise, the noise of soft whispers. I closed my eyes. My head swam for a moment. I smelt the strong odors of dust and decay. When I opened my eyes, I realized that I had somehow managed to come to the left wing of Falconridge, the wing that was closed up. The white objects were the sheets covering the furniture, and the whispering noise was made by the sheets as they rustled softly in the breeze. I sighed deeply, holding my hand over my heart. For a moment my imagination had gone wild.

I could still feel the eyes on me. This was not my imagination. I heard someone moving in the room. I could see a large, dark figure move across the floor, coming towards me. I leaned against the wall, trying to maintain some degree of calm.

"Who's there?" I called.

The figure stopped. There was no reply. I could see the dark shape standing several yards away from me. I knew that my eyes were not playing tricks, as they had done with the sheeted furniture. I could feel the presence of the person in the room, and I could feel something else, too. It was animosity. It was unmistakable. The animosity was there, directed towards me, filling the air with intangible waves. I felt cold chills on my bare arms, and I knew my instincts were not wrong.

"Who's there?" I called again, a pitch of hysteria in my voice. I bit down on my lower lip, fighting to keep control.

There was a loud rasping noise and then an orange flare as someone struck a match. The flame burned low for a moment and then a gradually widening glow of yellow took its place as it was held to the wick of an oil lamp. My eyes blinked at the sudden light. I saw first the hand holding the lamp and then, as the light grew, the face of Martha Victor. It was grotesque in the flickering glow of the lamp, half in shadow. The face seemed to be suspended there in the dark, like something in a nightmare. I could see the heavy jowls, the tight mouth, the dark eyes that stared at me with pure hatred.

"Why didn't you answer me?" I demanded angrily. "You gave me a terrible start."

"Were you frightened, Miss Moore?" she asked, her voice honied. I saw the large lips spread into a smile.

"You know I was!" I snapped.

"It is very easy to be frightened at Falconridge. There are noises you can't explain, little noises in the night, and shadows, always shadows. Sometimes they seem to be waiting for you, dark nests of shadows, waiting for you."

"Why are you talking like this?"

"No one sleeps well at Falconridge," she continued, ignoring my question, "with all the noise. It's a big place, full of twists and turns and corners and sudden stairways leading up into the darkness. Anything could happen to a young girl in a place like this."

"That will be enough, Mrs. Victor," I said. My voice was level now. I did not know why she had wanted to frighten me, but I was over the initial shock. I was merely angry now, coldly angry at the dreadful way she had acted.

"Why don't you leave, Miss Moore? Falconridge is not kind to people who do not belong. You do not belong. You are an outsider. You will not be happy here."

"That will be for me to decide," I replied.

She smiled again. She looked very satisfied with herself, as though she had done something very clever. We stared at each other, my own eyes as coldly angry as hers were flat and belligerent. I could not understand why she felt this way towards me, but I knew that there could never be anything but mutual dislike between us.

"Are you lost, Miss Moore?" she asked, still smiling.

"Would you tell me how to get to the dining room?"

She pointed. "Down that hall, through those doors. It is the first room on your left as you enter the main hallway."

"Thank you," I said icily.

I walked down the hall. I could feel the woman's eyes following my progress. They seemed to bore into my back, and I wanted to shudder. I flung open the door and entered the main hallway, stepping briskly on the parquet floor. Many lamps glowed in this part of the house, making a welcome contrast to what I had left behind me. I waited in the hall a moment before entering the dining room. I had brushed against a cobweb somewhere, and it clung to my skirt. I wiped it off, frowning. I had been in such a good mood when I left my bedroom. Now I was filled with anger. I didn't want my aunt and uncle to see me like this.

I took several deep breaths, arranged my dress and walked into the dining room with a smile on my lips. They were both at the table. A manservant was waiting to serve the food. Charles Lloyd stood up, nodding politely at me. Aunt Helena gave a sigh of relief.

"We were afraid something had happened," she exclaimed.

"I lost my way," I said quietly. "The lamp blew out in the hall upstairs and I took the wrong staircase down. I found myself in the closed wing."

"Oh, dear! That must have been frightful!"

"Mrs. Victor was there. She had probably gone to close a window. She was kind enough to show me the way to the dining room."

I had no intention of telling them what she had done or said. If Martha Victor and I were going to do battle, we would do it alone. I was not going to draw my aunt and uncle into it. Charles Lloyd helped me into my seat.

"You will soon learn never to walk the corridors of Falconridge at night without carrying a candle," he said. "The draft is terrible in every part of the house. It's nearly impossible to keep all of the lamps burning."

"The coastal wind," Helena said. "It's ghastly. Sometimes it's so bad I think the house will fall apart. Every shutter on the place banging, doors slamming...."

"Another attractive feature of Falconridge," my uncle said. His voice was heavy with sarcasm.

"I'm sure it won't bother me," I replied, "now that I know what to expect."

"I hope not, Lauren," he said.

The servant began to fill our plates, and I looked around at the room. It was spacious and elegant, the walls covered with rich mahogany wainscoting below, the remainder in embossed blue material. The carpet was dark gray, and the furniture was the same rich mahogany as the wainscoting, gleaming with a dark red sheen. The table was vast, far too large for three people, but the candles glowing in their heavy silver candelabras created an atmosphere of intimacy. Two large silver bowls contained pink roses, some of the petals scattered on the table. My uncle sat at one end of the table, Helena at the other. I sat in the middle.

"How do you like Lucy?" Aunt Helena asked.

"I find her adorable."

"I thought Lucy was in the pantry," my uncle said.

"She was. I promoted her."

"Did you consult Mrs. Victor?"

"Goodness, Charles, one would think I could promote my own servants without consulting the housekeeper. No, I merely told her that I wanted Lucy prepared to be Lauren's maid. She's a good child, perhaps a little imaginative, but very observant. She'll do wonderfully well, I'm sure."

"If you say so, my dear," he said.

Charles Lloyd smiled at his wife. It was a tolerant smile, the kind an indulgent parent gives to a spoiled child. He lifted his wine glass and drank, looking over the rim of it at Helena, his eyes full of some secret amusement. He wore an old brown velvet smoking jacket with brown satin lapels over his white shirt. His heavy blond hair was a little disarrayed, one of the locks fallen on his forehead. He was more mellow and relaxed than I had ever seen him, more at ease with himself and his surroundings, but the arrogance was still there.

"Lauren said you met Lavinia in Devon," Helena remarked.

"Yes, we did."

"What a coincidence," she said. "She had been visiting a sister? I didn't know she had relatives in Devon."

"I am sure there's a lot you don't know about the Graystones, my dear," he replied. "The relationship with them has never been intimate."

"I keep wondering how long you are going to keep that awful man. I don't like him at all. Neither does Norman."

"Norman doesn't completely run Falconridge yet," my uncle said. "Andrew Graystone does his job well. He collects the rent from all the tenants on time. He sees that they have enough seed and the proper tools and supplies. He is honest, so far as I know, and he does his work without grumbling about it."

"He's so surly," Helena protested.

"One does not evaluate one's employees according to their disposition."

"No," she said, an icy edge to her voice, "I suppose not. If that were the case, Martha would have been sent packing years ago."

"Poor Helena," he said, "after all these years you're still not at ease with the servants. I'm afraid you're hopelessly middle class at heart."

My aunt did not reply. We all ate silently. I could not help but be aware of the tension between the two of them. Charles Lloyd was condescending in his attitude towards his wife, and she was too intelligent not to see it. I wondered if it had always been this way between them. Helena was older than her husband, yet he treated her like a child, a not too bright child at that. Could they have ever been in love, I wondered.

I watched my aunt as she ate. Her lids were heavy with shadow and she looked tired, worn out by all the energy and emotion she had used so extravagantly during the day. She wore a lovely black dress, simple in cut, and a magnificent diamond necklace rested on the hollow of her throat. It was old-fashioned, matching the ring I had noticed earlier, but the diamonds were real, and sparkled radiantly in the candlelight. A perky red velvet bow was fastened among her silver curls.

She noticed me watching her and smiled.

"You look lovely tonight," she said.

"Thank you, Helena."

"I wish Norman were here. Then we would all be together. You'll meet him when he gets back. He's quite charming, in his way."

"Exactly where did he go?" Charles Lloyd asked.

"Oh, just to visit a friend."

My uncle frowned. "A woman, more than likely. He'd better watch himself, or he'll get into serious trouble."

"Norman is just a healthy boy," Helena replied.

"Norman is thirty years old, and he's an incurable woman chaser as you very well know. Remember the maid we had to discharge, and the girl in the village? I had to give her fifty pounds. It is always maids, always peasants. I don't know why he doesn't pick out a suitable young woman from among the local gentry and settle down. He could certainly have his choice. Their mothers parade them before him as though they were prize heifers, up for the highest bidder."

"Perhaps that's exactly why he doesn't want any of them."

"I thought you wanted Norman to marry?"

"Someday. Only if he is happy about it."

"He's too wild," my uncle said.

"He merely finds certain women irresistible."

"Well, at any rate he'd better be careful. Sowing a few wild oats is all well and good, but my nephew goes to excess."

"I'm sure he comes by it naturally, Charles," Helena said.

There was a barb to the remark, and it hit its target. My uncle fell silent, frowning. I wondered what my aunt's implication had been. Perhaps Norman Wade took after his uncle in his younger days. I could easily imagine Charles Lloyd chasing after women at thirty. He must have been even more magnetic at that age.

Aunt Helena made a few feeble efforts at small talk during the rest of the meal, but mostly we were silent. My uncle sat with his chin propped on his fist, staring sullenly at his plate, and Helena minced at her food, pushing it around with her fork. I was relieved when we rose from the table.

"Did you get the laudanum in London, Charles?" Helena asked.

"Yes, a good supply. It'll do you for quite some time."

"Laudanum?" I said. I knew it was a potion with an opium base. My mother had used it during her last days.

"Yes, dear," Helena said. "I'm an incurable insomniac. I can't sleep at all without a sedative. A few drops of laudanum in a glass of warm milk puts me right to sleep, and I sleep soundly the whole night through."

"Isn't it dangerous?" I asked.

She laughed lightly. "Not at all if it is taken in the proper dosage. The doctor prescribed it for me years ago, dear. I know how to use it safely." She touched my arm. "You are young and healthy. You will sleep beautifully and wake up feeling fit as can be. I used to be able to, but, sad to say, those days are gone for me."

We left the dining room and stepped into the main hallway. It was very late now, but Charles said he was going to read for a while in the library. Helena turned to me, taking both my hands in hers.

"I am going to putter about for a while," she said. "I want to check on the dogs, then I'll probably play solitaire if I can find my cards. Would you like to stay with me?"

"I'm very tired," I said.

"Of course you are. You've had an exhausting day. I'll get you a candle so that you can find your way back up to your room without any more mishaps."

I smiled, trying to stifle a yawn.

The bed was turned back when I reached my room, the yellow spread folded back neatly. My nightgown was at the foot of the bed, and Lucy was waiting, ready to help me undress. Her eyes drooped sleepily, and her head nodded, so I sent her away and made my own preparations for bed. The sheets were cool and crisp as I crawled between them. I blew out the lamp, lay there for a long time, watching the shadows and listening to the noises of the old house. After a while the wind died down and the house seemed to settle with a groan. I could hear the sea washing over the rocks below. It was a long, long time before sleep finally came.

VI

THE NEXT DAY WAS bleak and gray, with black clouds hovering low in the sky and thunder rumbling in the distance. Rain began to fall in heavy sheets, and the wind lashed at the trees outside and whistled through the cracks of the house. I could not help but be gloomy and depressed, but Aunt Helena was not content to let me mope about. She took me on a tour of the house. We went up and down, in and around, my mind soon losing track of the number of rooms we saw. Wearing a vivid red dress and smoking innumerable cigarettes, Helena kept up a bright line of chatter, pointing out treasured antiques, giving me a brief history of various pieces of furniture, and telling wickedly witty stories about people who had once lived at Falconridge. All the while the rain raged outside. Even Helena's vivacious personality could not ease the depression I felt, and I went to bed that night feeling tired, my head throbbing.

My second day at Falconridge, however, was a dazzling one. The sky was a luminous blue-gray, with strong white sunlight splashing over everything. The air, filled with the salty tang of the sea, was invigorating. Waking up very early, I flung open my bedroom window. I stood there feeling the touch of the delicious breeze on my cheeks. Full of energy and high spirits, the headache of the night before completely gone, I knew I could not stand to stay cooped up in the house. I wanted to explore the countryside; I wanted to go down to the seashore and watch the waves and collect shells.

I ate breakfast alone in the little room next to the kitchen, listening to the servants making noisy preparations for the day's meals. My aunt slept very late, I knew, and then had a tray brought up to her room. After finishing my ham and eggs, I nibbled on a biscuit spread with orange marmalade, waiting until it was time to send the tray up to my aunt. I heard a little bell jangle in the next room, and soon a servant came out carrying the tray. Taking it from her, I carried it up to my aunt's room myself. I knocked on the door and smiled to myself as I waited for her to admit me.

"Heavens, child!" she exclaimed. "Do you realize what time it is? It's positively immoral for you to look so bright and rosy-cheeked at this hour!"

"It's after ten," I said. "I've been waiting for you to wake up."

Helena groaned, sitting up in bed. She wore a white lace bed jacket trimmed with pink and blue rosebuds, and a frilly lace nightcap perched on her tousled curls. Simon, the brown and white spaniel, was curled up at the foot of the bed, nestled among the blue satin covers, his nose moist and twitching. It was hard to find room for the tray on the night table which was cluttered with all the things Helena liked to have on hand when she retired: a pot of rouge, a sleeping mask, the bottle of laudanum, a deck of cards, a horoscope chart, a box of chocolates wrapped in gold foil, a piece of rose quartz, several tattered French novels with the familiar yellow backs, a hammer, a glass and pitcher, a small blue vase holding half a dozen withered pink roses. I smiled at the profusion. If my aunt found it difficult to sleep, she was certainly prepared to get through the night in style.

"Just put it down anywhere," she said, somewhat irritably. "It's a beastly habit—food at this time of day. Do I look a fright? Hand me the rouge, will you? You'll find a brush and mirror and box of powder under the edge of the bed. No, no—don't open the drapes! Do you want to blind me!"

"It's a glorious day," I informed her.

"Bless you for your enthusiasm, dear."

"Didn't you sleep well?" I inquired.

"Tolerably. Just tolerably. I think I took a drop too much of laudanum. I had dreams all night long. I adore them, of course, but they are so tiring."

"Well, eat your breakfast. Then you'll feel better."

"Not for hours yet," she said. "Let me do my face first. I must look abominable...."

Aunt Helena made up her face, spilling powder on the bed, and merely picked at her breakfast, preferring to smoke a cigarette. There was a package of them in the pocket of her bed jacket, along with some matches. There was scratching at the door and I opened it to admit Adele and Philip who came bounding into the room and leaped on the bed. Simon growled, jealous of this invasion. Helena scolded all three of them and took great puffs of her cigarette.

"We must really see Lavinia about making you

some new clothes," she said, narrowing her eyes to keep the smoke out. "That dress is wretched, to say the least."

The dress was my oldest. It had once been jade green, but now almost all the color had faded. It was frayed at the sleeves, and there was a poorly repaired tear in the skirt. I was carrying an old wide brimmed hat of yellow straw, with a green ribbon around the rim. I explained to my aunt that I had put on these clothes because I wanted to go exploring.

"That's why I came to see you, actually," I said. "I wanted to know if you had anything planned for us for today."

"Nothing at all, dear. You're on your own at Falconridge. You may do anything you like, as long as it's within the law. I want you to feel free here."

"What are you going to do?" I asked.

"Fool around, putter. I'm going to have a look at Norman's rooms over the carriage house and see if they've been properly aired. He is supposed to come back today."

"Oh?" I said, trying not to show too much interest.

"Yes, the scoundrel. I'm eager for you two to meet. I'm sure you will like him."

"What kind of person is he? My uncle seems to think. . . ."

"Fiddlesticks! Charles and Norman have never gotten along. They're always at odds. Too much Lloyd in both of them. They don't see eye to eye about Falconridge, for one thing. Norman loves it. It is dear to him, in his blood. He's always wanting to make improvements on the place—open the closed wing and restore it to its former glory. Charles has let the place run down. Lack of interest, lack of money—Norman resents that."

"I see."

"Norman is perfectly charming. He may be a little hot tempered at times, at times a little too spirited, but he's a fine lad at heart."

"What time will he be back?"

"This afternoon—probably late. You run on and tromp about outside, dear. It will do you good. I'll see you later."

"You're sure you don't mind me going?"

"Oh, out with you," she cried, throwing up her hands in mock despair. "Run along, run along—you'll worry me to death."

I left my aunt's room, smiling, and went to get my sketch book. The long dark halls did not seem so grim now that I was familiar with them, and I could find my way about nicely in the parts of the house that were open. We hadn't gone into the closed wing yesterday, nor upstairs to the huge attic rooms, all locked and filled with discarded junk and trunks. I got my sketch book and crayons and hurried downstairs, going out the back way, onto the courtyard.

The sun glittered brightly on the flagstones. The sky shimmered overhead. The courtyard was neatly enclosed by a clipped box hedge, with the carriage house forming one side. It was a large building with a stone staircase leading to the rooms overhead. Strands of dusty green ivy clung to the gray stone. At the opening in the hedge three stone steps led down to the terraces and formal gardens. Some of the flowers were already in bloom, and I could smell the pungent odor of newly turned soil and manure and dead leaves mixed with the more pleasant aroma of blossoms.

I walked through the gardens, which were still lovely, though badly in need of work. Tall fruit trees spread shadows over the stone paths. Low stone fences separated the terraces, the sun bathing them. Roses were blooming, yellow and salmon and pink, and a swarm of tiny white butterflies fluttered over them. There was a large white stone pond, with leaves floating on the water and a cracked fountain in the center. Graceful willow trees, their yellow green branches dipping down, surrounded it. A narrow artificial stream wound throughout the gardens, bubbling over a bed of smooth round pebbles.

I passed through a grove of massive oak trees and walked down to the edge of the lawns. The grass was sparse here, the ground rocky. I looked down at the sea, at the huge waves washing over a narrow stretch of shore, churning over large gray stones, sending up flumes of foam. The water was green, turning bluer farther out, merging into a misty line of purple on the horizon. I could feel the power and magnitude of the sea, and it made me slightly dizzy. It dwarfed everything else, even the huge old house that stood far behind me now.

I stood there a long time, watching the water. A rough path, steep and rocky and dangerous, led down to the shore. I went down it carefully, holding on to the rocks and roots on either side. I scratched my knee on a rock, and once I almost fell. When I reached bottom, my head was swimming and when I looked back up and saw just how steep the path was I realized how foolhardy I had been. Yet it was wonderful to be so near the water.

The wind whipped at my skirts and hair, and I could feel the misty spray stinging my cheeks. I took off my shoes and walked in the damp sand.

Sitting on a flat gray rock in the edge of the water, and letting the waves wash over my bare feet, I felt at one with the elements. All the conflicting emotions of the past few weeks seemed to be driven away by the churning water and the brisk salty air. For the first time in months, I was almost happy, my mind completely free of worry. Here, with the elements raging, everything else seemed small and insignificant: my uncle and his belligerence, Martha Victor and her strange conduct, Falconridge itself with its shadowy halls and aura of mystery. I felt young and carefree, untouched by any of the solemn business of life.

I walked along the shore, the damp sand oozing between my toes. After a while I came up into the woods that bordered Falconridge. I sat on a stump and put my shoes on, deep in the brown and green interior of the woods. Tall trees spread their limbs in a tangle overhead, with only a few rays of sunlight stealing through to make pools of yellow on the ground. The trunks of the trees were covered with lichen and moss, and pinkish white mushrooms grew in little clusters at their base. The sound of the sea was distant now, hardly penetrating into this solitude. I wandered through the woods, pausing to listen to a bird, stopping to pluck the blossom of a wildflower. Thorns tore at my skirt, but I didn't care. I loved this sense of wildness and freedom.

Eventually I came to the road that led back to Falconridge. On the other side was a little clearing, overgrown with poppies. It was a lovely spot—the flowers violently red and golden orange, the grass long and yellow. I crossed the road and sat down in the clearing. Taking out my sketch book and crayons I began to draw a poppy. A bird perched on a branch of a tree, scolding me, and then soared away into the depths of the sky. It was all vivid blue now, with every trace of gray burned away by the sun. The heady odor of the poppies made me dizzy, and my eyelids began to feel heavy. I stretched languorously, yawning. I had exhausted myself with all the walking and climbing, and now I wanted to sleep.

The sound of horse's hoofs woke me out of my lethargy. I got up very quickly, fastening on my yellow straw hat and grabbing up my sketch book. Whoever it was was riding very fast. Standing at the edge of the clearing, I saw the magnificent black horse and the man who was riding him. The man saw me, too, and jerked the reins and pulled the horse to a stop, causing a cloud of dust. The horse was in a lather, stamping impatiently. The man sat casually in the saddle, one hand holding the reins, the other resting on his knee. He stared down at me, his eyes taking in every detail. Then he began to grin, his lips curling up slowly at one corner. I could feel a blush coloring my cheeks.

"It looks like I've been slipping," he said.

"I beg your pardon?"

"I thought I knew every pretty face in this country, but I've never seen yours before."

"I've just arrived in Cornwall," I said.

"That explains it then. Tell me, lass, what are you doing? Have you run away from your duties? Have you given the housekeeper the slip and taken an extra holiday?"

He had mistaken me for a housemaid. That wasn't surprising, as I must have looked like one in the old dress, thoroughly soiled with dirt now.

"Oh, no, Sir," I said. "It isn't that way at all."

"Don't try to alibi out of it, lass. I know the ways of you girls, always trying to get out of a little work, always getting into trouble. You'd much rather think about hair ribbons and country bucks than do a little work."

"Is that what you think?" I asked, my voice very cool.

"That's what I know, lass."

"You're pretty sure of yourself," I said.

"Do you know who I am?"

"No, and I'm sure I wouldn't care to."

"Ah, a saucy one. If there's anything I like, it's a lass with a little spirit. You and I are going to get along just fine, fine indeed."

"I'm afraid not," I said haughtily. "I don't care to associate with arrogant young men who go around insulting people they've never so much as been introduced to."

"La, la," he said, clicking his tongue. "Such airs! Delightful, absolutely delightful. Where did you learn to talk like that, lass?"

"That's none of your affair," I replied.

He slapped his knee and threw back his head, laughing. It was a rich, beautiful sound. He was a handsome fellow, with dark, dancing blue eyes and thick glossy black hair that fell in waves over his forehead and curled at the nape of his neck. His lips were large, and there was a deep cleft in his chin that gave his whole face a look of devilish merriment. He wore glossy black boots, tight black pants and a white linen shirt with full, gathered sleeves. It was open at the throat, exposing part of his chest.

He swung off the horse in one quick, graceful movement, and I saw that he was very tall, over six feet, with powerful shoulders and the fine muscular body of an athlete. He stood with his fists on his hips, his dancing blue eyes mocking me. He arched one thick black eyebrow, grinning. I backed away a little, not really frightened, although I could sense the strength and power of the man, and it disturbed me. I stared back at him, my chin held high.

"You've got a streak of dirt on your chin," he said, chuckling.

I wiped it away quickly, trying to keep my composure. He took a step towards me, holding his head down and looking up at me with his eyes. They were filled with mischief. I backed away, almost stumbling over a rock. My hat fell off, tumbling down among the poppies. I had already dropped my sketch book.

"You don't know who I am," he said. "I'll show you."

"Keep away from me," I replied.

"Are you afraid of me?" he asked, smiling.

"Not at all."

"Then why do you back away?"

"Go away," I said. "Get on your horse and go, or I'll...."

"You'll what?"

"Never mind. Just go!"

"I can't do that, not until I've taken a toll."

"A toll? What are you talking about?"

"You're trespassing. You're on my property.

You must pay a toll, or I won't let you go. Come here, lass, pay up."

I knew who he was then. I had sensed it all along. I was not going to let him know who I was, not just yet. I was certainly meeting my cousin in an unusual manner, and I wanted to see just how far he would go with his insolence.

"But I have no money," I said.

"It's not money I want," he replied, the grin broadening.

"Surely, Sir, I don't know what you could want then. I have no valuables...."

"We'll see," he cried.

He took my wrist and pulled me into his arms. He swung me around, holding me casually yet firmly against him. He was grinning as he covered my lips with his own. I tried to struggle, but his arms kept me imprisoned. He released me, laughing.

"There," he said, "paid in full."

I slapped him across the face as hard as I could. My hand stung with the force of it, but Norman Wade merely laughed. Then he seized me again, cupping his hand about my chin. "That calls for another," he said, and he kissed me again.

Then he let go of me. I stepped back, biting my lips. My eyes were blazing. I was angry with myself for letting the masquerade go so far, even angrier at Norman Wade for his intolerable conduct.

"Now do you know who I am?" he asked.

"You're the Devil!" I cried.

"With the ladies, yes. Ask the girls about Norman Wade. They'll tell you some pretty stories, lass."

"I'm sure of that!"

"La, la, such a temper. Now run along, lass, and you'd better not let me find you on this property again, or the toll will be much dearer, much dearer."

He walked back to his horse, swaggering a little. I watched as he mounted. He had the audacity to nod his head and wave before he rode away. I plucked a poppy and crushed it in my hand, consumed with anger. The day was spoiled for me, the peace and serenity gone. Norman Wade had destroyed it all, pulling me back into the world of emotions. Oh, yes, I knew who he was, and he was soon going to find out who I was. I was eager to see his expression when he did.

I was particular in my preparations for dinner that night. I wanted to look my best. I wore my best green taffeta and piled my hair in heavy curls on top of my head, fastening them with a black velvet ribbon. I had come back to Falconridge without meeting anyone, and now it was time to go down for the evening meal. Lucy fussed over me, chattering about the arrival of Norman Wade and how she knew I would like him. I tried to hush her up, but she smiled, looking pleased with herself.

"I know why you're dressin' so elegant," she said. "All the ladies want to look their best for 'im."

"How ridiculous," I retorted. "Do stop jabbering, Lucy. I am tired of listening to you."

"You look so lovely," she said, smiling happily. "Wouldn't it be nice if you'n Mr. Norman were to. . . ."

"That will be enough!" I said sharply.

I was deliberately late for dinner. They were already in the dining room, waiting for me. I paused for a moment at the door, holding my breath, then I sailed in, smiling, the taffeta skirts rustling. My uncle and Norman Wade were standing at the side table. Aunt Helena was fidgeting with her fan, glancing at the clock.

"Here she is!" she exclaimed. "Dear, I want you to meet Norman. He's been asking about you."

He turned around. He slowly arched an eyebrow, and his lips gave a little twitch, but other than that he showed no surprise. He was in complete control of himself. He bowed politely and took my hand, kissing it gallantly. I thought I noted a dark glimmer of anger in his eyes. He was very elegantly dressed in a suit of dove gray and a vest of sky blue satin, sewn with tiny black leaves. A lock of his glossy black hair had fallen across his forehead when he bowed, and he pushed it back. I could sense his animosity.

"Lauren has been tromping about in the woods today," Helena said. "She wanted to explore a bit, see the countryside."

"Oh? And did you meet anyone, Miss Moore?" he asked.

"No one worth mentioning," I replied sweetly.

"I do hope you two are going to get along," Helena exclaimed. "It's so nice for us all to be together like this."

"I am certain my cousin and I shall get along," he replied. "She is a charming, delightful creature, Aunt, full of the most unusual traits. Very accomplished."

"Accomplished?" my aunt said, slightly puzzled.

"Why, look at her. Such poise, such refinement.

One would hardly take her for a peasant."

"Not unless one were very foolish," Helena replied.

"Foolish is as foolish does," Norman Wade said, looking at me from under his long black lashes. "Men are strange creatures, Aunt. It's very easy to make a fool of them—once. But once you make a fool of them, you find it very hard to do it a second time."

"Unless that is their nature," I added, smiling politely.

"Let's stop this mysterious talk and eat," my uncle said, impatient with the conversation.

We sat down and the servants began to bring in the food. Norman Wade sat directly across from me, and although he talked charmingly with my aunt, he did not address a single word to me. Once, during a lull, I caught his eyes on me. I stared at him boldly. Seeing the dark blue flash in his eyes, I knew that he blamed me entirely for this afternoon's incident. I lowered my eyes demurely. He *had* made a fool of himself, but perhaps he had been taught a lesson by it. He would not be so likely to accost young women now, I thought, at least without hesitating first.

"We must have a party," Helena was saying, "a grand affair to celebrate Lauren's arrival. Don't you think so, Charles? We haven't thrown open Falconridge for a long time. We'll invite everyone, the Vicar, Lady Randall and that stupid husband of hers, Mr. and Mrs. Henderson, all the gentry. What fun. . . ."

"If it would please you, Helena," Charles Lloyd said, obviously quite bored by the idea.

"And the music—we must have music so that

the young people can dance. Yes, the ballroom hasn't been used in so long...."

"It would be quite expensive," Norman Wade said.

"Tish! Who cares about money if there is fun to be had?"

"All of us had better start caring," he replied. "I've been going over the books. Things are not well. If this year's harvest isn't good, we might be in a bad shape, really bad shape."

"Don't be a wet blanket, Norman. Very well, I'll draw on my personal account. There isn't much—but there's enough for a party, surely. If not—I'll hock the jewels!"

"I wasn't speaking in jest, Aunt," he said solemnly.

"Neither was I," she replied airily. She turned to me.

"It will be so exciting, making plans. It'll take at least a month to get everything ready. The first thing we are going to do is go see Lavinia about your clothes. Several dresses, I would think, and a grand ball gown, something spectacular to show you off to all the neighbors. I am wondering if white satin...."

"How is that?" Charles Lloyd asked, addressing himself to Norman Wade and referring to his earlier remark.

"You know how poor the yield was last year. There was the blight, you remember, those damn grasshoppers. The tenants are complaining this year. They're not happy with the seed—inferior grade, they say, and your man Graystone hasn't provided enough fertilizer...."

"So you two have been at it again?" my uncle said.

"No. I stopped by a couple of the farms on the way home. I talked to the men. I saw the conditions for myself. I saw just how slovenly Graystone has been in his duties. There was a lack of tools, for one thing, and on one farm the barn had been damaged by the winds and Graystone hadn't done anything about getting it repaired."

"He will in time," Charles Lloyd replied.

"In time!" Norman Wade answered heatedly. "How can you be so disinterested? The estate is going steadily downhill, and you sit there sipping your wine and won't even listen to me...."

"Falconridge doesn't belong to you yet, Norman," Charles Lloyd said coldly. I could see that he was not happy with his nephew's words. Both men were on the verge of anger. I could sense the tension between them. Helena stopped her chattering about the party, frowning.

"I'm well aware of that," Norman Wade replied. "If it did, Graystone would have been sacked months ago."

"Graystone is a perfectly good bailiff, Norman. He may not have a fine college education like you, but just because he didn't go to Oxford doesn't mean he can't run this estate."

"Graystone is a blundering, slovenly oaf! If I weren't here to look after the place, Lord knows where we would be. I simply can't understand why you keep the man on. Sometimes I think...."

"What do you think, Nephew?" my uncle asked. His eyes were black with anger, and his cheeks were a little flushed. His hands were balled into fists on the table in front of him.

"Sometimes I think he is holding something over you," Norman Wade replied, speaking very slowly.

"Sometimes I think you are afraid to let him go. That's the only reason I can think of for your keeping such an incompetent lout on the place."

My uncle stood up and tossed his napkin on the table. I could see him fighting to control his rage. A vein throbbed in his temple, and he was white about the lips. He looked formidable. Helena clasped her hands together, a deep furrow creasing her brows. I had gone a little pale myself.

"That will do," Charles Lloyd said. "That will do quite well for now, Nephew. I think you've gone a bit far this time. Yes, I think you've gone just a bit far."

He walked out of the room without losing his dignity. I had to admire the way he had handled himself. Norman Wade sat back from the table, one leg tossed over the arm of his chair. He had his napkin balled up in one hand, and he stared down at his plate sullenly, his hair falling over his forehead.

"Oh dear," Helena said. "Must you two always bicker like this, Norman? It's in deplorable taste—and in front of Lauren, too. What will she think of us?"

"I am sure my dear cousin would prefer to see the true side of the family," he said, tossing the napkin on the table. "We don't want her to have false ideas. She may have been sheltered in her private school, but this is real life."

"Real life needn't be filled with rudeness," Helena said, rising. She gathered up her skirts and walked to the door, very regal in her movements. "I am going up to my room now, children. Do either of you want anything before I go?"

"I think I'll take a walk in the gardens," I said.

"Some fresh air will do me good."

Helena and I left the room together, leaving Norman Wade sitting there with the candles guttering on the deserted table. I left Helena in the main hall and went outside. It was quite cool. Chilly zephyrs of breeze stroked my bare shoulders, but I welcomed the discomfort after the tension in the dining room.

The sky was banked with dark, restless clouds that moved slowly across its surface. Luminous rays of moonlight poured through, although the moon itself was temporarily obscured. The courtyard was very dark, spread with dark shadows from the hedge. In one corner was a patch of moonlight and there the flagstones gleamed dark blue, coated with silver. The hedge rustled in the breeze, and the sound of the sea was very loud. I walked down the steps and into the gardens.

It was calm here, restful. The gardens looked strangely eerie by moonlight, all moonlight-blue and gray with dark patches of black. The shadows were thick, moving across the pathway like live things. I went down to the pond where the water rippled in the breeze, very black, with shimmering streaks of silver. A moonbeam bathed the cracked fountain, gilding it, and a frog plopped off of it, splashing into the water. I shivered as the branches of a willow tree brushed against me.

I was strangely puzzled by all this talk about Andrew Graystone. I had only been here two days, and yet his name had come up over and over again. Lavinia's husband certainly made his presence felt around Falconridge. I wondered what kind of man he was. If he was such a brute, why did Lavinia continue to live with him? If he was so slovenly, why did my uncle retain his services? I thought about what Norman Wade had said. Could the man be blackmailing Charles Lloyd in some way? I found the idea highly unlikely. Charles Lloyd was not the kind of man to be blackmailed. He didn't care enough about what people thought to want to hide anything from them.

I thought about Norman Wade. He was undeniably handsome, and I was sure he had overwhelming charm when he chose to exercise it, but as far as I was concerned he was thoroughly unpleasant. He had seemed to resent my presence at the dinner table. Of course I had made a fool of him this afternoon, but that was hardly reason enough for those dark looks he had given me. It went deeper than that.

I found myself wondering if there really was something about Falconridge that touched those who lived within its walls. No one seemed to be happy. I knew that although she tried to hide them by her chatter, even my aunt had moments of deep depression, and she had to take laudanum in order to sleep at night. I wondered what it was about the place. Lucy had mentioned an evil spell. That was ridiculous, of course, but still there was a certain atmosphere that seemed to cause restless feelings. Perhaps it was the constant sound of the sea and wind.

I don't know how long I stood there, watching the strands of silver moonlight swimming in the dark water. The moon came out from behind the bank of clouds and poured radiant light over everything, only to be obscured a few moments later by wisps of cloud. Leaves rustled, and the wind moaned, sounding forlorn. I was sad, and I didn't know why. The gardens were suddenly depressing to me, the cracked fountain, the shabby borders. I turned to go back inside, and I gasped when I saw the tall dark form standing a few yards away from me.

"Thinking of something?" Norman Wade asked.

I had not heard his footsteps, and I wondered how long he had been beside the trellis, watching me. He was smoking a cheroot, and the dark orange butt glowed brightly in the shadows. I could smell the burning tobacco. He tossed the cheroot aside. It made a vivid orange streak as it flew across the darkness. Norman Wade stepped towards me.

"Maiden by moonlight," he said, "lovely picture."

"If you came out here to be rude to me . . ." I began.

"No," he said, "I didn't come to be rude, though I probably shall. It's a habit with me."

"I've noticed that," I replied.

"You've got a sharp tongue, Miss Moore."

"Have I?"

"Most assuredly. In fact, you're not at all what you should be. You should be shy and docile. You should lower your eyes when men speak to you. You should be inside now, working on your embroidery or reading a sentimental novel. You should faint frequently and always have a bottle of smelling salts on hand."

"I've never fainted in my life," I told him, my voice icy.

"I don't doubt it. I don't doubt it at all. You certainly succeeded in making a fool of me this afternoon."

"You had it coming, Mr. Wade."

"Yes, I suppose I did. You knew who I was all along, didn't you?"

"I suspected it."

"And yet you went right along with your little game? I don't think I owe you an apology for what happened. I think you had it coming. You were lucky to get off so lightly."

He laughed, a dry, short laugh that was not at all pleasant. I could see his face in the moonlight. It looked very solemn. The jaw was thrust forward and one brow was arched like a dark wing. The moon came out from behind the clouds again, scattering silver spangles of light over everything. Norman Wade looked beyond me, at the fountain. He seemed to be turning some problem over in his mind. For a moment he seemed to have forgotten my presence.

"Well, so you're at Falconridge," he said finally. "Now what do we do about it?"

"What do you mean?"

"I mean, how do we get you away from here."

"I don't understand what you're talking about."

"You don't? Then I'll explain. Falconridge is no place for a young woman, Miss Moore, particularly a headstrong young woman like you. It is big and dark and brooding. It's isolated. Falconridge is a place for losers in life. It's no place for youth."

"You want me to leave?" I asked.

"I never wanted you to come in the first place."

"Evidently my aunt did."

"Helena is a marvelous person, and I adore her, but she's very foolish at times, very foolish indeed. She lives in her own little world. She has drawn a self-protective shell around her. Nothing can penetrate it. I admire her for that. For her, that is the best way. She is blind to anything that does not fit into her self-imposed routine. When the letter arrived from London, I tried to keep her from sending for you. I told her you would not fit in at Falconridge."

"But she sent for me just the same."

"Yes. She felt it was her duty. She wanted to help you. She wanted a companion. I told her it would be better to send enough money for you to continue on at the school, but that wouldn't do."

"So now I'm here, Mr. Wade. There isn't much you can do about it."

"Perhaps not," he said. "I can try to make you see things clearly. I can try to talk some sense into you."

"Why don't you want me here?" I asked bluntly.

"Why? Because—because you don't belong. You will not be happy. I don't want to see you get hurt."

"Hurt?"

"Miss Moore, I have some money. I am willing to pay your expenses through the rest of the school year. You can go back and join all your friends. I will see that you are nicely provided for. I have some connections in London. I will see that you find some kind of suitable employment when you graduate. How does that sound to you?"

"It sounds perfectly loathsome, Mr. Wade. I have no intentions of leaving Falconridge. I have a right to be here. I am not going to leave just to satisfy your—your greed."

"Greed?" he said, surprised.

"Surely that's why you want me to go. You are going to inherit Falconridge. You are the sole heir.

You are afraid I might take something away from you. You might not get everything. Helena might leave me her jewels or some other valuables. I can see through your little scheme."

"Is that what you think this is all about?" he asked.

"That's exactly what I think!"

"You poor child."

"I am eighteen years old."

"Terribly young, terribly vulnerable...."

"I can take care of myself, Mr. Wade."

"I don't think so," he said.

"I certainly don't need anything from you."

"You don't think much of me, do you?" he asked.

"I'm afraid I don't, Mr. Wade. Now if you will excuse me...."

I started to walk past him. He reached out and took my arm. I tried to pull away, but his strong fingers gripped me firmly. He looked down into my eyes. His face was dark with anger, and for a moment I thought he was going to strike me. Then he shook his head, slowly, his mouth turned down.

"I'm sorry," he said, releasing me. "This has all been for your own good. You'll understand that some day."

"I think I understand perfectly," I retorted.

"No, Lauren, you don't. Until you do...."

"Until then I will stay out of your way, Mr. Wade," I snapped. "I shall try to keep my presence here from being a hardship to you. You do not need to worry about me."

"I only wish that were true," he said quietly.

He laid his hands on my shoulders, and he looked into my eyes, his head tilted a little to one side. There was a smile on his lips but his eyes were pensive. He seemed to be reflecting on something, thinking about another time, another girl perhaps. The moonlight fell across his face, sculpting it in silver. I stood rigidly, filled with anger, but I felt something else, too, something that I did not want to examine too closely.

"Too bad," he said quietly. "Another time—under other circumstances, we could have—perhaps...." He cut himself short, and his eyes grew darker. "If I let myself," he said, "I could...."

"You could do what?"

"This...." he replied softly.

He bent down and kissed my lips. His own were firm and hard, pressing against mine, and his arms wrapped around me, drawing me to him. I was lost to sensation for a moment. There was nothing but those lips on mine, probing gently, and those strong arms holding me against him. He released me abruptly. I almost fell. He held my arm, supporting me. I felt weak, too weak to strike out at him.

"Why?" I whispered. "Why did you do that?"

"You don't know? You really don't know?"

I shook my head. My lower lip quivered.

"Little girls should be kept in school. They should be kept away from great big men. Little girls should do embroidery and paint water colors and read proper novels. They should be kept locked up...."

His voice was cold, hard. I looked up at his face. It was lined with anger, the eyes dark, the lips turned down. It terrified me, and at the same time it was fascinating. I wanted to rake my nails across that face, and I wanted to reach up and stroke it gently.

"It would be so easy," he said.

"What would be?"

"I am a gentleman. I won't discuss it."

"Why did you kiss me?" I asked, my voice calmer now.

"Run away, little girl," he retorted. "Run away, before you find out."

"Before I find out what?"

"That little girls can get hurt—so easily."

"You...."

"Go!" he shouted.

I went past him and hurried up the steps to the courtyard. The wind was stronger now. The limbs of the trees creaked and groaned. Far below the waves crashed against the rocks. I stood in the courtyard, looking up at the huge old house. The wind tore at my skirts, whipping them violently about my legs. Falconridge was very still. The windows were like dark eyes, watching me. The house seemed to be waiting to swallow me up. I caught my breath, thinking of what Norman Wade had done. He had wanted to frighten me, just like Martha Victor. They wanted me to leave. I did not know why, but I intended to find out. They were both going to find that I had a will of my own. I was here at Falconridge, and nothing was going to drive me away.

VII

THE NEXT TWO WEEKS passed very quickly. Helena and I went to see Lavinia Graystone about new dresses for me, and we were soon caught up in a flurry of activity. We spent hour after hour choosing materials, deciding on patterns, leafing through all the fashion magazines to see what would be most flattering. There were many trips to and from Dower House. Lavinia was charming and very patient, but I felt that she was a little awed by Helena. She was reserved and a little distant when talking with my aunt, always polite, always respectful, yet never speaking unless she was first spoken to. She was far more relaxed and natural on the occasions when I went to Dower House alone.

In addition to all the dressmaking activity, Helena was going ahead with her plans for the party. The servants were in the process of a full scale cleaning job. Windows were washed until they glittered, floors were waxed until they shone with a golden brown sheen, rugs were dusted, furniture was taken outside and revarnished. A troop of men had come in to touch up the gilding on the walls and ceiling of the ballroom. It was a gorgeous room with ivory walls and a sky blue ceiling, both adorned with a profusion of gilt swirls and leaves and flowers. Now it was a swarm of men and paint buckets and cloths and ladders, with Helena in the middle, giving orders, making threats, shouting, smoking too many cigarettes. I had to use much persuasion to keep her from scrambling up a ladder and doing the job herself.

When she was not bothering the workmen or harrying the servants, she was stationed in the front parlor where she sat at the tiny rosewood desk making out invitations on cream colored stationery and compiling endless lists of things that must be done before the big night. I was afraid so much activity would tire her, but she scoffed at the idea. It was good for her, she claimed. She had never felt better. Indeed, she seemed to thrive on the work. Her blue eyes sparkled and her step was light as she flew from one part of the house to another, always chattering and ordering people about. Lucy told me that the Mistress had not looked so well in months.

My uncle kept out of the way as best he could. He went riding every day and when he was at home he kept himself closed up in the library with a pile of leather bound ledgers, going over accounts and adding figures. In the few occasions when I saw him, he was grim and unpleasant, preoccupied with serious matters. Once I almost collided with him on the stairs. He caught me by the arm to keep us both from falling, and then he looked at me for a long time, holding my arm, not saying a word. Then he told me I must be careful of accidents, as he wouldn't want anything to happen to me. I laughed pleasantly, but Charles Lloyd did not even smile. He went on down the stairs, slapping the side of his leg with his riding crop. I tried to avoid him as much as possible.

I saw Norman Wade only once. He got up early every morning and rode out to inspect the tenant farms, coming in after sundown. He no longer took the evening meal with us, claiming he was too tired to dress for it. He would prefer a simple meal in his lodgings over the carriage house, he said, until he was finished with his tours of inspection. I suspected the real reason had to do with me. He did not want to sit face to face with me every evening and be forced to make polite conversation. I was glad he had excused himself. The ordeal would have been as bad for me as for him. I dreaded the evening meal as it was, for my uncle sat with a frown most of the time, speaking gruffly if at all.

One afternoon I went to the courtyard to watch the sun set. I had had a day full of fittings, and after that I had helped Helena select the menu for the night of the party. I was very tired, and it was relaxing to watch the dark golden streamers of sunlight dissolving slowly into a dark blue sky. The sea made a gentle, whispering sound as it washed up on the shore, and the air was very still. All three spaniels were with me. They scampered about, sniffing at the hedges and playing with one another. I was lost in thought when I heard footsteps on the flagstone. The dogs began to bark happily, and I turned around to see them rushing to greet Norman Wade.

He was evidently just coming in from the fields. His boots and his tight brown pants were covered with dust and his white linen shirt was soiled with perspiration. He knelt down to fondle the dogs. His face was tanned from being out in the sun every day, the dark skin making a startling contrast with the vivid blue eyes. The dogs clamored about him, vying for his attention. He looked up at me, still petting the dogs. Then he stood up, throwing his shoulders back. He seemed exhausted, and I knew he really had been working hard.

"Good afternoon, Lauren," he said. He smiled. The smile seemed sincere. "How have you been?" His voice was pleasant.

"Just fine," I said, my own voice cold and haughty.

"Still mad?"

"Not at all," I replied.

"Then you are cold by nature, not by choice," he said, laughing to himself.

He made a little bow and went on up the steps to his lodgings. I was sorry I had spoken so harshly, and I wished I had not been wearing my oldest dress. I stayed there in the courtyard until the last streak of gold faded away and the sky grew misty purple. When I went inside, the crickets had begun to chirp under the stones and I was chiding myself for weakening in my attitude towards the man. I must be on my guard against his charm. I knew to succumb to it would mean trouble for me. He was a scoundrel, I told myself, regardless of how handsome he might be, and I must never forget that.

Martha Victor was civil whenever I happened to see her. She spent most of her time in the servants' quarters, overseeing their duties. She nodded to me when I passed her in the hall, but I could still feel her animosity. Once or twice I caught her staring at me but when I looked up she averted her eyes quickly, pretending to examine a spot of dust or a crack in the woodwork. Helena assured me that Martha was nasty to everyone but the Master of

Falconridge and just laughed when I told her I thought the housekeeper didn't like me.

If Martha was unfriendly, Lucy made up for it. She was like a merry little magpie, coming into my room every morning to wake me up and chatter. She kept my things in perfect order and would have waited on me hand and foot had I allowed it. She gossiped blithely, and I soon knew everything about the servants' private lives and the habits of half the county. Lucy had a vivid imagination, and I discounted most of what she said. One morning she told me she had seen someone in a black cloak moving across the front lawn, leaving the house, and when I told her it must have been a shadow, she swore it was a mysterious figure and that she had not been able to sleep for the rest of the night. I laughed at her, giving her a new blue ribbon for her long blonde hair.

I had grown accustomed to the noises in the night at Falconridge. I could identify the shutters flapping, the creaks in the floorboard, the wind coming down the chimneys, the branches scratching against the windows. For a while I had lain awake nervously, listening intently to all the strange sounds, my imagination summoning up all sorts of fantasies, but after a few nights I no longer paid any attention to them. After spending the days trying to keep up with Helena's pace, I was generally much too tired to do anything but climb in bed and go to sleep.

I was making preparations to go to the village one morning two weeks after I had talked with Norman Wade in the gardens. Lavinia needed some thread and lining material, and Helena had a whole list of little things she needed. I wanted to go myself rather than send one of the servants, as I had never been to the village before and would enjoy the outing. I would drive the light phaeton with the gentle dappled gray horse, and it would be pleasant.

Eager to be gone, I hurried downstairs to find Helena. I wore one of the dresses Lavinia had already finished—a rustling white silk with tiny blue and pink print flowers. It had puffed sleeves and a very full skirt that billowed as I darted down the hall and into the living room. Helena was at her desk, sorting through piles of paper. She looked irritated about something, a frown on her face. She took an angry puff on her cigarette and looked up at me with snapping blue eyes.

"Oh dear, I've lost the list," she exclaimed. "I had it here or at least I thought I did! Have you seen it, Lauren?"

"No, Helena. Are you sure. . . ?"

"I may have left it in the library," she said. "I went in there to get a new pen. Would you be a dear and run look? It would be somewhere about the desk, probably, if it's there at all."

I smiled at her irritation and went down the hall to the library. It was one of my favorite rooms. The shelves were varnished golden oak, and they contained thousands of books, all of them in uniform sets of orange and brown and burnt gold leather, their bindings gleaming. The carpet of dark gray, the huge fireplace of gray marble, and the comfortable sofa and chairs of brown leather gave it an informal, relaxed atmosphere. I could smell the pleasant aromas of tobacco and leather and paste and the musty smell of old paper. My uncle's desk sat in a corner, piled with papers and ledgers and a tray full of cigar butts. He had forbidden the servants to touch his desk, which explained the disorder.

I looked through the papers, but I could not find Helena's list. I moved the ledgers and looked under them, trying to put everything back as it had been as I knew my uncle would be furious if he thought someone had been prowling about his desk. I opened the top drawer to see if Helena had accidently dropped the list there when she got the pen. I moved some papers, and then I saw the curious scratch pad. I took it out, examining it.

My uncle had written his name several times in his strong, forceful handwriting, shaping the letters boldly. Then he had written the name Andrew Graystone and crossed it out. Below this there were a few illegible scribbles and marks, the kind a man will make when he is thinking, and then he had written his own name over again several times in an awkward, almost illiterate scrawl, deliberately making the handwriting poor and messy. I held the sheet up, puzzled by it, wondering what he had been thinking about when he had made these scrawls.

I was startled when the door opened. I dropped the sheet back into the drawer hastily and turned around. Martha Victor was standing just inside the room, her large face expressing disapproval. I do not know why I should have felt guilty, but I did as she stared at me with those sullen black eyes. She moved towards me slowly.

"You know your uncle doesn't allow anyone to fool about his desk, Miss Moore," she said.

"I was looking for my aunt's shopping list. She said she may have left it here." I felt exactly like a child who has been caught in some small misdemeanor, and I was irritated with myself for the feeling.

Martha Victor was standing beside me now. She had an unpleasant odor, some sharp, sour smell which probably came from the ointment she used on her iron gray hair. She looked down and saw the opened drawer, with the scratch pad on top. After rearranging the papers in the drawer, she closed it. Then she sorted through the things on top of the desk, pulling out Helena's list. It had been stuck in one of the ledgers, and I hadn't seen it.

"Is this what you were looking for?" she asked primly.

"Thank you," I said, taking it from her.

"Your uncle will be very displeased if he finds out that you were going through his things, Miss Moore. Very displeased."

"Do you intend to tell him?" I asked.

"Not this time," she replied, her voice low.

I left the library, turning at the door to glance back at the woman. She was standing at the desk, her face hard. She seemed angry as though she had caught me doing something criminal. I closed the door behind me, trying to rid myself of the sensation of guilt.

Helena was elated that I had found the list. She made a few hasty additions to it and then handed it back to me. The phaeton was waiting for me in front of the drive, the groom holding the horse by the bridle. He helped me into the seat, handed me the reins, and I drove away from Falconridge, the wheels crunching on the crushed shell drive. It was delightful to be out in the open air after the scene with Martha. I reveled in the fresh air that touched my face and the warm sunlight that sparkled brightly.

The drive to the village was pleasant. I drove slowly, letting the horse take his own pace. I passed through the woods and saw the clearing where I had had my first encounter with Norman Wade. The memory of the event caused me to smile bitterly. Only two weeks had passed, and yet it seemed to have happened in the distant past. There had been so much activity since then. I wondered if Norman Wade would ever forgive me for my little deception, and I wondered if I would ever forget the sensations I had felt when his lips were on mine.

The road curled out of the woods and into the open countryside, all bathed in the radiant sunlight. There were large rugged fields behind the split wooden fences. The fields rolled over hills, the rich furrows of soil reddish brown, some of them emerald green with growing crops. I saw men working in the fields pushing primitive plows behind slow moving oxen. I passed farm houses, shabby little dwellings on the side of the hills, not nearly as nice as the large red barns with their tall, round silos. I knew this was where the tenants lived. It was hard to believe that all this land and all these farms were a part of Falconridge.

I reached the crest of a hill and started down towards the village. It rested in a little cove, the buildings clustered around a sparkling blue harbor. A fleet of small fishing boats bobbed on the water, and there was an enormous naval vessel anchored there, the sun making bright bursts of light on its wales. Her Majesty's flag fluttered proudly from its mast. The tall bronze spire of the church steeple rose above the roofs and the tops of gigantic oak trees, towering up to touch the steel blue sky.

I could sense an atmosphere of festivity in the air as I drove into the village, caused, no doubt, by the naval vessel. All the villagers were out, greeting the sailors and hoping to sell goods to them. I drove past the village green where children played around a tarnished bronze statue. Farm wagons were parked around the square, and old men in straw hats sat on the benches, chewing tobacco and talking. I left the phaeton in front of the hardware store and did my shopping quickly. One of the shopkeepers told me that the ship was on its way to America on some mission or other, and this would be one of its last stops before it moved across the ocean. Few ships ever stopped at the humble little village and it was quite an event.

My shopping done, I strolled along the streets, shaded by the limbs of the oak trees. The little shops were white and blue and pale green, all neat and clean. The sidewalks were narrow, the cobbled streets taking up most of the room. Blond haired sailors in crisp uniforms thronged about the streets in small groups, laughing, pointing, all blue-eyed, with fresh, boyish faces and muscular bodies. The village girls were in their best dresses, strolling along in pairs and openly flirting with the sailors. My arms laden with packages, I paused to admire some hats in the window of the milliner's shop, then walked on down to the piers.

There were even more sailors here, watching the fishermen patch the salt-encrusted nets that were strung up on poles at the edge of the water. Some of the nets were still wet, with glittering fish scales caught up in them catching the sunlight. The men had seamed, weathered faces, and they worked silently, mending the nets and ignoring their audience. Women with baskets of fish stepped over coils of rope and poured the fish into briny barrels. A girl with long black hair was surrounded by sailors. She wore a vivid red dress, and large golden earrings dangled from her ears. The sailors whooped with laughter at something she said, and she threw back her head, smiling at all of them.

A man was selling salt water taffy at a little cart, and I stepped over to buy some. As I did so, I noticed a young man watching me. He was wearing a pair of faded blue denim pants and a sleeveless blue and white striped jersey that exposed the tanned, muscular arms folded over his chest. He leaned against a pole, his sun bleached hair falling in waves over his forehead, his dark brown eyes following me as I bought the taffy. The man nodded at me. He was obviously a fisherman, a burly lad who loitered about the pier when there was no work to be done. I gave him a haughty glance, turning to go back toward the phaeton.

As I did so, I saw something that made me stop abruptly. My uncle was at the other end of the pier talking with a sailor. Charles Lloyd had a letter in his hand, and I saw him give it to the sailor, who nodded vigorously and stuck the envelope in his pocket. Then my uncle took out some money and thrust it into the lad's extended palm. They talked for a moment longer before the sailor turned and walked away. My uncle watched him leaving, a look of satisfaction on his face.

I wondered what in the world he could have been talking to the sailor about and what kind of letter he could have given to the boy. My uncle hated the village, I had heard him say so several times, and he avoided coming here. Yet there he was, an incongruous sight on the crowded pier. He was wearing glossy brown boots, a handsome brown suit, and a vest of yellow satin stitched with small brown designs. He wore a tall brown hat and carried his riding crop.

I did not want him to see me. I started to hurry away, but I was stopped by the man who had been leaning against the pole. He stood in my path, blocking the way. His hands were on his hips, a broad grin on his face. There was a long pink scar across his cheek, and his brown eyes were full of mischief. When I moved to go around him, he moved too, still in my way.

"Let me help you with those packages," he said. "That's a big load for a little girl like you to handle alone."

"I can manage quite well, thank you," I replied frostily.

"Where did you come from, little girl? I ain't never seen you down here before."

"Will you please step out of my way," I said.

"Now, don't be rude. I was just bein' friendly."

I tried to move around him again, and again he blocked my way. He smelled of ale. I clutched my packages, suddenly very nervous. I did not know what to do.

"There's a nice little tavern just down the pier," he said. "Why don't you come have a drop with me? You're a pretty little thing, you know, and a stranger in town. Jake here will show you around."

"No, thank you," I said, my voice trembling a little. "Now get out of my way."

"You ain't bein' friendly," he said, menace in his

voice. "I ask you to come have a little drop and you ain't friendly at all. Come on, now. I ain't goin' to hurt you. . . ."

He took my arm. I dropped my packages, trying to pull away from him. He laughed huskily. His eyes were sparkling now. The smell of ale was overwhelming.

"Let go of her," Charles Lloyd said.

The man looked up, belligerent. Charles Lloyd stood quite calmly, his eyes flat. The man released me and stepped back, an ugly look on his face. He doubled up his fists and narrowed his eyes.

"You stay out of this, Mister," he said. "It ain't none of your affair."

"Come along, Lauren," my uncle said, ignoring the man.

I gathered up my packages, looking up at the two men nervously. I saw the man called Jake rear back, ready to strike. As he did, Charles Lloyd struck him violently across the face with his riding crop. The man cried out, stunned. There was a large red gash on his jaw, and he touched the blood, his eyes full of amazement. My uncle waited calmly, ready to deal another blow if necessary. The man backed away, unprepared for such a cool, vicious adversary.

Charles Lloyd took the packages from me and led me away from the pier. His face was inscrutable. He seemed calm and collected, walking in long, self-assured strides as though nothing had happened. He never once looked back to see if the man were following us. He did not acknowledge the stares of those people who had witnessed the scene and watched us with curiosity. I hurried along beside him, my cheeks pink with shame over the incident. I felt that he blamed me for it. We were on the shady sidewalks of the village proper before he spoke.

"You came alone?" he asked.

"Yes, in the phaeton. It's in front of the hardware store."

"I'll drive you home. I'll send a servant back for my horse."

"You don't have to do that," I protested. "I can manage. . . ."

"But it seems you can't, Lauren," he replied acidly. "I might add that respectable young women do not wander about the pier unescorted. It's fortunate for you I had business here today."

"I'm sorry. I didn't. . . ."

"You attract trouble. You seem to have no idea how to conduct yourself in the proper manner. That's most unfortunate. It seems I'll have to keep a tighter rein on you in the future. You are not to come to the village again without my permission."

"But, Aunt Helena said. . . ."

"Don't argue with me, Lauren. I've had enough trouble with you for one day. I am the Master of Falconridge. As long as you stay there, you will do as I say."

Neither of us said a word during the drive back to Falconridge. My uncle drove slowly. I felt that he was deliberately holding himself back and that he wanted to whip the horse into a lather and race madly. I could feel his anger. Strangely enough, I felt that the anger was not caused by the incident with the man on the pier. It was directed against me, but I felt there was some other explanation for it. He was angry not because he had had to rescue me from the advances of a stranger, but for some other reason I could not fathom. I sat beside him, my eyes straight ahead, holding the packages in my lap. My uncle gripped the reins very tightly, and I saw his knuckles were white. It was all very puzzling, very puzzling indeed.

VIII

LUCY LOOKED PERTURBED the next morning as she came into my room. Her thin face was pale, and there were shadows around her downcast eyes as though she had just been scolded. She moved about in a doleful manner, all her bright vivacity gone. Her pale blonde hair had not been combed, and she was not nearly so neat as she usually was. Curious, I asked her what was wrong. She looked up with large blue eyes, hesitating before she answered.

"Ma and I've been quarreling," she said. "She hit me, called me a meddler and a chatterbox and told me to keep my mouth shut."

"What brought all this on?"

"I'd better not say, Miss Lauren. Ma just got mad when I told her. She didn't believe me. You won't either. I'd better not say."

"Don't be tiresome, Lucy. Tell me what happened. And stop fussing around the dressing table. Look at me and tell me what caused the quarrel."

Lucy put down her dust rag. She looked very pathetic in the old black dress that had clearly been handed down to her. It was too short, badly frayed at the sleeves, and the material was shiny from too much wear. Only her apron was new, crisp and white. Lucy perched on the window seat, looking down at her thin hands. She seemed very nervous. I was impatient with her, but I knew I shouldn't try to hurry her.

"Last night," she said, "I was in my room—the little room behind the servant's staircase. I couldn't get to sleep. I was that tired, all my bones aching. Ma made me scrub all the pots and pans when I was finished helpin' you. It was real late. A spot of moonlight was playing on the wall of my room, making it all silvery...."

"Yes?" I said, urging her on.

"I'm like that a lot," she continued, not to be rushed, "can't get to sleep. I just lay there in bed, tossin' and turnin'. Ma says it's because I'm growing. Anyway, I looked out my window, and I saw that thing again—that thing in the black cloak. Only it wasn't leaving the house this time. It was coming towards the door by the staircase."

"You're certain you didn't imagine it?"

"I'm certain, Miss Lauren. But wait, let me finish. In a little while I heard someone on the stairs. They go right over my room, you know. I couldn't mistake it. Someone was going up the stairs...."

"It was probably one of the servants," I told her, finding nothing particularly unusual about her story. One of the servant girls probably had a boy friend and had been coming back from a rendezvous. Naturally she would slip back in the house after dark, making as little noise as possible.

"No, Miss Lauren. It wouldn't have been. No one uses that staircase anymore, not since the left wing of the house was closed up. The staircase leads up into that part of the house. We all use the back stairs, the ones coming down from the main hallway. There would be no reason to use the servants' staircase anymore, not unless you wanted to get up to the left wing—and it's all closed up."

"Well, Lucy, I don't know quite what to make of your story."

"I was scared, Miss Lauren, real scared. I didn't sleep a wink for the rest of the night. I told Mrs. Victor what happened. She's the only one who has a key to the left wing. There's a little door at the top of the staircase, and it's kept locked, just like the main one. Whoever it was—on the stairs—had to have a key."

"You didn't hear anyone coming back down?"

"No, Ma'am."

"You're quite sure?"

"I'm positive, Miss Lauren."

"Then—perhaps you did imagine it all."

"That's what Ma said. Mrs. Victor went straight to her and told her she'd have to keep an eye on me. Said I was tellin' stories again. Ma wouldn't believe me when I told her what happened. She boxed me on the ear."

"Well, I'm sure there's some reasonable explanation for what you saw and heard, Lucy. Now cheer up. You look much too glum. I'm to have the final fitting for my ball gown today, and if Mrs. Graystone finishes with it I'll bring it home and show it to you this afternoon. Won't that be nice?"

"Yes, Miss Lauren," she replied quietly.

"Come, Lucy, I must get ready for breakfast."

I found Helena in the sitting room later on in the morning. She was wearing an old blue smock and, strangely enough, her diamond earrings. A box of paints was open on the desk in front of her, and she was painting little gold borders around the invitations to the party. She dipped the brush into the paint, bit the tip of her tongue, then spread the gold paint evenly around the squares of cream colored stationery. The dogs played at her feet, and a cigarette slowly turned to gray ash in a tray beside her. She glanced up when I came in, gave me a vague smile and went back to her work.

"It's nonsense, of course," she said, "but I want them to look especially nice. I wish there had been time to get proper engraved invitations, but these will do nicely, yes, nicely."

"They look lovely," I said.

"At any rate they're nicer than the ones Lady Randall sent out for her ball last year. Scraps of paper—mere scraps of paper. I wouldn't have made out a grocery list on them."

Helena put her paint brush down and took a final puff on her almost diminished cigarette. She crushed it out, yawning a little. She had been getting up much earlier these past days, claiming there was too much to do for her to stay in bed. The workmen were gone now, but the servants were still busy with the house. It was beginning to shine with a new luster, although the effect was rather like that of an old woman who tries to disguise her age with too much paint.

"Haven't you got a fitting today, dear?" Helena asked. "Lavinia should be almost finished with your gown."

"I'm going to Dower House after lunch," I informed her.

"I'm anxious to see the gown. You'll look lovely in it. I'm going to take my old blue satin out of moth balls today. It'll do quite well for the party. It should—it did well enough for my Presentation!"

Helena rattled on about her presentation to Her Majesty several years ago. She continued to paint as she talked, flicking spots of gold paint over her smock. I was anxious to ask her a question, and it was some time before I found the right moment.

"Helena," I began, "do—uh—do any of the servant girls have a boy friend that you know of?"

"Boy friend? I shouldn't think so."

"You're quite sure?"

"Well, let's see—there's Millie. She's over thirty and as dried up as a prune. Agnes is pushing forty, and her husband's the gardener. Jane, perhaps, but she's the butler's niece. I would imagine he keeps an eye on her. That leaves Cook, and she's a widow, and, of course, Lucy. Martha Victor is out of the question. Why did you ask?"

"Just curious," I replied.

"I would probably know about any romance below the stairs. We had that awful Agatha last year—red hair and as forward as could be. Quite a little hussy! We had to dismiss her because of Norman. Young men will be young men, you know."

"I know," I said, thinking of the incident at the clearing.

"Martha has always kept a pretty tight rein on all the girls who have worked here. She wouldn't tolerate any goings on."

"I shouldn't think so," I agreed.

"Now, what is this all about? You surely had a reason for asking me."

"Oh, nothing really," I said, trying to make light of it. "Lucy thought she saw someone coming into the house last night and heard them going up the servants' stairs. I fancied it might have been one of the servant girls coming in from a rendezvous."

"Lucy must have imagined it," Helena said, lighting a new cigarette. "No one uses those stairs anymore. Besides, they go up to the left wing, and it's closed."

"Lucy seemed quite certain," I said.

"Poor child. I'm afraid her imagination is a bit too lively. She has always been that way, even as a small child. Nervous, unable to go to sleep. Perhaps it's because her father died when she was a baby. She used to mope around and burst into tears at the least provocation. Then she started telling these stories—Cook says it's because she wants to draw attention to herself."

"I see."

"I must say, though, she's perked up quite a bit since you've come here. I think that's just what she needed—a responsible job and someone to look after. She's like a new person. I'm fond of the child, always have been."

"You wouldn't pay too much attention to what she says?"

"None at all, my dear. The child had a nightmare. It's as simple as that."

I did not disagree with her. Her explanation was probably the most reasonable one. Lucy had thought she saw something, had told her mother about it and been scolded. She no doubt exaggerated the account to me, hoping for a little sympathy. I stayed for a while with Helena, talking about inconsequential things, until lunch time. I put the incident firmly out of my mind. I had far too much to think about to let what a child imagined in the night bother me.

The walk to Dower House was always a pleasant

one. A well worn path led through the woods, lush green now and dappled with yellow sunlight. A rustic wooden bridge crossed over a brook, the water rushing over small rounded gray and white pebbles. I paused at the bridge for a moment, looking down at the water. It made me a little dizzy, and I gripped the rough wooden railing. A bird swooped down from a tree to dip its beak into the water. It was peaceful and serene here. I tried to pull my mind away from the enormous house I had just left and the dark brooding atmosphere of the place.

I slowly walked on down the path. The trees were all twisted overhead, making a dark green canopy over the path, with spots of sunlight dancing through, making yellow splashes on the worn ground. I could hear the birds calling, hear the swoosh of their wings as they flew through the thickets in search of food. A spray of blue flowers grew beneath the trunk of a tree, and I stopped to examine them. Their delicate blue blossoms were just uncurling, and I touched one of them with a gentle fingertip.

As I did so, I heard a great crash in the underbrush behind me and a large gray mastiff leaped towards me, his fangs showing. I jumped up, a look of terror on my face. The dog stopped a few yards away from me, his strong legs spread wide apart. He growled angrily. His fur was bristling, and his yellow eyes were filled with vicious lights. I backed against the trunk of a tree, searching frantically for a stick or some object with which to ward the dog away. The strong body leaned forward, ready to leap at me. My heart pounded, and my throat was dry.

"Back, Hugo!"

A man stepped onto the path. He held a shotgun loosely in his arm. The dog acknowledged his presence by a brief turn of the head, then he continued to growl at me, moving a little closer. The man stepped over to the mastiff and kicked it violently in the side. The dog whimpered, curling its tail between its legs and moving away.

"He don't mean no harm," the man said. "Just don't like strangers hanging around."

"He—he frightened me."

"He never attacks unless I tell 'im to. Then he's real mean. Tore the arm off a poacher last year, tore it clean off. Folks around here know Hugo. They know to keep away from where they don't belong, mind their own business."

I looked at the dog. He was still whimpering, huddling behind the man, his large yellow eyes mournful. He didn't look vicious now. He merely looked abused. The kick had been powerful enough to break a rib or splinter a bone. The man swung his gun to the ground and rested his hand on its butt, leaning forward a little and studying me with smouldering brown eyes. Helena had said they were smouldering. I could see now what she meant.

Andrew Graystone was a large, loosely built man with large bones and too much flesh. While not stout, he gave the impression of being heavy, lumbering. His hair was shaggy, the color of tarnished gold, falling over his deeply tanned forehead. Heavy brows arched over brown eyes that seemed to be banked with black fires. His nose was large and fleshy, his thick lips loose and sensual. He wore a leather jerkin over a soiled white shirt, the full sleeves hanging down over his wrists. His light brown pants were stained with mud, as were the heavy brown boots. There was an air of the animal about him, something slightly untamed. He looked as vicious as his mastiff had, and just as dangerous.

"Do you want to explain yourself?" he asked. His voice was guttural, very husky.

"Explain myself?"

"What are you doin' here, Miss?"

"I am on my way to Dower House to have my fitting," I said, my own voice quite superior, putting him in his place, I hoped.

"You're the new girl, aren't you? I heard you was here. Heard you come from London. Lavinia said she was makin' some fine new dresses for you. I ain't never been there when you come to Dower House before. Been out doin' my job. Some of us has to work."

That last remark, uttered in a sneering tone, told me quite plainly what he thought about those people who did not have to work to earn a living. I could sense his resentment. Perhaps that explained why he and Norman Wade had so many differences of opinion. Andrew Graystone was crude, a peasant. Three hundred years ago he would have been the leader of a revolt, bearing a pitchfork and a flaming torch, leading his men against the castle. I stared at him coldly.

"I am Lauren Moore," I said.

"Andrew Graystone," he said, nodding slightly, "the bailiff. You better make friends with Hugo, Miss Moore, in case you ever meet up with him again. Here—pet his head. He likes that. Don't be afraid. . . ."

"I—I'd rather not," I said, eyeing the dog.

"You got to," he said, "if you intend to roam around these parts." He grinned. "He'll tear you apart if you don't. . . ."

Andrew Graystone took my wrist roughly and pulled my hand down until it touched the dog's head. He guided my hand over the dog's skull, his fingers gripping my wrist firmly. "Friend, Hugo," he said, "friend." The dog looked up at me, his eyes curious now. After a moment, he licked my palm. Graystone released my wrist and stood back while I stroked the dog's ears, scratching them a little. Hugo wagged his tail, a friend now.

"He won't never bother you again," Andrew Graystone said. "Once he knows a person, he's like a pup, wantin' 'em to pet him. He likes that. Yeah —he likes the pretty lady."

I straightened up, brushing my skirts. Andrew Graystone was grinning, pleased with himself. I did not like the way he was looking at me. His eyes seemed to labor as they looked me over, taking in every detail. I rubbed my wrist that ached from the pressure of his fingers. I felt as though his touch had left me soiled. He seemed to sense what I was thinking, and he grinned all the more.

"You're a fine lady, ain't you?" he said.

"I beg your pardon."

"Think you're pretty grand with all them fine airs. I can tell. You don't like me, do you?"

"Really, Mr. Graystone. . . ."

"I can tell." His eyes suddenly grew very dark, almost inky black, and he frowned. I could tell that he was thinking of something else, something completely unconnected with me. He stood there leaning on the butt of his gun, and he suddenly looked vulnerable, almost like a child whose pretense of ferocity had been stripped away. His face was very serious, heavy and grave.

"Not many people like me," he muttered under his breath, "but I'll show 'em. They think they can use me. They think they're gettin' away with something, that I'm a fool 'n they can use me like a fool. It ain't going to be that way much longer, not much longer...."

I parted my lips, ready to ask him what he meant, but something about his face caused me to hesitate. He seemed to be in a brown study, a deep mood completely different from his previous belligerent manner. I wondered what he could possibly have been talking about.

Andrew Graystone stared down at his feet. When he lifted up his head a shadow seemed to pass over his face. He curled his lips, all his former belligerence coming back. The strange mood that he had lapsed into was gone.

"You ain't any better than them," he said. "All your fine airs 'n snooty words. I may not be gentry, but I can tell you right now I'm as good as a lot of fine people as thinks they're so high and mighty. Yeah, I'm as good as some...."

"I don't understand, Mr. Graystone."

He was talking in riddles. There was a mystery behind his words. I could sense that he had been talking about something else besides my own haughty manner. He was a sullen brute, staring at me with a sneer on his face, but he knew something important, something he had hinted at just now. I wondered if it had something to do with Norman Wade and all the arguments they had had.

"You gonna tell your uncle I was fresh with you?" he asked.

"I don't think there's any reason for me to do that," I replied as calmly as I could.

He smiled slightly. "You're smart," he said.

"Smart?"

"To keep your mouth shut. That's the best policy around here. Just keep your eyes open and your mouth shut. That's the best way. Be dumb, then you won't need to worry none."

I wondered if these words were meant to frighten me. They were laden with meaning, but I didn't know if they contained a threat or a warning. I was thoroughly perplexed by this crude man. He was crafty, sly. I sensed that he had knowledge of some secret, and this knowledge gave him a feeling of power and superiority.

"Go on and get your dress made now," he said. "Vinny'll be glad to see you. She gets lonely, she says. She's always glad to see someone who ain't crude. She ain't so happy to see me, 'cause she's stuck with me and I won't put up with her fine airs. I put her in her place and it makes her angry."

He snapped his fingers at Hugo and shambled on down the path, his shoulders swinging. The dog bounded after him. I watched the man leaving, my eyes focused on the back of that tarnished gold head. He turned off the path and went into the woods, holding his gun in his arms. My head ached, and my wrists felt a little limp. I stood under the shade of the oak tree a long time before I continued on my way to Dower House.

IX

DOWER HOUSE SAT in a clearing, about a mile from Falconridge. It was made of the same gray stone, but there were charming dormer windows and dark blue shutters that gave it an individual character. An oak tree grew in front, its sprawling limbs touching the weathered blue slate roof. There was a shabby herb garden at one side of the house and an old wheelbarrow and a stack of cordwood at the other. Dower House was small and run-down and there was a certain air of sadness about the place, set off here all by itself in the middle of the woods.

When I first knocked at the door there was no answer. I thought that curious because Lavinia had known I was to come for my fitting. I knocked again, then peered through the window. The frayed muslin curtains kept me from seeing much. When I knocked for a third time I could hear the sound echoing inside, and I felt very foolish standing on the doorstep, knowing there was someone inside. I could sense a presence in the front room. I could feel someone hesitating, listening to my knock.

"Mrs. Graystone," I called. "Lavinia. . . ."

There was a slight shuffle. I heard footsteps. Then Lavinia opened the door, holding it back for me. The front room was dim, all the curtains pulled to keep out the sunlight. In the dimness I saw a table with two bowls and a half a loaf of bread on it. On the old iron stove there was a pot of stew. I could smell the odor of cabbage and boiled beef. Lavinia went to the windows and pulled back the curtains. Sunlight flooded into the room, making me blink a little after the dim half light.

The room was a combination sitting room and kitchen, and it was very untidy. Dishes were piled on the drain board. The fireplace was littered with cold ash. Stacks of fashion magazines were piled on an old chair with a broken wicker bottom. The room was ordinarily very neat, but today the old straw broom leaned against the wall and dust and bits of scrap were scattered over the floor.

"You must forgive me..." Lavinia said. Her voice sounded strange. It was very weak, as though she had to make a strong effort to speak. "This mess," she said, "I haven't had time to clean up— He didn't go out this morning as he usually does. He just left a short while ago...."

Lavinia was always neatly groomed, fresh and crisp and ready to begin with her duties. She was always gracious and polite and a little reserved. This afternoon she wore a flowered cotton wrapper that had clearly seen its best days. Her hair, always so beautifully brushed and shining, fell in untidy waves about her too pale face. There were heavy mauve shadows about her sad brown eyes, and I noticed a swelling on her jaw, as though she had suffered a physical blow. It was obvious that she had been crying, too. The dried tears were still salty on her cheeks.

"What has happened?" I asked, my voice quiet.
"Nothing," she replied.

"But—you've been crying."

"Nothing," she repeated. "I'll be all right."

"I can come back for my fitting another day," I said. "You're not up to it now. I can see that. I'll come back tomorrow."

"No," she protested, raising her hand as though to prevent me from leaving. "I'll be all right. I'll just make a little tea. You will have some with me, won't you? Then—then we can work on your dress. It's almost finished."

"If you're certain...."

"Please," she said. Her voice seemed to entreat me. I nodded. She smiled sadly, brushing a lock of raven hair from her temple. She put the tea on and asked me to excuse her for a few moments. She went into the next room, and I sat down, looking around at the messy room. Mrs. Graystone was not at all herself today, and I knew the reason why, as surely as if she had told me.

She had been quarreling with her husband. He had not gone out to his duties this morning. He had stayed in, something he didn't ordinarily do. They had argued, and he had struck her. Helena had told me Andrew Graystone beat his wife. I did not doubt it after my own encounter with the man. Evidently he had just left Dower House when I met him on the path. There were two bowls on the table. Lavinia must have cooked lunch for him. The tea kettle began to whistle shrilly. I took it off the stove and prepared the tea. It was ready when Lavinia came back into the room.

She looked much better now. She had brushed her hair into its usual neat cascade of waves, and she had changed into a dress of subdued orange linen adorned with small brown velvet bows. She had applied lip rouge and powder and her face did not look nearly so ravaged. She came into the room with her customary poise, and a smile on her lips. But the smile was an effort, her lips tremulous, and her eyes could not hide the incredible depths of sadness.

"You must forgive me," she said, trying to sound light. "I have been feeling—very poorly this morning. A headache. Ghastly. I did not sleep well last night, and, of course, with Andrew being here all morning my day has been disrupted. I see you have the tea ready. How nice of you. Tell me, how is your aunt?"

"Helena is fine," I said. I admired the woman for her ability to dissimulate so smoothly. She had had a wretched experience with her husband. He had struck her, and yet she was able to gloss it over with a few casual gestures, a smooth bit of chatter. Putting the tea pot and two blue cups on a tray, she led the way into the sewing room. She moved gracefully, smiling still, and only her eyes betrayed her true emotions.

Lavinia Graystone made pleasant small talk as we drank our tea. She talked about the dresses she had made for me and the gowns she had made for other women in the community. She discussed the newest trends in fashion from Paris and chatted on about her one brief visit to that capital. I listened politely and answered when an answer was required but all the time I studied the woman and wondered how she could possibly be married to someone like Andrew Graystone.

Lavinia was an attractive woman, beautiful in her way, poised in manner, charming. She was intelligent, and she had finesse. She was skillful in her work as a seamstress, very adept with a needle and always tasteful in her own choice of clothes. She had all the graces so admirable in a woman of breeding, and yet she was married to a man who should have repelled her. She lived in a shadow of sadness, and that shadow was thrown by the man whom she had agreed to love, honor, and obey.

After the tea things were put away I changed into the ball gown and stood up on a small round table so that Lavinia could work on the hem. The gown was lovely, all cream satin, the skirt belling out over a large hoop skirt. Lavinia moved around the table, adjusting the hanging of the material, putting a pin in here, taking one out there. I was still brooding over the enigma of the woman, and I decided to see if I could find out anything that might answer some of the questions that kept bothering me.

"Tell me about your shop in Liverpool," I said. "Helena told me you had one before you married."

Lavinia did not answer for a moment. Her hands worked skillfully on the hem of the dress, gathering up the rich satin, smoothing it, putting in pins. "It was very nice," she said finally. "My parents left a little money when they died, just enough for me to open the shop. It wasn't easy at first—there seems to be a conspiracy against women in business—but I managed to survive. I had a friend. . . ." She hesitated, looking up at me as though debating whether or not to reveal more. "He helped me quite a bit, sent customers to me, helped with the finances. I couldn't have done it without him. I—I was very young, only a little older than you are now."

She did not need to tell me what her relationship

had been with the "friend." I was not shocked, although as a student of Mrs. Siddons' School for Young Ladies I should have been. I had already begun to learn that the world of real people was quite different from the one seen from within the cloistered confines of a proper school.

"He taught me a lot, too," she continued, her voice quite low. "He taught me how to speak properly and how to walk, how to dress with taste and how to conduct myself in society. I was very raw and unlettered—he had a lot of work on his hands. For three years. . . ." She paused. Her eyes seemed to be turned inwards, looking back on that period of her life. Her mouth drooped sadly, and after a moment she shook her head, as though to shake away unpleasant memories.

"Something went wrong. It always does. I found myself in trouble. My friend was married. He left me to my own devices. That's when I met Andrew. He was a sailor, or had been. He was in Liverpool looking for work of some kind. He found me— quite overwhelming. I found him a solution to my problem. He married me so that the child would have a name. When it was born, he—he made me give it away. We left Liverpool. He took all kinds of jobs, but he wasn't satisfied with any of them. It is hard for him to get along with people."

I wondered why Lavinia Graystone was telling me this story. She was a reserved woman who quite plainly suffered in silence and kept her own counsel, but I had caught her in an awkward situation this afternoon. She was not herself after the quarrel with her husband. Perhaps she needed to talk and found me a trustworthy audience. Perhaps she sensed my curiosity and was discreetly trying to answer the questions I hadn't the temerity to ask.

"I met your husband as I was on my way to Dower House," I said.

"Oh?"

"He saved me from his dog."

"Hugo is quite vicious with strangers but he's a fine animal. I feel safer with him around. He's a good watch dog, and it's so isolated here at the house. Did—did Andrew mention me?"

"No," I lied. "He just introduced himself."

"Andrew is—moody. He's—really not so bad. He just wants so much from life, and he doesn't know how to get it, so he rebels. He rebels against authority and against people in general. He can be quite nice at times."

I wanted to tell her that she did not have to justify him to me. She finished with the hem of the dress and I got down from the table and went to take the dress off. When I returned, Lavinia was gathering up all of her sewing things: the tape measure, the pins, scissors, bits of ribbon. She looked a little embarrassed, afraid that she had talked too much. She told me that she wanted to work on the dress a little more and would have it delivered tomorrow. She was very reserved now, her charm the careful professional charm of a paid employee.

"Thank you so very much for—putting up with me," she said. "This has been a bad day, as I said earlier. And, Miss Moore. . . ."

"You don't need to say it," I told her, smiling. "I don't carry tales, Lavinia. What you have told me is between us, between friends."

Lavinia returned my smile, relaxing a little. Her eyes seemed to shine, and for a moment I thought she was going to cry.

"One needs friends," she said. "I am happy to have found one in you."

The sun was already going down when I left Dower House. The afternoon had vanished away, and I quickened my step as the evening shadows began to spread. The sky was a deep blue gray when I reached the clearing before Falconridge. I stared up at the towering pile of gray stone so massive and so formidable. One of the curtains parted on the second floor. I saw a hand holding it back and the white blur among the shadows that would be the face of whomever was watching me.

It was a moment before I realized that the window was one of those in the left wing. The hand moved and the curtain fell back. Who could it have been, I wondered. Martha Victor? What would she be doing in the left wing at this hour?

I barely had time to change for dinner. Helena and Charles Lloyd were waiting for me, as usual. I wondered how long it would be before Norman Wade joined us for dinner again.

My uncle was in his usual irritable mood. He snapped at one of the servants because the soup was not warm enough, and he seemed to find any number of things wrong with the meal. He was tense, and he kept drumming on the table with his fingertips, as though he were waiting for something and could not bear the suspense. Helena looked tired, and her conversation was not as animated as it usually was.

"Did you get the dress finished?" she asked.

"Lavinia wanted to make a few minor alterations. She'll have it delivered tomorrow."

"So it is 'Lavinia' now?" Charles Lloyd said. "You seem to have become fast friends with our Mrs. Graystone."

"She is a charming woman," I replied.

"Charming? I suppose so. The woman irritates me. She is too downcast and humble for my taste. Needs a little spirit."

"I should think being married to Andrew Graystone would take the spirit out of any woman," Helena commented. "Beastly man."

"I met him today," I remarked.

"Oh? How pleasant," Helena said. "Did he growl at you?"

"No, but his dog certainly did. He almost attacked me. Mr. Graystone had to restrain him. It seems dangerous, having such an animal roaming about."

"The animal is necessary," my uncle said. "He keeps poachers away. There used to be a lot of that, until I bought Hugo."

"You bought the dog?" I asked.

He nodded. "I trained him myself. He was a friendly, playful pup, too eager to lick your hand, but all the right instincts were there all right."

"The right instincts?"

"The instincts to kill," he said flatly.

"Every animal has them?"

"Of course. So does every man. It just takes the right amount of pressure to bring them out—in an animal or in a man. It took a lot of work to train Hugo to attack. Had to starve him and use the whip. He's a proper beast now, though, the best breed."

"I think the whole thing is abominable," Helena said.

"Abominable, my dear, but necessary. Hugo won't kill unless he's told to do so. There are only three people who can command him, Graystone and I, and Norman."

"Norman?" I asked.

"He was quite fond of the dog, still is. Frequently Hugo will go out with him on a hunting trip. Norman kept the dog in the downstairs of the carriage house when I was training him, pampered the beast. He would have kept him for his own if I hadn't assigned him to Graystone."

"Norman is certainly keeping to himself lately," Helena said. "I hardly see him from day to day. The tenants must be taking up a lot of his time. One of the servants told me she saw Norman working on one of the fields, pushing a plow behind an oxen while the farmer was working another lot."

"He coddles them," Charles Lloyd said. "He treats them as equals, and they take advantage of that. You need a strong hand with these people, to keep them in line."

"Like yours?" she inquired, a touch of acid in her voice.

Charles Lloyd arched an eyebrow and looked at his wife. "Yes, my dear, like mine," he said.

"Isn't it almost time to collect the rents again?" she asked.

"Graystone is going to do it next week."

"I do hope there's no unpleasantness," Helena remarked. "It has been a bad time for them. Some of them could hardly scrape up enough for the rents last fall. I'm sure it will be worse now."

"They can always leave," Charles Lloyd said.

"Most of the families have lived on the land for generations. They are as much a part of Falconridge as we are."

"Hardly, my dear. The land belongs to me. So long as they work it, they must pay. The sum isn't much."

"It is when there's no income," Helena replied.

"Would you have me run a charity?" he asked testily. "The men are able bodied. The land is good. There only needs to be a little sweat, a little backbone to make it produce."

"But Norman says...."

"I don't care a hang what Norman says," he said violently. "Norman doesn't run Falconridge—yet. I think you would do better to stick to your dresses and your party, my dear, and leave the business affairs to those who are qualified to discuss them. Now, if you will excuse me, I think I'll go to the library."

He left the table, bowing to both of us. Helena sighed, throwing up her hands and shrugging her shoulders. A servant brought our dessert and Helena began to chatter about the Japanese lanterns she was going to have strung up along the drive and on the terraces for the party. We spent half an hour or so discussing the party, Helena telling me about the musicians she had hired and the extra servants who would come in to help for the affair. It was almost ten o'clock when we left the table, and I went up to my room immediately, quite exhausted.

Lucy was disappointed that I didn't have the dress to show her. I told her that it would be ready tomorrow, and her eyes widened at the prospect of seeing it. She had picked a bouquet of flowers for me—yellow roses and golden white daisies with long stems overflowed in a small green vase. She looked much better than she had this morning, although her eyes were still shadowed and she was not as vivacious as she ordinarily was. I slipped into my nightgown and let her brush my hair for a while before I sent her away.

When I blew out the lamp and climbed into bed, I thought that I would go to sleep immediately. I was so weary, yet it eluded me. Try though I might, I could not sleep. Moonlight streamed in through the window, gilding the furniture with a soft silver sheen and throwing the rest of the room into misty blue shadow. A gentle breeze rustled the bed hangings, the thin yellow curtains billowing about me. I tried to pretend I was in a boat, sailing away into the darkness, the sound of the sea whispering me into oblivion, but the harder I tried to induce sleep the wider awake I grew.

An hour passed, perhaps two, and I lay there in a state of semi-consciousness, my mind going around in curious circles. I saw all the faces of the people of Falconridge. They seemed to be floating around me, Martha Victor's grim and threatening, my uncle's frowning, Norman Wade's smiling, Helena's looking puzzled. They merged into one another and they seemed to be whispering. I listened closely. One of them was trying to tell me something, something important, and the words were there, hanging in the air, waiting for me to comprehend. I closed my eyes, hoping to shut off the phantoms, but the words were still in the air. I had the feeling that there was something I must know, something that would save me from danger. The old grandfather clock downstairs struck one.

The noise was vibrant, echoing through the house in waves of sound. I sat up, rubbing my eyes.

If sleep wouldn't come, then I wouldn't try to sleep. I lit the lamp, and the phantoms disappeared as the warm yellow glow brought the room into its proper perspective. The sea still whispered, the waves washing over the rocks with a gentle, monotonous sound. The house creaked and settled, the wind rattling the window frames. I pulled on my blue dressing gown over the ruffled white nightgown, fastening the sash at my waist. I was wide awake now, atune to every noise, my senses magnified with the feeling of isolation, of being the only person awake in the massive old house.

I thought that if I read for a while I might grow drowsy enough to go to sleep. There were two books by my bedside, a novel by George Eliot and a travel book written by a prim lady who had gone tromping off through darkest Africa in a pair of high button shoes. I had read both books already, and there was nothing else in the room to read. I would go down to the library and find something, a book of dull sermons or a history of Parliament, something dreary enough to make me sleepy. I turned up the wick of the lamp and left the room.

It was cold in the corridors, and the heels of my slippers made a loud rapping noise that echoed against the walls. I slipped them off, not wanting to awaken anyone with my nocturnal wandering. My bare feet tread silently down the hall. The lamp flickered, casting large black shadows over the walls. The house seemed empty, deserted. I might be the only person alive, wandering about in a tomb. The sensation was a spooky one, and I tried to laugh at myself. I paused at the head of the staircase, looking down into the nest of shadows. A draft of cold air came shivering up from below, as though a door had been left open somewhere. I had the sensation of cold fingers stroking my cheek.

I walked down the stairs slowly, holding on to the railing. I made no noise except for the soft, silken rustle of my nightgown. I stood in the main hallway, looking around at the vast black walls and the high ceiling, all shadowy and dark. The tapestries fluttered, flapping on the walls. There was a tapping noise at one of the windows that sounded like someone trying to get in. I looked up, seeing the pane silvered by the moonlight. The branch of a tree scratched against it. I smiled at myself. Lucy was the imaginative one, not me, I told myself, and then I wished that I had not thought of Lucy and her fantasy. It had been a fantasy, of course, but I would have preferred not to think of it at that moment. I walked on down the hall, holding the lamp high. The library door creaked as I pushed it open, and I paused, sure that the noise was loud enough to awaken everyone.

No one came and the noise died away, leaving an even deeper silence in its wake. The library was close and stuffy, all the windows tightly shut, with the heavy draperies pulled across them. There was a smell of stale cigar smoke and the musty odor of books, stronger now that the room was so still. I set the lamp down on a table. It gave only a little light, just enough to fill one corner with its yellow glow. The rest of the room was dark, the furniture like squat black figures that crouched down, trying to conceal themselves in the shadow. The lamp illuminated one section of books, the gold stamped titles gleaming. There was a volume of lectures on

Ancient Greece, and I thought it would do nicely for my purpose. It was heavy, bound in calf, and a cloud of dust rose in the air as I pulled it off the shelf.

Suddenly there was a gust of wind and the library door slammed shut with a mighty bang. The lamp flickered wildly for a moment and then went out. I leaned against the shelf, startled, my lips parted in a silent cry. I stood very quietly for a long moment, listening to the sound of my own breathing. It was absurd, of course, but I felt that there was someone in the room with me. It took a moment for me to pull myself together and rid myself of the idea. My nerves were on edge. That was all.

I had brought no matches with me. That had been foolish. The lamp had blown out that first night I was in Falconridge, and Helena had warned me of the drafts and sudden gusts of wind that played havoc with candles and lamps. I should have had the foresight to bring matches. I felt terribly foolish, standing there in the darkness, panting just a little. I still held the heavy book in my hand.

There were matches in my uncle's desk. He kept them to light his cigars. I groped my way across the room and found the desk. The surface was icy cold to the touch. I drew open the top drawer and felt for the matches. My hand slid over several objects, a pen, a knife, a stack of papers, a small paperweight, and finally I found the box of matches. I struck one, smelling the sharp smell of sulphur. I held my palm cradled around the tiny flame and took it over to the lamp. In a moment the lamp was burning nicely, and I sighed with relief.

I tugged open the door and left the library, the

lamp in one hand, the book in the other. I was a little weak from fear. Although I tried to scold myself out of the notion, I felt that eyes were watching me, that someone was listening to my movements. I stopped once, straining to listen to a sound. It was a creaking floorboard, nothing more. The wind had come up strongly since I left my room, and the house was full of all those familiar noises I had grown accustomed to.

I paused at the foot of the staircase, listening again. I thought I heard footsteps passing on the floor above. No, it was just the wind flapping the tapestries. I started up the staircase, and I was half way up when I heard the sound again. Footsteps. There would be no mistake this time. They were passing down the hall, towards the closed wing. There was a great curve in the staircase before one reached the second floor, and the lamp light was weak. It was unlikely that whoever had passed had noticed the light. I blew it out, huddling against the wall. I could feel the damp wall behind me, and my knees were weak. There was someone on the floor above. I was sure of it.

I stood there for several moments but the sound was not repeated. I could hear the tapestries, and there was a strange rustling noise, but the footsteps were gone. Perhaps I had imagined them. I was in a highly nervous state—sleepless, restless, exhausted after a trying day. How foolish to be standing here with a palpitating heart, surrounded by darkness, listening for a sound that had never been, and to have been so hasty to have blown the lamp out made it even worse. Now I would have to go all the way back to my room without any light at all. I had calmed myself down and was ready to go on up the staircase when I heard the whisper.

"This can't go on. It's too dangerous, too dangerous. . . ."

The whisper was hoarse, barely audible. I could not recognize the voice, but it was the voice of someone in torment. Those strange words seemed to hang in the air, vibrating, only to disappear in the ensuing silence. I shut my eyelids very tightly, trembling, and a moment passed, two, several more. The pulse in my temple throbbed, and my body arched against the damp wall.

This is absurd, I told myself, absurd. I imagined the whisper. It was like the phantom faces in my room earlier in the night. It was the product of an over stimulated imagination. It must be. The words had come out of the emptiness of silence, like things with a life of their own, disembodied. They had not been in the house at all. They had been only in my mind. I couldn't stand here all night in the cold air, too frightened to move. It was absurd.

I walked on up the staircase, holding my shoulders straight, determined to win control of myself. I turned down the hall and went in the direction of my room, dreading the long walk. I felt along the wall for the turning that led to my room, and I stumbled, dropping the heavy book. The crash as it hit the floor sounded like an explosion. I let out a little cry. There were tears of frustration on my cheeks. I was acting like a child, a child frightened of the dark and imagining all kinds of terrors.

The footsteps were real this time. So was the glow of light. It flickered against the walls from another passage of the hall, and I was not imagining it. The glow grew wider and brighter, and Charles Lloyd stepped into the hall, holding the lamp in front of him. He was wearing a black brocade robe with quilted blue satin lapels. His heavy blond hair was all disarrayed, and his face was lined, disturbed. He held the lamp up in front of me, and his dark brown eyes looked black with anger. I stared up at him, too intimidated even to speak.

"What is the meaning of this?" he demanded. "It's two o'clock in the morning."

"I—I didn't know the time."

"I heard a noise. It sounded like an explosion."

"It was my book—I dropped it. Lectures on Ancient Greece. I—I was unable to sleep. I wanted a book. Something dull. I went down to the library. . . ."

"Why isn't your lamp lit?"

"I—blew it out."

"Blew it out?"

"I—I thought I heard someone. I didn't want them to see me."

Charles Lloyd looked down at me, one eye brow arched like a wing. I felt like a small child under the gaze of a stern parent. He was plainly disgusted with me. He shook his head slowly from side to side. I felt his seething anger. I knew I must look like a fool, and I knew what he must be thinking.

"I suppose you heard voices?" he said.

"Yes. No. I—I thought I did."

He smiled wryly. He did not believe me. I didn't know now if I had heard the whisper or not. It was a nightmare, like Lucy's. She had told me only this morning about what she had imagined she saw and heard and it had been in the back of my mind all day, lurking there, bothering me. I had let it prey on my mind until I, too, had begun to imagine things. Now under the harsh gaze of my uncle I could see all this, and I wanted to shrink away from his sight.

"I'm sorry," I said, entirely calm now.

"I should think you would be, my dear."

"Did I awaken my aunt, too?"

"I wouldn't know," he replied. "Helena's room is down the hall from mine. Her laudanum generally insures a sound sleep. Some of us do not rely on drugs. We can be aroused, certainly by an explosion of noise in the middle of the night."

"It—it won't happen again."

"I should hope not. It was quite foolish of you to wander around in the house at this hour. You could have had an accident. You could have fallen down the stairs. I strongly advise you not to do it again."

"I won't," I replied tartly, affronted by his manner.

"You're shivering, my dear. Come, I'll escort you to your room. I hope you have the good sense to stay there."

He took my elbow and led me down the hall to the door of my room. He paused to pick up my slippers where I had left them, and he handed these to me, smiling wryly. His eyes were full of mockery, and there was something else, too, something I could not recognize. I closed the door and listened to his footsteps going on down the hall. I did not light up the lamp. I sat down before the window, wondering. I watched the shadows swirl in darkness, slowly turning from black to gray. The first meager strains of yellow had begun to stain the horizon before I even tried to sleep again.

X

JAPANESE LANTERNS made soft splotches of color on the drive as carriages continued to drive up, letting out splendidly dressed men and women who stepped into a Falconridge that was ablaze with candlelight and full of the subdued sound of music and the tinkle of hushed laughter. The last rays of sunlight had just disappeared, and the house was surrounded with swirling gray mists. There was a distant rumble of thunder, as there had been all day, but as yet the storm was a mere threat and had done nothing to dispell the gaiety of Helena's party.

Helena had been frantic all day, rushing about to see that everything was in order, scolding the servants, fussing with the decorations, stopping to fix tea for the musicians when they arrived in their attractive uniforms. She had stopped to dress only half an hour before the first guests arrived, yet she had been there in the front hall waiting to greet them with every curl in place, all regal grace and charming poise. She looked lovely in her soft blue dress with its low cut bodice and billowing bell-shaped skirts. She wore long white gloves and carried a white lace fan. A diamond and sapphire pin, her single adornment, rested among her sculptured silver curls. She was every inch the grand dame, self-assured, calm, gracious.

My uncle looked bored and irritated as he moved among the guests. He had been gone all day, leaving early in the morning. I supposed it had something to do with collecting the rents, which had begun yesterday morning. Charles Lloyd had come in around five o'clock, slightly disheveled and in a foul mood. He had looked upset about something when he passed me in the hall. I noticed that his boots were muddy, something quite extraordinary with a man as fastidious about his dress as he was. He was handsomely dressed now, as resplendent as he had been that first night in London. Many a feminine eye followed him as he strolled about, and many of the women fluttered girlishly when he paused to speak to them. He was a little too recklessly handsome to be quite respectable, I thought as he stopped to fix the Vicar's wife with a stern eye. I saw her blush as he spoke to her in his deep voice.

I was a little timid in front of all these strangers. They had come to be introduced to me, the guest of honor, and I felt strange eyes following me as I passed through the brightly lit rooms. I felt I was under inspection, and it made me rather nervous. The lovely gown gave me some confidence. The creamy satin skirts billowed over the hoop, swaying as I walked, and the bodice was cut fashionably low to display my shoulders and bosom. Helena had insisted that I wear her emerald necklace, one of the few really valuable pieces of jewelry she owned besides the diamonds. The dark green stones with their deep blue lights glittered at my throat and set off the simple, unadorned lines of the gown. Lucy had spent over an hour on my hair, arranging it on top of my head with three long ringlets dangling down. I could tell by the admiring glances of the men that I met with their approval, yet that did little to ease my nerves. I was apprehensive lest I make some slip in front of these fine people.

Helena was talking with Lady Randall, a plump brunette in a poorly fitting red satin gown. Helena summoned me over and introduced me to the Lady, who fussed with a string of obviously artificial pearls and talked in a broad, countrified accent. She had large bovine brown eyes and a little bow shaped mouth that seemed out of place in her chubby face. She toyed with the pearls and fluttered her eyelashes and exclaimed over me, telling Helena what a marvel I was.

"Where's my Billy?" she said, glancing over her shoulder. "Billy must see her. He'll be dazzled, he will. He's on leave, you know. We just have him for another week before he goes back to London to join his regiment. He has the most fascinating stories about India! You must meet him, child. Oh, there he is! Billy!" she yelled in a voice more appropriate for calling pigs than for summoning one's son.

"I want you to meet this delicious creature, Billy," she said, her voice slightly cloying now. "Isn't she a joy! She's Helena's little niece, just come from London. You be sweet to her, you hear? Now, you two go amuse yourselves while we old women gossip!"

Billy Randall was not at all the striking military figure I had imagined. He was a tall, lanky boy in his early twenties with sandy hair and a prominent

Adam's apple. He wore the handsome uniform awkwardly, as though it were an unaccustomed masquerade costume. He seemed to be entirely flustered at meeting me. He clicked his heels together smartly as he bent to kiss my hand, and I had to smother a giggle. He was like an embarrassed little boy.

"Would you care to dance?" he asked, stammering a little.

"I would be delighted," I replied, smiling.

He escorted me to the ballroom, moving stiffly. The room was all illuminated with candlelight which glimmered on the newly refurbished gilt. The chandeliers dripped their rainbow-hued crystals over the heads of countless couples who whirled to the strains of soft waltz music. The soft pastel skirts of the women fluttered like flower blossoms against the dark trousers of the men. It was an enchanting scene, all light and color and movement, and I paused for a moment to watch before Billy Randall took me awkwardly in his arms and swept me into the midst of it. I looked into his watery blue eyes and smiled charmingly. I did not grimace when he stepped on my feet, nor did I frown when he stumbled. He was a touching fellow in his eagerness to make a good impression on me, and his own nervousness was so intense that it made mine disappear entirely. I was relaxed and at ease when the dance was over.

Billy had just begun a long, laborious story about a tiger hunt in India when his father came over and asked me to dance. Lord Randall was stolid and slow, puffing his cheeks out with the effort of dancing. His face was a little red, and he had an improbable walrus mustache. When the dance was over, another man asked me to dance, the son of a local merchant, and he was followed by a whole series of eligible young men who talked ponderously about their business affairs or foolishly about their social pursuits. I thought about the dark, handsome Cornish men Clarissa had predicted for me in one of our conversations. None of these men would qualify, although most were charming enough. They treated me like some rare bird whose plumage they were afraid to ruffle, and I was a little put off by their countrified mannerisms.

Between dances there were glasses of champagne, and the fizzling golden drink soon began to go to my head. I was slightly dizzy, and the room seemed to revolve in a whirl of blurring color. I smiled politely at my current partner and listened patiently to his description of a new thoroughbred horse he had purchased. I saw Helena talking with a group of women at the foot of the stairs, and Charles Lloyd standing at the French windows that opened out from the ballroom onto the terraces. He was smoking a cigar, one hand jammed into his pocket, looking very superior to the creatures who swirled around him. My escort asked me if I was feeling well, and I nodded to reassure him and asked if he would excuse me for a moment.

I knew why these young men seemed pale to me, and I knew why I was searching the room, looking for one face I had not yet seen. He must be here. We had successfully avoided one another for a long time, but tonight it seemed inevitable that we meet. Although I had not admitted it to myself, that was the major reason for my uneasiness earlier in the evening. That was the reason I had gone to such pains with my grooming, why I had been so careful to appear charming and at ease, having a good time. I wanted to look well in his eyes. I wanted Norman Wade to see that I was enjoying myself. I had cast furtive glances over the shoulders of my partners, looking around for him. He appeared to be nowhere in sight.

My head was spinning now, and I walked carefully away from my partner. I had had too much champagne, too quickly, and everything was a little hazy. I felt almost as though I was walking under water, moving in slow motion while the room swayed with my movements. I thought some food would help.

I left the ballroom and went through the large arched door that led to the dining room. Helena had prepared three elaborate buffet tables, heavily laden with food. Gleaming china platters held glazed hams, a golden brown turkey, succulent roasts dripping in juice. There were side dishes of vegetables, green asparagus, tiny peas, small potatoes, sliced red tomatoes, golden corn. There were platters of fish, a pail of oysters, small pink shrimp in red sauce. Servants in crisp white aprons heaped platefuls of food for the people who flocked around the tables like so many starving peasants. I saw Lord Randall wolfing down a plate of glazed cakes, and I felt quite ill, suddenly in need of some fresh air.

A hundred candles burned in the main hallway, and little groups of people stood about, eating their food and chattering much too loudly, I thought. Billy Randall waved to me, indicating that I join him beside the potted plant, but I shook my head and smiled and walked on. I saw a cluster of young girls sitting on the steps. They held plates on their knees and seemed to be convulsed in giggles. They were large, buxom girls with big bones and rather gawky mannerisms, all dressed in the finest gowns they owned. A brown eyed lass with untidy flaxen hair leaned against the stair railing, her brown and yellow velvet gown a little too tight, as though it had been made three years earlier. She giggled with a tall brunette in purple who fluttered a fan of tattered blue feathers. The attention of the girls seemed to be focused on one point, and I followed their gaze to see Norman Wade deep in conversation with one of their friends, a strapping lass with pink cheeks and large green eyes. Her red hair fell in rich ringlets about her shoulders, and the pink velvet gown was an unfortunate choice for one with her particular coloring.

Norman Wade was at his most charming, looking deep into her eyes with an intense gaze. He whispered something in her ear. She blushed vividly and then giggled. He clenched his fist into a ball and tapped her gently on the chin. The girls on the stairs burst into gales of horrified titters, nudging one another. I hurried on down the hall and out onto the porch, little spots of anger on my cheeks.

There was no reason why I should be angry. It was foolish, but I was consumed with rage. The man was outrageous. He was scandalous. He was abominable, and I was angry because he chose to devote himself to the healthy, robust Cornish girls while ignoring me completely. I held on to the railing, leaning forward to breathe deeply of the fresh air. I was still slightly drunk, or I would not have had such feelings. Norman Wade meant nothing to me. He was just a nuisance, and I was delighted that he had not seen fit to bother me tonight, no matter how I looked in the elegant gown and emeralds. Billy Randall was a much more preferable companion. I wished that I had not snubbed him just now. I would have liked for Norman Wade to have seen me laughing with Billy and admiring his fine uniform.

I leaned against the railing, looking out over the drive. The thick gray mists swirled around Falconridge, pressing closer and closer, but the Japanese lanterns glowed beautifully in the darkness, making pools of the color on the crushed shell drive, blue, red, green. They swayed gently in the wind, moving to and fro like fairy lights. Thunder rumbled, louder now, and there was a touch of moisture in the air. I hoped the storm held off until the party was over and the guests safely departed.

The effects of the champagne were wearing off with the fresh air. My head was clearing. Behind me I could hear the muffled noise of the party, the laughter, the music, the voices shut off by the great door. I should go back inside soon, I thought, but it was relaxing to be out here, listening to the wind creaking the tree limbs and watching the colors of the lanterns glowing against the encroaching mists.

There was a sudden surge of noise as the door was opened, shut off again when the heavy door closed. I saw the man silhouetted against the night, his profile sharp. I could not see his face, but I knew who he was. He didn't say anything for a moment. He took out a cigar and lit it. In the glow of the match I could see his eyes, lowered to his task, intent on lighting the cigar. I turned away from him, catching my breath. I did not want to talk to him.

"The guest of honor shouldn't run away," he said quietly.

"I haven't run away," I replied. "I wanted some fresh air."

"Yes, it is rather stuffy inside. Also, it helps clear the head."

"What do you mean?"

"All that champagne."

"You drank too much?" I asked.

"I never touch the stuff. It's too light. Whiskey is my drink. No, I was referring to you. Seven glasses, or was it eight? I may have missed one."

"You—you were watching me?"

"Observing you, my dear."

"I didn't see you."

I was sorry I had said that. It indicated that I had been searching for him. I didn't want him to think that, even if it were true. Norman Wade gave a little chuckle, as though he could read my thoughts. He took a step towards me. I stiffened. He was standing behind me now. I had an overwhelming sense of his presence. I could feel him there, his eyes on me. I could imagine his amused, slightly mocking smile.

"Little girls shouldn't drink too much champagne," he said.

"I am not a little girl."

"No? No, I suppose not. Not tonight, at any rate. You seem to have made quite an impression on the local swains. The gown, the hair, the poise—all that of a woman. A very beautiful woman, I might add. They were quite smitten with you. Little Billy Randall, for example."

"He's a sweet boy," I retorted.

"A boy, yes. A mere lad. Tell me, did any of the

gentlemen ask you out? Tea at the family manse, perhaps, or riding, or an offer to escort you to church? All properly chaperoned, of course."

"What concern of yours is that?"

"I must watch out for my little cousin."

"I'm not your cousin," I replied, irritated.

"Technically, no. Still, I must watch out for you. I wouldn't want to see you get mixed up with a local blackguard, although I suppose Billy Randall is innocent enough."

"What I do is my business. You might look out for your own affairs. The young ladies seemed to be very interested. That little redhead in the awful pink dress. . . ."

"So you noticed me talking to Arabella?"

"I—I happened to pause in the hall on my way out here."

"Long enough to notice that her dress was awful," he said, chuckling softly. "You're right. It was."

"And those girls on the stairs. . . ."

"Children of the local aristocracy, quite charming, all of them. Uncultured perhaps—they haven't had the advantage of private schools and a cosmopolitan background—but endearing, every one of them. Very healthy lasses, all of whom can cook a hearty meal, shoe a horse, milk a cow and ride to the hounds with the best of them. They spend more time in the stables than in the parlor, I'm afraid, and I doubt if any one of them has read a book from cover to cover. They'll make fine wives."

"Arabella, perhaps?"

"Oh, yes, she'll make a marvelous wife. She can even pitch hay, and her family is one of the wealthiest in the county. Our aristocrats are quite down to earth. Earthy. It's only the pretenders who cultivate fine airs and grand manners."

I knew that he was mocking me, holding me up to ridicule in comparison with the Cornish girls. I was too angry to reply to his comments. He had been very affectionate with the girl named Arabella. I wondered if he was interested in her. Once again he seemed to read my thoughts.

"But, alas, when you spend so much time in the stables you carry the smell of the stables with you. A quite bracing smell, not at all unpleasant, but not to my taste. I prefer the perfume of the parlor. Your hair has a very lovely aroma, Lauren. Like spring flowers, fresh, clean. I find it delightful."

"I—I had better go in now," I said, my voice not at all level. I half turned to leave, but he blocked my way. I could see his face in the faint glow of moonlight. The lips were grinning, the eyes mocking. He was teasing me, as one would tease a child. I was infuriated with him. I wanted to slap that arrogant face. He sensed my anger, and the grin broadened.

"Afraid?" he asked.

"Is there anything to be afraid of?"

"There could be. There just possibly could be."

"Your arrogance is overwhelming."

"So is your charm, my dear. I hadn't realized before just how much charm you have. The little peasant girl among the poppies was delightful, of course, but the woman in satin and emeralds is—how shall I put it?—delectable."

"You're making fun of me," I said defensively.

"Not entirely," he said, his voice low pitched. "No—I'm not just making fun of you. You haven't had much experience with men, have you?"

"None whatsoever!" I retorted, "And I'm not sure I want any if you are any example of the men I shall meet!"

Norman Wade laughed loudly. He stepped back, holding out his hands as though giving up. He continued to laugh while my cheeks burned hotly. I wanted to run into the house and be swallowed up by the crowd, but he was still standing between me and the door, and I was afraid of making an even greater fool of myself. Norman Wade tossed his cigar over the railing and folded his arms over his chest. His laughter subsided, but his eyes were still full of amusement.

"You're quite right," he said. "I mustn't let the clothes fool me. You're still an innocent school girl, despite the air of sophistication. Far be it from me to be the one to indoctrinate you into the mysteries of the adult world. You stick to your novels and your sketch book for a while. That's the safest course."

"You—you're intolerable," I said.

"Do you find me so?"

"Entirely!"

"I'm delighted. It's refreshing after all that primping and fawning from the local lasses."

"Intolerable!" I repeated vehemently.

I started to go past him. He put his hand on my shoulder, restraining me.

"Not just yet, Miss Moore," he said. His voice was serious now, no trace of mockery in it. "Have you been behaving yourself?"

"What do you mean?"

"Have you been minding your own business?"

"I don't know what you're talking about."

"My uncle mentioned that he found you prowling around the house in the middle of the night last week. That isn't wise. You've also been going to Dower House quite frequently. I wouldn't. I would stay away from there. You ran into Andrew Graystone, I understand. Helena said Hugo almost attacked you. He never attacks unless he's told to do so. You are causing entirely too much bother around here."

"What I do is my affair."

He clenched my shoulders angrily.

"You little fool!" he said passionately. "Can't you see—no, you can't. I don't expect you to. You're an innocent little thing with no idea what you're up against. You stay in your room, and stay away from Dower House. Do as I say. You just tend to your own business."

"And just what is that, Mr. Wade?"

"I wish I could say," he replied. He released me. He seemed wary now, as though exhausted from so much emotion. "You are a little girl. You must act as proper little girls do. You must be a companion to Helena and occupy yourself with innocent things. I wish you would take up embroidery."

"Don't count on it, Mr. Wade," I retorted.

I swept past him and went into the house, closing the door firmly behind me. I leaned against it for a moment. My temples were throbbing, and I was in a wretched mood, but my head was quite clear now. Billy Randall saw me, and he hurried over. I permitted him to bring me a plate of food and then I danced with him again. The color and movement of the party engulfed me, and I tried to forget Norman Wade and his strange words. Several men asked me to dance, and I whirled around the floor, my head held high. I chatted and smiled and flirted politely and laughed when they said something they thought amusing. I gave myself up entirely to the sound and movement. An hour passed, two, and I was exhausted from the effort of being charming and gracious.

"Mrs. Henderson drank too much champagne and passed out in the cloak room," Helena said. "Her poor husband had to take her home. She's dreadfully common, for all their money and position in the community."

We were standing by the French doors. I begged off dancing for a while, and it was a relief just to stand there and watch the couples glide over the smooth parquet floor. My head ached, and my whole body felt sore. I had thrown myself into the activity with too much abandon and it was beginning to tell. Helena looked slightly agitated, although she smiled and nodded to friends who passed.

"You look a little pale," she remarked.

"I'm exhausted," I told her.

"Yes, you've done nothing but dance for two hours, and with so much vivacity! All the young men are quite beyond themselves with eagerness to know you better. Several of them have asked me about you. Did you find any who suited you?"

"I'm afraid not."

"Not even Billy Randall?" she asked, smiling wickedly.

"Him least of all."

"Oh dear, I so wanted you to meet a nice young man who could become your beau. I adore playing Cupid, but there's not much to work with. Oh, I don't mean you dear. I mean the men. A rather drab lot, for all their respectability. I don't imagine any of them would make a maiden's heart flutter. Can you imagine poor Billy on a charging white horse?"

"Hardly," I replied, smiling at the thought.

"The party is a smashing success," she said, waving her fan. "No doubt about it. It's the event of the season. Everyone's delighted with the music, and the ballroom has never looked so grand, not even in the old days. And the food! My dear, there isn't a crumb left. Not a crumb! They went after it like a hoard of starved ruffians."

"Where's my uncle?" I asked. "I haven't seen him in over an hour."

"Oh, Charles has closed himself up in the library, quite bored with everything. I told him how rude it was, but he's been disgruntled since morning. I wish I knew why. What a night. . . ."

The candles had burned down and were beginning to splutter when the guests began to leave. The musicians folded up their music and put their instruments away in black calf cases. Carriages began coming up the drive to pick up happy but wearied guests. I stood beside Helena on the front porch, shaking hands and bidding good night. The thunder rumbled loudly and there was a streak of lightning. The first drops of rain began falling as the last guests scurried to their carriages. The drive was at last empty. Only the Japanese lanterns waved wildly like living things as the rain began to pour in torrents.

XI

HELENA AND I were both far too overstimulated to sleep after the guests had departed. We sat in the front sitting room, weary but wide awake. Helena slumped on the sofa, her feet propped up on a stool. She smoked a cigarette voraciously, casually flicking the ashes into a tray. Her lovely blue gown was rumpled, and her careful coiffure had fallen into a mass of silver curls. I stood at the window, holding the curtain back and watching the rain. It splashed and whirled and completely enveloped Falconridge, making it seem even more isolated. Lightning bolts crashed with savage silver-blue anger, and the thunder was deafening. We were in the midst of a terrific storm, the worst since I had come to Falconridge over a month ago.

"I hope all the guests get home safely," Helena said. "Some of them will undoubtedly be caught in the middle of the storm, those who have a long way to drive. I'd certainly hate to be out in it. Listen to that wind. It's vicious."

"I've never seen it this bad before," I remarked.

"Oh, this is nothing compared to what I've seen," she replied. "I remember once when I thought the whole house would come toppling down. I was younger then and hadn't lived in Cornwall long."

"The house seems strangely deserted now, doesn't it?" I said. "After all the noise and activity and movement of the party filling it up with life—it seems empty."

"Like a room that has just been vacated by a group of people," Helena added. "Yes, I get that feeling. It's sad. This poor old house. It's seen so much life in its day, and it's been so empty recently, no swarms of young people, no parties, just two middle-aged people rattling about in all these rooms. Tonight was like the old days—Falconridge was a jewel then, every door open, every room throbbing with life. Now it's like an old maid that life has passed by."

"You really love it, don't you?" I said quietly.

"With all my heart. I hate to see it like this. Someday, perhaps, when Norman inherits it, it will revive some of its lost youth. He has the same love for the place. He and his wife and children will fill it up and live in it like it's meant to be lived in."

"He seemed very interested in that redhead," I said, "Arabella, I think her name is."

"The little Treveleyan girl? No, I'm afraid not. None of these girls around here seem to interest him, not the suitable ones anyway. I think he wants someone special. . . ." She scrutinized me with narrowed eyes, her head held a little to one side.

"He must be very particular," I said.

"Oh, he is, my dear. Haven't you noticed that?"

I did not reply. I thought about Norman Wade. I had not seen him again after I had left him on the front porch. I had looked around for him, but he had been nowhere to be seen. He had not put in an appearance when the guests began to leave, and I had thought that Arabella had looked disappointed when she left and did not see him. Perhaps he had gone to his lodgings early, before the party was over. I was certain that he had not gone off with one of the girls. I had counted them, irritated at myself as I did so.

"I think I'll go watch the storm from the back door for a moment," I said. "I imagine the water is in waves on the courtyard. Can I bring you anything when I come back?"

"No, thank you, dear," Helena said, looking at me with a curious expression, half-inquisitive, half-smiling.

I walked through the halls to the back of the house. The ballroom looked ghostly now with only one or two candles burning, the floor littered with little scraps of debris: a dance card, a faded rose, a bit of ribbon. The buffet tables were barren, the gleaming white linen tablecloths soiled and grayish in the gloom. The servants had cleared away the dishes earlier, and they would all have a busy day tomorrow cleaning away all the signs of the party and putting the house in order. They had all gone to bed, even Lucy, who had wanted to wait up for me and hear all about the dancing. I passed down the back hall and stood in the little foyer that looked out over the courtyard.

The rain swept in waves over the flagstones, splattering in great gusts. The wind tore at the box hedges, that waved dark green arms in protest of the violence. The carriage house was dark. I had come to see that, of course. If Norman Wade was there, he had gone to sleep already. I stood watching the rain come down in mighty sheets that slammed against the house and splattered loudly against the window panes. I was ashamed of myself for coming for such a reason, and I turned to go back and join Helena.

By rights I should be bone-weary and longing for bed, but I was in a strange restless mood. The storm added to it, and I was certain that I would not be able to sleep at all tonight. I had an overpowering feeling that something was about to happen. I could not explain it, but it was strong, impossible to shake. I walked on down the hall towards the lamp that glowed in the front part of the house. I had brought no lamp of my own, as the lightning constantly illuminated the halls with its violent phosphorescent blasts.

It felt strange to be wandering the halls still in my evening gown. The skirt made soft, silken noises as it swayed over the hoop, and my bare arms and shoulders were exposed to the chill. An explosion of thunder rent the air, and I thought I could feel the house tremble. I went hurriedly towards the lamp.

Martha Victor was standing by the front staircase, still in her neat black uniform. She was immobile, like a statue, but her dark eyes watched my progress as I came down the hall. The grandfather clock that stood in the hall struck, one loud clang. Martha nodded to me as I came past her. I thought there was a wry smile on her lips, but her face was in the shadows, only her eyes and broad forehead really visible. I wondered why she was still up. There was no reason for it, surely. It was as if she was waiting for something, I thought.

I hurried on down the hall, wishing I did not have that feeling of inferiority when I was around the woman. There was something about her that intimidated me, made me feel small and foolish, though I tried to hide the feeling with a haughty bearing around her. It was not fear. I was not afraid of her, but she made me feel—vulnerable, I thought. I had never been able to find the right word for it before. Yes, she made me feel vulnerable.

I had just passed the library door when I heard it open. Charles Lloyd stepped into the hall. He had changed from his evening clothes to a pair of black trousers and a dark yellow smoking jacket with black velvet lapels. His forehead was lined and, seen unguarded, his face looked worried. A lock of hair had fallen over his forehead, and his eyes were dark with introspection. There was a bottle of port on a table behind him, an empty glass beside it. I wondered how long he had been drinking. His shoulders were slumped a little, and looked older. When he saw me, his whole manner changed. A dark frown came onto his face, and he straightened up, looking at me angrily.

"Still up? Roaming again?"

"Helena and I are staying in the sitting room. I am on my way back there."

"It's one o'clock."

"Neither of us can sleep in this storm."

"Where have you been?"

"I just wanted to watch the storm from the back windows. The courtyard is like a lake." I wondered why he was so curious about my whereabouts.

"I've spoken to you about prowling," he said sharply.

"I wasn't prowling," I replied testily.

"Helena is still up? She hasn't taken her laudanum?" This seemed to disturb him.

"We—we plan to talk. Would you care to join us?" I asked, hoping he would refuse.

"I've had my share of gabbing females for one night," he replied, his voice gruff. "You two had better go on up to bed soon. This storm may last all night."

As I left, I noticed Martha Victor going to the library. She and Charles Lloyd stood in the doorway for a moment, talking quietly, and then they both went in, closing the door behind them. What could my uncle want to see the housekeeper about at this time of night? I wondered. I assumed that she had been waiting for his summons. Perhaps he wanted to go over some household accounts, but at this hour? It was very strange, but then this was not a normal night. There was something in the air. The whole house seemed to be holding its breath, waiting. For what? What was wrong?

I went on to the sitting room. Helena had lighted a small fire in the tiny white marble fireplace, and the flames were beginning to lick the logs like tiny orange and blue tongues. The fire helped a little, but there was a chill in the room. Helena smiled when I came in.

"Was there a light?" she asked.

"Where?"

"Why, in the carriage house, of course."

"I—I didn't notice," I lied.

Helena laughed to herself. It was a pleasant sound, but I found it irritating. She missed nothing, I thought. Helena was shrewd and observant, and she probably knew all about my feud with

Norman Wade. She probably knew that that was the reason he had stopped taking the evening meal with us. I went over to the window, making no comment. The storm seemed to have abated somewhat. The thunder rumbled in the distance, but not as loud. The lightning was not as frequent nor as bright. The rain, still falling heavily, did not fall with such fury.

I told Helena about seeing Martha Victor going into the library to see my uncle. I said I thought it strange that they should be together at this time of night. Helena merely smiled, somewhat bitterly.

"Martha is like a broody old hen where Charles is concerned. If he was in the library—with a bottle of port, no doubt—it's only natural that she would be up and that she would go see if he needed anything. Her devotion to him is—quite touching, I suppose one should say. I find it rather irritating."

She lit a fresh cigarette, took two long puffs and then crushed it out in the tray. Helena looked tense, not at all herself. She stood up, her blue eyes filled with a strange emotion I could not read.

"I think I'll go up now," she said. "The rain is slacking. The storm should die down in a little while." She smiled at me, but it was a forced smile. I wondered why my mentioning her husband and Martha Victor had affected her in such an unusual way. She looked upset, and there was not any apparent reason for it.

"I'll go up with you," I said, concerned. "I know I won't be able to sleep, but I will read for a while."

"Come, then," she said. "It is terribly late. I hadn't realized I was so very tired."

We stepped into the main hallway. Only one candle gleamed, and it cast a faint light. The dark parquet floor gleamed with a dull shine and dark shadows climbed to the high beamed ceiling. The sound of the rain was a dull, monotonous background noise. Helena clasped my hand, and we stood in the dim half light, watching the candle flame flicker. Again I had the eerie sensation that the house was holding its breath, waiting for something to happen. Helena seemed to feel this way, too.

It happened as we started down the hall. There was a crash of thunder and then a moment of complete silence. Someone pounded on the front door, violently. The dogs, somewhere in the back of the house, began to bark. Helena squeezed my hand tightly, and we both stared at each other in silence. The library door opened and Charles came out, looking pale. From the back regions of the house Martha Victor materialized, her face as blank and expressionless as a mask. The four of us stood in the hall a moment, listening to the frantic knocking.

My uncle threw a quick glance in our direction. He pressed his lips together very tightly, his eyes narrowed as though he was debating the wisdom of opening the door. Martha Victor glided up beside him. She looked into his eyes and nodded almost imperceptibly. My uncle moved to the door and flung it back. A gust of rain swept in, wetting the floor. Lavinia Graystone stood in the doorway, her fist still raised to knock again. She stared at my uncle, her eyes wide with fright. She made no effort to come in. The rain swept past her, making puddles on the floor. She seemed paralyzed, unable to move. My uncle gripped her arm and pulled her into the house. He closed the door behind her, shoving against the wind to get it shut. It slammed loudly. Tiny pools of water stood in front of it.

Lavinia was drenched to the skin. She wore a black cloak that clung to her shoulders like wet wings and a vivid pink dress that was molded against her body, every inch of the material soaked. Her skirts were streaked with mud, and her hair hung in wet ringlets about her face, one dark strand plastered against her cheek. She pushed it aside, her hand quivering like a small white bird as it moved. Her large brown eyes were filled with fright, and the corners of her mouth trembled. She was panting, as though she had been running. None of us made a move toward her. We were too stunned.

My uncle was the first to compose himself. He seemed to be in a towering rage, but he banked it down, as one will bank down a fire. I saw him draw his shoulders up and pull the lines of his face together into a mask of calmness. He held his rage in check when he addressed her.

"What is the meaning of this, woman?"

"I—I had to come...."

"Why did you come here?"

"It was—Andrew is...."

"Yes? Yes? Don't stammer."

"Charles," Helena interrupted. "Can't you see she's...."

"You keep out of this," he said firmly. "Now, Mrs. Graystone, compose yourself." It was a command.

Lavinia looked up at him with brown eyes dark with fear. I could see that he terrified her. She pushed another lock of hair from her temple, and the trembling of her lips ceased. I could see her summoning up all her natural dignity. That was hard to do under the circumstances, but her native poise came to her aid. She stood very still, her eyes lowered, and when she finally spoke her voice was level, beautifully modulated.

"My husband is gone," she said quietly. "I thought at first it was just another of his sulky periods, but I began to grow anxious when he didn't come back for dinner."

"He hasn't come back at all?" my uncle asked.

"No," she replied.

"He has been collecting rent money from the tenants all day."

She nodded. A flush glowed on her cheeks like a pink stain.

"You think something has happened to him?" he questioned.

Lavinia looked at him calmly. Then she slowly shook her head.

"No. I think he has run away—with the money."

Charles Lloyd said nothing. I could see the dark fires in his eyes. He stared at Lavinia with pure hatred, and then he turned away. He hit his fist in the palm of his hand, cursing under his breath.

"I was afraid this would happen someday!" he cried suddenly. "The man is a thief!"

My uncle had always taken up for Andrew Graystone before, and I wondered why he was so violent in his condemnation now, so quick to accept Lavinia's supposition without further questioning.

"I waited and waited," she said, "and he still didn't come. I had to come tell you."

"In the middle of this storm?" Helena asked.

"I didn't think about that. I was—afraid to stay

there, waiting. I knew Mr. Lloyd would want to know. I knew he would want to try to find my husband before it was too late."

"Where could he have gone?" Helena asked.

"I—I don't know," she said, hesitating just a little. My uncle noticed the hesitation. He whirled around, facing her with venom. Lavinia met his gaze calmly.

"Has he ever taken off like this before?"

"No. Never with someone else's property."

"But he has spent the night away from Dower House, hasn't he?"

"Once or twice. . . ."

"Where did he go?" my uncle demanded.

"He—we quarreled once. He stayed away for two days. He told me later that he had been at the lighthouse."

"The lighthouse?"

"The old deserted lighthouse on the other side of the cove. No one goes there, but there is a little room beneath the observation tower. Andrew has gone there several times."

"You think he might be there now?"

"I—I wouldn't know."

"Did he take the horse?"

"No. He took it this morning, of course, but the horse came back early this evening, the saddle empty. That was when I really began to worry. I thought Andrew might have had an accident. But surely someone would have known if that had happened. I would have been informed. Then I—I began to think about the money he had been collecting."

"Does he have access to a boat?"

"There was a little rowboat he found deserted on

the sand one day. He repaired it and used it to fish sometimes, and when he went to the lighthouse. I don't know if the boat's still there or not."

"He wouldn't have gone into town," my uncle said. "He would have been seen. He would have gone somewhere to hide for a day or so until a ship came in that he could board. He's bound to be still around here somewhere."

"Charles. . . ." Helena began.

"I'm going after him!" Charles Lloyd said, fierce determination in his voice. "I'll go down to the boathouse and take out *The Falcon*. I'll go to the lighthouse, and if he isn't there I'll search every inch of this county until I find him."

"Charles," Helena said, her voice trembling, "you can't go out now. Not in this storm. It can wait until morning. If he's at the lighthouse he'll still be there. Wait. Please wait."

He ignored her. He turned and went upstairs, his footsteps ringing loudly. After a moment Martha Victor followed him, moving silently, her black uniform looking like a shroud. The one candle flickered, threatening to go out. Lavinia stood very quietly, her wet pink dress clinging to her, her brown eyes fixed on that turn of the staircase where my uncle had disappeared. Helena stood with her hands clasped together. Outside the rain picked up in momentum. It sounded louder, pounding on the drive, lashing at the house.

My uncle came downstairs. He wore a black suit, heavy black boots and a sturdy black cloak that enveloped his enormous shoulders. He had his riding crop with him, and he strode across the hall without even looking at us. He flung open the door, letting in sheets of rain. The cloak billowed

about his shoulders like the wings of a bird of prey.
He was drenched before he even stepped outside.
He pulled the door shut behind him. The three of
us stared at that closed door, wordlessly. There was
no sound but the storm, increasing now in fury.

XII

THE SKIES WERE swollen with rain that would not fall. Ponderous gray clouds hung low, tormented by a lashing wind. There was one line of blue on the horizon, half concealed by the clouds. It had been like this all day. All day we had waited. Lavinia was still with us. She sat by the window, looking out, not speaking. For once Helena was silent. She had not said a dozen words all day. Falconridge was like a tomb, and we the living were trapped within its walls. Even the servants were quiet, moving about their tasks with hushed voices and stealthy movements.

It was after five o'clock when the men came. They had found the boat—*The Falcon* had been washed up on shore two miles down the beach and there was a huge hole in its bottom. The hull was smashed. It had undoubtedly crashed against the rocks in the fury of the storm. A fisherman found the mast splintered against rocks further on down the beach. The body had not been recovered.

Helena took the news with dignity. She was polite to the men and thanked each of them separately. When they left she stood for a long time watching the fire dying in the fireplace. When the ashes had turned from pink to gray and the room was permeated with a clammy chill, she turned and smiled. It was a vague smile, a mere upturning of the corners of her lips. She said she would go up to her room now. She nodded to Lavinia and me and left, holding herself erect, her shoulders straight. She had never looked so regal.

Lavinia went back to Dower House. There was no news from Andrew Graystone. A week passed, and still she had had no word. Her husband did not return, and none of us believed he ever would. I thought it was the best thing for her. She could begin a new life, and she would be much better off without him. She came to Falconridge once or twice to see Helena during the first week, bringing a bouquet of flowers once, a loaf of newly baked bread another time. She stayed for only a short while, grave and graceful in manner. Then she stopped coming, and we did not hear from her. I supposed she had her own private grief to nurture.

Norman Wade collected the rest of the rents. He went out every morning and did not come in until very late. He worked twice as hard as he had done before. He and Helena had agreed that everything must go on as normally as possible. There would be time to work out all the plans later. For the present, routine must be followed, and it was routine that saved us all. Tragedy had struck, but we were not allowed to sink under its weight.

Helena carried on much as before, but there was a new gravity in her manner. She busied herself about the house, doing little jobs, inventing jobs to do when there were none that needed to be done. She painted and cleaned and polished and scrubbed. She relined the pantry shelves with new paper. She made new curtains for the kitchen and put them up herself. She spent a great part of each day in the gardens, weeding, hoeing, talking with the gardener and making plans for new shrubs.

She did not talk about the accident, but I knew she still had hope. Perhaps he had been miraculously rescued. Perhaps he had gone on in his search for the missing bailiff. The hope was slender, but it was strong, at least during the first days. She would look up anxiously if there was the sound of hoofbeats on the drive. She would sit by the window during the rare moments when she was not busy. She stayed up late every night, sitting in the front parlor and listening for the sound she knew in her heart would not come. After a while, even this slender hope died away, and she had a look of resignation that I found very sad.

A pall hung over Falçonridge. We were all restless, waiting for something that we could not explain. I felt it in the air. It was a real thing, as tangible as the moist old walls and the drafty halls. We seemed to be in a state of suspension. Even Lucy noticed it. She was glum, silent, not at all her cheery self. She seemed to be harboring a terrible secret, and keeping it to herself was draining away all her spirits. Martha Victor kept to herself, spending most of her time in the servants' quarters. One night as I was going to my room I saw her standing by the door of Charles Lloyd's room, as though she had just come out of it. I wondered what she could have been in his room for. She was grimmer, more silent than ever, and I couldn't help but shudder when I saw her.

I did not sleep well. Every night when I closed my eyes I saw a whirlpool of images, all of them revolving around rapidly, and once again I felt that they were trying to tell me something. I could hear the whispering voices. The words seemed to be urgent, but I could not quite understand them. I saw my uncle and Andrew Graystone and Lavinia, and all three of them seemed to be telling me of a conspiracy. It was always very late when I finally went to sleep, and every morning I was pale and weary, with dark shadows under my eyes.

Helena noticed this and commented on it. I told her about being unable to sleep properly. I told her that I heard noises that should not be there, that I saw faces and heard words that were always just out of reach. She said this had all affected my nerves and suggested that I get out more, go for walks. She offered to let me take some of her laudanum, but I refused that.

One morning, almost three weeks after *The Falcon* had been found, I walked down to the boathouse. It was a foggy day, the pale blue sky half obscured by puffy gray clouds that hung low and moved slowly in the breeze. The mists were thin, not quite obscuring anything but covering every object with a hazy veil of moving white vapors. As I walked along the beach, I had the sensation of walking in a dream landscape. The waves washed over the sand with a soft swooshing sound and out in the water the large gray boulders were enveloped in swirling white vapors. I walked at the edge of the water, my feet bare, the waves splashing the hem of my light blue dress. My shoulders were wrapped in a dark sapphire blue shawl, and my hair flew free in the wind.

The boathouse was built out over the water. The waves slapped against the flimsy wooden frame. The boards were encrusted with salt, and barnacles clung to the lower slats. It was a shabby structure, needing much repair. One of the window panes was broken and the roof sagged. The door stood open, banging monotonously in the wind. Half hidden by fog, it looked almost sinister. I thought about my uncle coming here the night of the storm.

I pushed back the door and went inside. A platform was built around three sides, the fourth open to the water. In the middle there was a place for the boats. One old rowboat bobbed in the water, hitting against the side of the platform. There was a large empty place where *The Falcon* had been. There was a rusted anchor on the platform, beside it a coil of rope that was rotting. Fishing gear was hung on the walls, covered with delicate silken cobwebs that vibrated in the breeze that came through the broken window pane.

The place made me uneasy, but something had compelled me to come here. I had set off this morning with no destination in mind, and my feet seemed to have brought me here of their own volition. I had been guided here by some power that I could not comprehend, and now that I stood looking down at the empty space in the water, I felt a shiver go down my spine. Something was wrong. What? What? If only I knew, I could answer all the questions that had been haunting me ever since I first came to Falconridge. Something did not fit, and I felt that it should be obvious to me what it was. Something I had seen. Something I had heard. Something was there in the back of my mind, but it would not come to the surface.

I had sensed an aura of mystery about Falconridge from the first night I had come here. My aunt had been the only one to welcome me.

The others had clearly not wanted me. Martha Victor, my uncle, Norman Wade—all in various ways had shown their resentment of my presence. I was an intruder. I should leave. Falconridge was not the place for me. Why? Why had they wanted me to leave? There had been little warnings all along, and now one man had disappeared and another was dead, his body churning somewhere in the treacherous waters. I felt that the mystery was still present. It was there, permeating the very walls of Falconridge, even stronger now. In my present nervous state I was even more aware of it. I could not sleep, I could not rest—not as long as I felt this uneasiness in the air around me.

The waves slapped against the sides of the boathouse. The floor swayed a little under my feet, the old warped planks groaning. Behind me the door banged open and shut, the broken hinge creaking with a shrill, raspy noise. I could smell the rotting rope and the dried salt and the unpleasant odors of decay. Several minutes passed, and I was suddenly aware of my own fear. I hardly dared breathe. Something had changed. Something was wrong. The door had stopped banging. It was silent, and the silence was terrifying. I whirled around. Norman Wade was leaning in the doorway, his thumb hooked in his belt, watching me with one dark brow arched inquisitively.

I had no idea how long he had been there. He was wearing a pair of boots and tight navy blue pants that clung to his calves and thighs like a second skin. His white cambric shirt had full sleeves that were gathered at the wrists. It was open at the throat, and the material was a little damp from the vapors. His hair was damp, too, the dark black ends curling about the nape of his neck. He looked menacing as he stood there, casually blocking the door. I stepped back, and the boards creaked. The water behind me slapped loudly against the wood. I tried to hide my fear, but he could see it. He frowned darkly.

"Two more steps back," he said quietly, "and you would be in the water. It would carry you out to sea. No one would ever know what had happened to you."

I stood nervously on the edge of the platform, my knees weak. I was afraid I would lose my balance. I stared at him defiantly, making no reply. He moved towards me slowly, not saying a word. He stood in front of me, his chest heaving a little. He put his hands on my shoulders. He was breathing heavily, and his eyelids drooped as he looked down at me. There was a drop of moisture in the cleft of his chin. His fingers gripped my flesh.

"Or someone could push you," he said. "Just one little shove and you would be gone. You could never swim in those skirts, not in this water. It would be so easy," his voice was beautifully modulated. It seemed to caress the air. "So very easy. . . ."

"And—what would it accomplish?" I asked, my voice trembling.

"No more little girl who asks too many questions. No more little girl who is always in the wrong place at the wrong time. The corners of your lips are trembling. Are you afraid, Lauren?"

"Yes," I whispered, unable to lie.

"I could kill you. So easily, so neatly."

His face was very close to mine. I looked into the dark blue eyes and saw the darker blue lights there.

I seemed to be lost in them, to be held captive by their magnetic power. I watched his lips moving as they formed his words. The corners slowly curled up into a smile, and the dark lights flickered in his eyes.

"You are afraid?" he repeated.

I nodded. I could not speak. My throat was dry.

"Good," he said, the smile playing on his lips.

"What—what do you intend to do?"

"Frighten you," he said. "Frighten some sense into you."

He released me and stepped back a little. I closed my eyes. I was aware of the dark wings fluttering inside my head, and then I stumbled. His strong arms flew about me, catching me as I tottered. Norman Wade held me to him. I could feel the pounding of his heart, and it seemed that it was as quick as my own. With his arms still around me, he led me away from the edge of the platform.

"There," he said quietly, letting me go.

"That was a—dreadful thing to do, Mr. Wade," I said, barely able to enunciate the words.

"I suppose it was," he replied calmly. "I've done a lot of dreadful things in my time."

"You followed me here?"

"I saw you climbing down the side of the cliff. I was crossing the courtyard and could not believe you would do anything so foolhardy on a day like this. You could have fallen so easily."

"I held on to the roots. The path is safe."

"I beg to differ with you. It has never been safe, and it's twice as dangerous when everything is shrouded with fog. Where are your shoes? Have you lost them?"

"I left them at the foot of the cliff. I wanted to

walk barefooted in the sand."

"You'll catch pneumonia. You have no sense at all. You need a nursemaid."

"Is that your opinion?" I asked sharply.

"That's it," he retorted, "and don't contradict me."

"Well...."

"Why did you come here?" he asked, his voice gruff.

"I don't know. I—I wanted to see where *The Falcon* had been. Something—led me here."

"What kind of nonsense are you gabbling about now?"

"It's true. I didn't know I was coming here. Something led me. I saw the boathouse rising out of the mists, and I knew that I had to come to see it. I hadn't known it before. Instinct. Some kind of instinct led me here."

He did not reply. He looked at me with a frown on his face. It was clear that he was irritated with me. His very stance showed it. He held his legs spread wide apart, his fists on his hips, his head held forward with the brows lowered, the eyes glowering at me through the forest of thick, sooty lashes. I pulled myself up haughtily, throwing the ends of the shawl about my shoulders as though it were an ermine cloak. Norman Wade continued to stare at me in that infuriated manner.

"I don't expect you to understand," I said.

"And I don't expect you to understand what a little fool you are. I suppose I'll have to keep my eye on you every minute. And if you say 'I can take care of myself,' I'll slap you. I'm going to move my things into the house tonight. I'll take my uncle's room. It's mine by rights now, I suppose. Now come on. Let's see if we can get you back to the house without anything happening to you."

He took my wrist and practically dragged me out of the boathouse. I staggered along behind him as he marched along the shore, holding on to my wrist as a parent would hold on to a child who strayed when not kept secure. I stumbled once and fell to my knees in the damp sand. Norman Wade let out an exasperated sigh and waited while I stood up and brushed the sand from my skirt. Then we continued on our way. He stopped while I gathered up my shoes and put them on. He led me much further on down the beach where the land made a natural curve up the slope.

The grass was dark green and damp with moisture. I looked back at the ocean. I could barely see the edge of the shore through the fog. I could see the tongues of water lapping at the sand, leaving foam as they slid away. The rest was obscured by fog that rose up in wavering white columns that swirled in the breeze. Ahead of us, I could see the roofs of Falconridge rising out of the mists. Only when we reached the courtyard did Norman Wade release me. He still seemed to be in a towering rage, and he left me there without another word.

He moved his belongings from the carriage house that night. A manservant carried piles of clothes down the hall. I stood at the door of my bedroom and watched. The servants came back with another load as one of the maids did the room. Martha Victor stood in the hall. Her eyes were dark with resentment, and she watched the proceedings as she would watch an execution. When Norman Wade himself came down the hall, Martha did not try to hide the hatred that glittered in those eyes. He nodded to her and said some light word of banter, but she did not reply. Her lips were pressed together tightly and they looked a little white around the edges. She watched him until he disappeared down the hall, and then she left, moving as silently as a raven in her black dress.

Helena was delighted. There was a flush of pleasure on her cheeks when he came to the table that evening. She wore a pale lavender dress and her diamonds in honor of the occasion. Although more subdued than before, some of her old spirit seemed to have returned. She and Norman talked pleasantly. I sat quietly in my chair, peeling a peach. Norman Wade, sitting at the head of the table, seemed to have taken on a new authority. He gave orders to the servants in a cool voice, and when the meat was not cut properly he reprimanded in the same cool tones. For the first time I could see a resemblance between him and Charles Lloyd. It was in manner, not in appearance. He was the Master of Falconridge now. It was what he had always wanted. I watched him with lowered eyes, and I wondered. I wondered.

The body was recovered three days later. It had been found twelve miles down shore, washed up among the rocks. It had begun to decompose, and it had been badly battered. Only the thick blond hair and the black onyx ring carved in the shape of a falcon made identity certain. It was to be sent back in a closed coffin. Helena took the news calmly. The last ray of hope had long since died, and her light blue eyes were clear of any emotion. She did not cry. She gave instructions in a level voice, and then she walked slowly down the hall, ignoring the three dogs who went scurrying after her.

XIII

THE OLD GRAYSTONE church stood on a barren tract of land two miles from the village. Gnarled, ancient oak trees grew in the yard, reaching out to touch the roof with skeletal limbs, and all the surrounding land was flat, deserted, covered with brown grass that was seared by the wind. A drab sky hung low over the church the day of the funeral. Several carriages stood in the church yard, and inside there was the stifling odor of too many wax candles and too many people. Every pew was filled with grim, sober faced people, the same people who had been so gay the night of the party. The old gray walls were damp. Smoke from the candles rose to the oak beamed ceiling.

The black coffin rested on a dais with a single spray of lilies on it. Behind it the Vicar stood, his lips speaking the words I found impossible to concentrate on. They were solemn and depressing, spoken in a monotone with an occasional thundering flourish. The atmosphere in the church was suffocating. Light came in through the green stained glass windows, bathing everything with a greenish hue. I had the unpleasant sensation of being caught up in a subterranean nightmare. None of this seemed real.

Helena, Norman Wade and I sat in the family pew with its cushions of faded red velvet. The dusty old family escutcheon hung on the wall beside us, a fierce black falcon flying over a field of green. There was a black border about the shield, and I thought it appropriate now. The pew was of heavy oak, with high back and sides which afforded us a little privacy from the eyes of the curious. Norman Wade sat with his eyes fixed on the Vicar. His profile looked stony, the jaw thrust out a little, the mouth tight, the blue eyes hard. He might have been in a trance. Helena had a black veil over her face, and she seemed restless. She moved her hands about in her lap, twisting her gold wedding band. Her stiff black dress rustled crisply and she looked up to see if I had heard the noise. She did not cry. She had not cried once. I felt that all her tears for Charles Lloyd had been shed many years ago.

When the services were over we filed out before all the people who stood assembled on the front steps. No one spoke. They stood in little groups huddled together as though fearing that death would touch them too. An ancient black coach adorned with plumes of black ostrich feathers took us to the graveyard. It was a long drive through the barren countryside. The graveyard stood in the middle of the fallow fields, without a single tree to afford it protection from the wind. It was enclosed by a rusty iron fence, the tombstones yellow and crumbling behind the bars. I saw the newly dug grave with a pile of earth beside it. An old man with a shovel stood waiting.

Not more than a dozen people followed us. The cemetery was too far, and Charles Lloyd had not been popular. Those who had felt it their duty to show their respects had come to the church, and they would send cards of condolence. Only a few had come to the burial. They stood quietly as the coffin was brought to the graveside. Helena, Norman Wade and I stood under a green awning that flapped in the wind. Helena's face was hidden by her veil, and Norman Wade stood with his hands behind his back, his head lowered. He seemed to be examining the highly glossed toes of his boots. My eyes wandered over the faces of those present.

Martha Victor stood with two other servants. She was shrouded all in black, and her face looked as though it had been chiseled out of granite. The wind whipped at her black garments. Lavinia Graystone wore a dress of dark green and a bonnet with a long semi-transparent black veil that fell over her face. She clutched a handkerchief in her hand, and when she raised it to her face, I saw that she was crying. Her brown eyes were filled with tears and they ran down her cheeks in sparkling rivulets. I thought it strange that she should be the only one crying. Perhaps Lavinia felt that she was responsible for my uncle's death. If she had not come to Falconridge that night, he would not have gone out in the storm. I felt great sympathy for the woman and wished that there were something I could do or say that would make her feel better.

A stranger stood a little apart from the other people, and there was something vaguely familiar about him. He wore soft gray trousers, a plum colored frock coat and a tall gray hat. One white gloved hand rested on the tip of a sleek ebony cane, the handle carved ivory. The man had the unmistakable look of the city about him. It was evident in his carefully trimmed mustache, in his elegant clothes, in the slightly nonchalant way he stood. I searched my memory, trying to place him, and then I realized that this was Mr. Stephens, the man Charles Lloyd had gone to see about some insurance when he was in London to pick me up. I had met Mr. Stephens at the restaurant and had been impressed with his well groomed hands and his beautiful manners.

When the ceremony was over and the old man had begun to toss shovels of dirt over the coffin, Mr. Stephens came over to Norman Wade as we were on our way to the coach. He and Norman talked quietly for a while as Helena and I got into the coach. When Norman joined us he did not say anything about the conversation. It was only after we had left the cemetery and were on our way back to Falconridge that he mentioned Mr. Stephens. He told Helena that the insurance man wanted to talk with her briefly about a policy and had asked permission to visit her the next day. He was staying at the inn in the village and would ride out to Falconridge. Norman Wade had given him permission to come.

"Is there some question about the policy?" Helena asked.

"I don't believe so. I think he just wants to confirm a few things before he writes up the papers. I wrote to him about the accident, knowing my uncle had taken out a policy and that the firm should be notified. I believe a lot of money is involved."

"Charles was always so vague about the policy," Helena said. "I have no idea what it entails. He kept some papers in the safe. Perhaps there is a copy of the policy there."

"I'll check tonight," he replied. "I want to go

over some of those papers anyway. I'll take care of everything, Helena. All you will have to do when Mr. Stephens comes is answer some questions and sign a statement. It won't tax you too much." He spoke in a tender voice, and he patted her hand.

Helena looked up at him sharply. "I'm not afraid it will tax me," she said. "I'm quite strong. You're not dealing with a nimble-witted old woman, Norman. All I need now is a good strong glass of brandy."

Norman Wade sat back in the seat, his arms folded across his chest. He smiled at her tenderly, as though humoring a child. Helena gave him an exasperated look and turned her attention to the fields we passed. The rest of the drive was silent. I felt that Helena thought her nephew just a little presumptuous. What she had said was true. She was not a nimble-witted old woman. She had shown great strength of character throughout this whole business, and if anything she was sharper and more resourceful than before.

The sun had already gone down when we reached Falconridge. None of us were hungry, and Helena told the servants to forget about the evening meal. Norman Wade went into the library and closed the door, ready to go over all my uncle's papers. Helena and I went into the front parlor. She threw herself down on the sofa and called the dogs. They came bounding into the room, happy to see her attentive again. Helena rang for one of the maids and told her to bring in brandy and glasses, then she took off her veil and tossed it casually on the floor.

"I refuse to wear mourning," she told me, patting her silver curls. "Charles wouldn't have wanted it, and besides, I would feel like a hypocrite. This has all been a great tragedy, and it distresses me, but I shall not mourn Charles. It should be no surprise to you that we shared absolutely no affection for one another."

I made no comment. The maid came in with the brandy. Helena poured out a drink for herself. I refused. She took a sip of the liquor and lit a cigarette. She smoked in silence for a while, long blue-gray plumes of smoke rising to the ceiling. Her eyes were reflective, and I could see that she was thinking about things past, about days when there had been love. I did not pressure her to talk about it. I felt it would be good for her, but it would have to be of her own volition.

"Things weren't always that way," she said after a while. "I loved Charles passionately when we were first married. That love lasted through a lot. I knew that he had grown tired of me, but I tried to carry on. I looked the other way when he started going to other women. Oh, there were many, many—but I endured. I blamed them, not him. He was so very handsome, so magnetic. I knew they couldn't resist him. Then when your mother came. . . ." she paused, looking at me. "You never knew why we were estranged, did you?"

"No," I replied quietly.

"Louise came to Falconridge. She was eighteen and a dazzling beauty. She was already engaged to your father and seemed very much in love with him. She was so young, so fresh, so full of life and vitality. I could not really blame her for falling under my husband's spell. He really put everything into it—all those little tricks, all that virile charm. She was captivated, helpless. She forgot all about her fiance. She woke up every morning with only one thing in mind—my husband."

"Did—did anything happen?" I asked, my voice a whisper.

"I called her a silly goose. I told her to go back to her handsome young soldier and leave my husband alone. She told me that she was going to run away with Charles—they were going to the continent. I didn't understand him—I need not go into all the details. Charles came into the room while we were arguing. Louise asked him to take her away with him. She had the foolish notion that he would throw her over his saddle and gallop away into the sunset. He didn't. He laughed at her and took my part in the argument. Louise left the next morning. We never spoke to each other again. I knew her heart had been broken. . . ."

"I'm so sorry," I said, sitting down on the sofa beside Helena. I was on the verge of tears.

"It was my fault," she said. "I should have handled her differently. I should have known she was an impetuous young girl, and I should have treated her like one, not like a woman. I never forgave myself, and I never forgave Charles. The love died then, all of it. We lived in the same house and got along quite well, but our marriage was a marriage in name only from then on. I liked Charles, I was very fond of him, but I no longer loved him."

"It must have been dreadful," I said.

"Oh, no," Helena replied. "I haven't been unhappy. Life is too rich, too full for unhappiness. I have had this house, and I've had so many joys, little things, things that compensate when the big things don't go as you would have liked. I've felt so bad about Louise for all of these years—I longed to make it up to her. I have you now."

She patted my hand and stood up, smiling brightly. Much of her old sparkle had returned, and I felt that now that the morbid business of the funeral was over she would be all right. "I shall go take off this hideous dress and burn it," she said. "I will grieve Charles, of course I will. I will miss him —even though things were as they were. You are too young to realize this, my dear, but life must go on. We live, we suffer, we are disappointed, we grieve—but life goes on."

Helena was true to her word. There was no sign of mourning when she received Mr. Stephens in the drawing room the next day. She wore a dress of white linen printed with yellow daisies, and there was a yellow ribbon in her hair. She was grave and polite, but the sadness had gone out of her light blue eyes and they sparkled with interest as Mr. Stephens explained the policy and asked her questions about Charles Lloyd's death. The sun was brilliant today. It poured through the open windows and made pools of wavering light on the pearl gray carpet, gleamed on the golden oak furniture and made a vivid sunburst on the silver pen set on the desk.

Helena sat quietly on the sofa. A small blue bowl on the table beside her held a loose bouquet of daisies that were the same color as the ones on her dress. Norman Wade stood by the window, his hand holding back the sweeping white drapery. He listened intently to everything that was said, occasionally asking a question of his own or making a comment. He had gone over the policy thoroughly the night before and seemed to fear that something was wrong with it. He seemed nervous, a frown stamped on his brow in a deep line. I sat in the chair covered with light blue satin, the blonde Adele at my feet. Helena had insisted that I be here when she learned that I had met Mr. Stephens in London.

"It seems everything is in order," Mr. Stephens said, taking out a sheet of paper from his leather portfolio. "Now if you will just put your signature on this line, Mrs. Lloyd. . . ."

Helena signed the paper and Mr. Stephens took it. He waved it a little to let the ink dry. He was smiling, a rather wry smile. When he had replaced the paper in the portfolio, he sighed deeply, shaking his head. He seemed both bewildered and amused.

"It's not often that the firm hands out such a large sum of money under such circumstances," he said.

"Everything is all right?" Norman Wade asked, rather tense. His eyes were worried.

"Yes, yes, everything is legal now that your aunt has signed the paper. She will receive the money as soon as arrangements can be made in London."

"It won't be put in the bank?" Helena asked.

"No, that's what's so unusual about the terms. The money is to be paid in gold and is to be delivered to you at Falconridge. No checks, no bonds, but cash. Ordinarily, it is deposited in the beneficiary's bank, but Mr. Lloyd wanted it put in a safe here, where you would have immediate access to it."

"Charles never trusted banks," Helena said.

"So it would seem. You won't be uneasy about having such a large sum of money in your possession?"

"It will be quite safe, Mr. Stephens," Norman Wade said in a voice of dismissal. "I want to thank you for all your trouble and consideration. I hope you have a nice trip back to London."

Mr. Stephens looked at him with an unusual light in his eyes. He arched one eyebrow slowly, and his lips were curled in that same wry smile I had noticed earlier. I could sense that the man did not like Norman Wade. He nodded briskly and then turned to make his farewells to Helena and me. Helena walked him to the door, and in a moment we could hear his hired rig driving away. When Helena came back into the room there was a pensive expression on her face.

"So puzzling," she said quietly. "I didn't know that Charles had taken out so large a policy. I certainly had no idea the money was to be delivered here. Do you really think it's wise to keep it in the safe here, Norman?"

"It will be perfectly all right, Helena," he said smoothly. "I'll take care of everything."

I watched Norman Wade as he slid his hands into his pockets. He had a very satisfied look on his face. He looked around the room, his eyes lingering on every piece of furniture. Falconridge belonged to him now, and everything in it was his. The money that would soon arrive was Helena's, and he had no right to it. He had told her that he would take care of everything. I did not doubt that he would.

A letter came addressed to Lavinia the next day. What mail the Graystones had was always delivered to Falconridge and carried on to Dower House by a servant. The envelope was crumpled, much handled. It was addressed in an awkward scrawl, and there was no return address but it was postmarked from New York City in America. As the servant took the letter from the tray and left for Dower House, I wondered who could be writing Lavinia from that part of the world. The answer was soon forthcoming.

Lavinia herself came to Falconridge that afternoon. She brought the letter and showed it to Helena. It was from Andrew Graystone. He had boarded a vessel on its way to America and had worked his way over on the ship, saving the money to invest in "business." He told Lavinia that he intended to stay in that country and that he would never be in England again. He told her to forget him. The letter was short and poorly worded. He made no apologies for taking the money or for leaving his wife. The letter was crude and blunt, like the man himself.

Helena handed the letter back to Lavinia. "What do you intend to do now?" she asked in a quiet voice.

"I have a little money," Lavinia said, "not much, just the little I've managed to save from my sewing. I am going to go back to Liverpool. I have one or two friends there. Perhaps I will be able to open another shop. I will try to, anyway."

"I'm so sorry about this, my dear," Helena said.

"Please don't be," Lavinia replied. "Perhaps it was best. I will be better off without him. We were never happy, you know. I am only sorry that—that it all had to happen this way. I thought you would want to know my plans."

"When are you leaving?" Helena asked.

"A ship leaves for Liverpool from the village tomorrow morning. I shall be on it. I've already seen to most of my packing. Most of the things in Dower House belong to you. What few personal possessions I had I will leave behind."

"You don't have to go, you know," Helena said. "You could stay on at the Dower House until you had more definite plans for the future."

"It is best this way," Lavinia said. "I—you can understand. I can't stay, not after all that's happened."

Helena nodded. "You are very brave," she said.

Lavinia looked up. Her large eyes were sparkling with tears and a smile quivered on the corners of her lips. She shook her head slowly from side to side. "Not brave," she said, her voice so low it was barely audible. "Just—just. . ." She could not complete the sentence. She turned and quietly left the room. Helena and I exchanged glances, both thinking about the relentless fate that had pursued the woman, making her life one long echo of unhappiness.

We drove with her to the village the next day, her bags piled in back of the carriage. Everything had been seen to. Servants had gone to help her close up Dower House. Norman Wade had ridden over early in the morning and taken Hugo, bringing him back to Falconridge. The dog had been ecstatic. Lavinia had already purchased her ticket. There was nothing to do now but board the ship and wait for it to sail. We were silent as we drove through the countryside.

Lavinia sat on the front seat by me. Her eyes

wandered over the rolling green hills bathed now in glittering sunlight that picked out every detail and sharpened it. There was a line of gray trees on the horizon, and a faint mist hung over them. The air was heavily laden with salt, and once we passed a curve of the road and could see the ocean below, the water lapping in large waves over the white sand. She seemed to be saying silent goodbyes to all this. I knew she would never come back. Cornwall for her would always be the scene of heartbreak and tragedy.

The ship was in the harbor, almost ready to set sail. The gangplank was down and brawny men with bronzed muscles rolled barrels up to the deck. Others carried heavy boxes balanced on their shoulders. The heavy sails flapped in the wind, and men climbed up the rigging, adjusting the ropes. The harbor was a hive of activity, and the air rang with shouts, curses, the crash of wood, the clang of metal. A man took Lavinia's bags on board. We stood by the carriage, none of us speaking for a while, as we watched all the bustle and hurry. For us it had an aura of sadness.

"I want to thank you for all your kindness," Lavinia told Helena.

"I've done nothing," Helena said, trying to sound light.

"You have been wonderful," Lavinia said. "Whenever I think about Falconridge—and I will think about it often—I will remember you. You are a great lady, Mrs. Lloyd."

Lavinia turned to me and smiled. "Goodbye, Lauren," she said. "I will write to you both." But I knew these were just words. She would not write.

When the ship left, we would never hear from Lavinia again. I was sad, but I knew that she had to leave.

I remembered the first time I had seen her, standing on the platform in Devon. I remembered how sad she had looked and how lovely. That seemed so long ago. She was sad and lovely now as she stood waiting for the men to finish loading the cargo. She wore a dress of mauve colored silk with a short white cape of velvet trimmed with mauve ribbons. Her face seemed thinner, and there was a slight hollow under each cheek bone, a delicate molding that made her look sadder than ever. Her eyes were a lustrous brown, moist and shining, and her lips drooped down at the corners. She brushed a lock of raven hair from her temple, and her lashes fluttered. I would always remember her like this.

The men had finished loading the crates and barrels. The ship was ready to leave. The captain, handsome in his blue uniform with its gold braid, stood on deck, checking off items on a list. Lavinia went up the gangplank and smiled down at us from the railing as the men took the gangplank away. The sails flapped loudly in the wind. A sailor in a red and white striped jersey began to haul the anchor up. The chain came up out of the water festooned with seaweed and barnacles. In a few moments the ship began to move ponderously out of the harbor. Lavinia waved, her hair blowing across her face, and then she disappeared. I hoped she would find happiness. There had been so little of it in her life.

I was restless during the days that followed. The tragedy had upset me, and I was sad, but there was something else that I couldn't identify. I found it difficult to sleep properly, and I lost some of my appetite. I seemed to be the victim of strange longings that I couldn't completely understand. I wasn't sick, yet I wasn't charged with the vitality that should have been there. I sat before the mirror for long periods at a time, examining myself, wishing I were older, wishing I had golden hair and slanted eyes and worldly poise. I wanted something, but I was not quite sure what it was.

I tried not to think of Norman Wade. The man's arrogance irritated me beyond endurance, and a blush colored my cheeks when I remembered that night in the gardens and the liberty he had taken. I remembered that night far too often, and I wondered if he ever thought about it. I was a child to him, a little girl who was a nuisance, and yet that night he had not treated me like a little girl. It was foolish even to think about it. He was arrogant and much too sure of himself, and now that Falconridge was his responsibility he certainly wouldn't have time to think about a girl he kissed one night in the moonlight.

One morning I woke up at four thirty after a restless night, and I couldn't bear the thought of staying in bed any longer. I lit a candle and dressed slowly, slipping a light green dress over the frilly white and pink striped petticoats. I sat at the mirror and brushed my auburn curls until they gleamed, and then I made my way downstairs, careful to make as little noise as possible. No one else was up yet and I didn't want to disturb anyone. I went along the back hall and stepped outside so I could watch the sun come up over the water. For some reason it seemed imperative that I be outside to welcome the new day.

The sky was dark gray, gradually lightening, and there was a soft mist that evaporated as I moved through it. I moved to the stone railing and looked at the grayish-green water lapping the shore with gentle waves. Everything was silent, still. I felt that I was the only person on earth, and it was a desolate feeling. At that moment I needed something desperately, but I could not have said what it was. I felt very, very young, very vulnerable.

The mist evaporated, and a few gold stains began to appear on the horizon. The dark gray sky lightened, shade by shade, until it was a pearly hue, not white but no longer gray. The gold soaked into the pearl, and everything around me began to take on shape and form. The shadows vanished. Trees came out of the mist. I could see every leaf of the shrubbery, dark green, distinct. I leaned on the railing, watching the gray-green water suddenly sparkle with chips of gold, every wave capped with shimmering gold. It was a beautiful sight, and I wanted to cry because it was so beautiful, and because there was no one to share it with.

I had not heard Norman Wade come down the steps of the carriage house. I had not heard him cross the courtyard. I was not even aware of him until his voice interrupted my sad reverie.

"Beautiful," he said.

I turned, startled. He was standing right beside me, and his face was strangely reflective. He was no longer the arrogant young aristocrat. He was a man who saw beauty and appreciated it. He looked almost humble, and I was puzzled. This wasn't the Norman Wade I knew so well. This was a stranger.

"I—I didn't hear you," I said.

"You're up quite early, aren't you?"

"I—wanted to watch the sun rise."

"Yes," he replied, as though he understood completely, as though there was no need to ask why I needed to be out here.

"It's hard on you, isn't it?" he asked.

"What?"

"All this. . . ." He extended his arms to take in all of Falconridge. "Such a sudden change in your life, so much unhappiness—I'm surprised you've been able to bear up so well."

I stared at him with suspicion, wondering what he was up to. His lips curved in a quiet smile, and his dark eyes seemed sincere. I was puzzled, and I almost wished the arrogant young lord would come back. At least I would be prepared to deal with him. I did not know how to deal with this quiet, pensive stranger.

"I'm perfectly capable of. . . ." I began.

He laid a hand gently over my mouth. "No," he said. "Not this morning. No arguments. Poor child, so defensive, so suspicious. One day you will understand." He took his hand away from my mouth and laid both hands heavily on my shoulders. "I'm asking you again to go away," he said quietly. "I'll make all the arrangements. . . ."

"Why?" I protested. "Why do you want me to go? Am—am I so very disturbing?"

"Indeed," Norman Wade replied. "You are—disturbing."

I started to pull away from him. He swung me into his arms, holding me loosely. For a moment his eyes studied my face, and then he kissed me. When he released me I was unable to speak. I glared at him, my cheeks crimson, and I wanted to lash out at him. Too, I wanted to have those arms around me again. I wanted to rest my head on that chest and feel warm and protected.

"I. . . ."

"Will you go away?" he asked quietly.

"I hate you!" I cried.

"No," he said, his voice almost a whisper. "No, I think not. I wish you would be reasonable, but I can see you won't. I had hoped I could deal with you gently, but it seems not." He shook his head, and he frowned, a deep crease between his brows. "Stay out of the way, little girl," he warned. "Stay out of the way."

He turned abruptly and left. He strolled across the courtyard with long strides, swinging his shoulders jauntily. The pensive stranger had disappeared, and he was the same arrogant Norman Wade as before. I was trembling with rage, and with other emotions I refused to identify. I looked at the sea, the gold melted now, the water dingy gray. The sky was white, and dark clouds were forming. The wind blew fiercely, whipping my skirts against my legs. I hate him! I cried silently. I hate him! I repeated the words over and over again, hoping the passion and the fury would convince me the other emotions did not exist.

XIV

NIGHT FOLLOWED NIGHT and I was still unable to sleep properly. The sound of the sea was a constant monotony, and I had the feeling that it was a breathing demon waiting to suck Falconridge into its depths. My nerves were on edge, and I could not understand it. I kept remembering the day of the funeral. Something had not been right. I could not understand why I had this feeling but it would not leave me. During the day I tried to keep busy and cheerful, but it took more and more effort. During the night the feeling was even stronger. I was a slave to it. Norman Wade had told me Falconridge did things to those who lived under its roof. I wondered if that was his version of Lucy's "evil spell." I wondered more and more if it were true.

I thought about Charles Lloyd. I could not believe that he was dead and no longer a part of this house. His presence had been so strong. It had permeated the place, and I had always been aware of him, even when he was in a distant part of the house. Now that he was gone, I could still feel his presence. Martha Victor had taken all his clothes and his personal effects, and Norman Wade had transformed my uncle's old room to suit his own tastes, but I still felt Charles Lloyd in the house. In the library the odor of his cigar smoke still hung in the air, and when we ate in the dining room it seemed that he was there, watching us with disapproval. At night I fancied I could hear his boots tramping on the floor in the hall, and sometimes when I would go into a room it was as though he had just left it.

I was strongly tempted to try some of Helena's laudanum, but I was too afraid of the narcotic. I hoped that this feeling would eventually wear off of its own volition. Nothing seemed to help, and certain things made it worse. Martha Victor moved about the house like a black wraith, never speaking but always appearing in different parts of the house as if she were guarding some secret. Lucy had changed, too, all her vitality drained away. Her blue eyes were enormous in her thin, pale face. She did her tasks obediently and skillfully, but she no longer chattered and gossiped. Several times she would look at me with a deep frown between her brows, her lips slightly parted as though she were about to be the messenger of some dark tidings, but she never spoke. It was no longer a joy to have her around, and I was sorry, for I was very fond of the child.

"Miss Lauren, do you believe in ghosts?" she asked once.

"Of course not, Lucy," I replied. "Such things don't exist."

"Are you sure?" she whispered.

"Of course. That's all nonsense."

"Teddy Lane—he's stable boy for the Randalls—he says he's seen a ghost at the old cemetery, all white like fog, and I. . ." She hesitated.

"Yes, Lucy?"

"Nothing, Miss Lauren. You'd think I was lying. I've learned my lesson. I'll keep my mouth shut, just like Mrs. Victor told me. They say they'll whip me if I carry any more tales."

"Who said that?"

"Ma—and Mrs. Victor. But—there are ghosts, Miss Lauren."

I sighed. It was ghosts now, not mysterious figures in black. Her vivid imagination and downcast mood depressed me. I wondered what had happened to the child. I longed for her old vitality and zest to return. It would be a comfort to me.

Helena was busy with the gardens, which had already taken on a new beauty. Two extra men had been hired to help the gardener and under the supervision of my aunt they were working wonders with the shabby borders and lethargic plants. Norman Wade spent every day in a bustle of activity. When he was not going to the farms and seeing to improvements, he was in the library working over the ledgers and making plans for further improvements on Falconridge itself. He and Helena had several interviews about finances, and I hated to see her agreeing to turn all the insurance money over to him to use for his ambitious plans. The money would be arriving any day now, and it would not remain in the library safe for very long. Both Norman Wade and Helena seemed pleased with all of their plans. Falconridge would be like it was in the old days, Helena said. I wished I could share her enthusiasm. I was dubious.

Each day seemed longer than the next. I wrote copious letters to Clarissa, who was back at Mrs. Siddons'. Clarissa wrote to tell me all the gossip of the school, but it all seemed incredibly childish to me. I could hardly believe that I had once been part of that life, that the rather giddy, carefree young woman who wrote such vivacious letters had once been my best friend. I seemed removed from Clarissa by many years. Nevertheless, I made plans to visit her in late summer when she would be with her parents at their country home. Perhaps the visit would help me forget some of the gloom of Falconridge and restore some of my color and spirits.

At Helena's suggestion, I started visiting the tenant farms, making friends with the farm wives and seeing something of their way of life. They were a little reserved with me at first, but after I sat in their kitchens by the old stone fireplaces and watched them grind corn, they began to grow accustomed to me, even friendly. They found it flattering to have someone from the big house showing an interest in them, and I soon knew all the families by name. The children would come running out of the shabby farmhouses when they saw me crossing the fields, and their mothers would brew a pot of weak tea or put a batch of cookies in the oven. I enjoyed watching these women at their chores. They were all strong, rather grim in manner, their lives filled with work and sweat. But they seemed happy. The children were wild, like carefree little animals, their knees skinned and scratched, their faces dirty, their flaxen hair tangled and falling over freckled foreheads.

Helena had suggested that I take one of the horses and ride over to the various farms, but I preferred walking. It was good to be out in the fresh air and to wander through the woods and across large fields where the grain was beginning to turn golden brown. I climbed over the primitive wooden fences and frequently stopped to gather up bunches of wildflowers in my skirts. I saw the cows with large sad eyes grazing on the horizon, and sometimes I passed farmers who pushed their plows through the soil, turning over rich furrows of earth. There were pig pens and chicken yards around every farmhouse, and I soon grew familiar with all the sounds and smells of this rustic life. It made a great contrast to the brooding, shadowy atmosphere of Falconridge.

When one of the farm children came down with the flu, I sent word down to the kitchen to have some broth made. I would carry it over to the farm myself, as the little girl who was ill was one of my favorites. It was a rather cloudy morning, two and a half weeks after Mr. Stephens had been here. A messenger had arrived to say that the money would come the next day. I put on an old dress of yellow cotton, the hem slightly tattered, and took down the broad-brimmed straw hat. I felt tired and languorous after yet another night of only fitful sleep. My cheeks were pale as I brushed my long auburn hair. At least it hadn't lost its rich color.

The kitchen region was suffused with the delicious fragrances of baking bread, but the noise I heard as I neared it made me stop. There were yells and a loud shrill scream, then the sound of something hitting the wall. I hurried into the kitchen in time to see Cook, her arms white with flour, holding a protesting Lucy by the ear. The child was terrified and her cheeks were wet with tears. Cook was yelling with rage. Martha Victor stood in a corner by the gleaming copper pans, her arms folded across her bosom, and a grim expression on her face.

"What's going on here?" I demanded.

"The child's a thief!" Cook yelled. "She's been taking...."

"No, Miss Lauren," Lucy cried. "It isn't true."

"I tell you it is!" Cook said, her voice trembling with anger. "My pantry shelves are half-empty! Someone's been stealing the food. Lucy is the only one who knows where I keep my key—she's been stealing things. Probably been sneakin' off to have picnics with that no good Teddy Lane! My canned peaches and a whole cured ham—just yesterday they were there, and this morning...."

"I didn't take them," Lucy said. There was a red welt across her face, and her shoulders were trembling. I stood in the doorway with a look of disapproval on my face. Cook stopped yelling, and Lucy huddled against the wall. I came into the room, looking around at the disorder. Cook had been in the midst of baking bread, and all the mess of her labor was strewn over the kitchen. A row of golden brown, newly baked loaves was on the table, their crusts golden brown and flaky, and from the oven came the smells of more baking. Flour had been spilled on the floor and dishes were piled on the drain board.

"Did you take the food, Lucy?" I asked quietly. "Tell me the truth. I will see that you are not punished anymore."

"No, Miss Lauren," the child said, her voice sincere. "Honestly, I didn't. I don't know what happened to it."

Martha Victor smiled slowly. She stepped over

to the table. There was malice in her eyes. Lucy edged slowly away from her, moving towards me. I took her hand, holding it firmly.

"This has all been a misunderstanding, Cook," Martha Victor said. "A band of gypsies came last night. I didn't like the looks of them, and I wanted to get rid of them. They were camped just over the hill. I gave them enough food to do them for a while and sent them away. I threatened to have the sheriff after them if they didn't clear out."

"See!" Lucy cried. "See, Ma. I didn't take it."

"Why didn't you tell Cook this before, Martha?" I said. "Why did you stand there and let her accuse the child?"

Martha Victor did not answer me. She drifted out of the room, moving silently. I had seen the smile on her lips. I shuddered. The woman had become even more intolerable since my uncle's death.

"Food's been disappearing all along," Cook said, still not thoroughly convinced. "It didn't all just go at once. I've been missin' one or two items every day."

"I'm sure there's some explanation for it," I said. "I don't want you to strike Lucy again, Cook. If she needs reprimanding, you come to me and let me know. I'll see to it."

Cook looked resentful, but she did not argue with me. She gave me the broth she had prepared for the sick child. "You won't tell Mr. Wade about this, will you?" she asked, her eyes worried. I shook my head. Cook wrapped up a fresh loaf in a blue and white checked cloth and told me to take it to the farm as well. I left the kitchen, puzzled by the incident. Lucy trailed after me, staying close beside me until we were out of the region. She was still crying, sparkling tears rolling down her cheeks.

I stopped just inside the main hall, near the staircase, while Lucy made an effort to stop sobbing. She looked so frail and tiny standing there in the shadows, her face pale with the red welt across it. I pushed a strand of pale blonde hair away from her temple, and she looked up with light blue eyes still filled with tears. I patted her shoulder and told her everything would be all right. She gave one last sob, then sniffed quietly for a moment.

"It's not true," she said. "I didn't touch them things. She took 'em—Mrs. Victor did. I saw her doin' it. She wanted to get me in trouble. That's why she did it. There weren't no gypsies. She took the food herself and blamed it on me. She just said that about the gypsies because you came in. She hates me."

"No, Lucy. . . ." I began. "Why should she hate you?"

"Because I know. . . ."

"Know what?"

"Miss Lauren, there's something I've got to tell you. I've been on the verge of tellin' you several times but—but I was too scared. I've got to tell you now, because. . . ."

She hesitated a moment and looked over my shoulder. Her eyes grew wide with fear, and she put her hand to her mouth. I turned around. I saw the hem of Martha Victor's skirt disappearing around the bend in the staircase. She had evidently been standing there, listening to us. Lucy was trembling visibly. She had seen Martha Victor, and now she was too frightened to speak.

"What were you about to tell me?" I whispered,

concerned. I did not like the look on the child's face. It unnerved me. It was genuine. There was a twitch at the corner of her lips, and her brows were tightly contracted.

"Not now," she replied. "Later—tonight. Tonight, when I come to your room. . . ."

Lucy scurried on down the hall, her light footsteps making hardly any noise at all. She disappeared in the shadows like a frightened little sparrow. I looked up at the staircase. I could sense Martha Victor hovering there, just out of sight. She made no sound, but I knew she was there. I left the house, going out the back way. My brain was in a turmoil, dozens of questions pleading to be answered, and I hoped the walk would ease some of the tension I felt.

Hugo was chained up in the courtyard with a long leash. When Norman Wade did not have the animal with him, he kept him leashed, as the dog terrified the servants. He barked now, leaping up to greet me. I stroked his head, wondering how such an affectionate animal could, at the same time, be so vicious. Hugo looked up at me with yellow eyes, his strong body stretching with pleasure. The servants refused to cross the courtyard while he was here, even though the chain restrained him from going far. Hugo was friends with me, but he would bare his fangs and growl menacingly if anyone else besides Norman Wade came near him.

The low gray clouds wallowed in the sky as I walked to the farm. A moist breeze ruffled the fields of grain as I passed, and they looked like seas of golden brown. I passed a little girl who led three noisy geese down the road, prodding them with a long stick. The child waved at me. The geese honked angrily, ill tempered fowl that they were. I climbed over the wooden fence and crossed a fallow field. A deserted barn stood in its midst, the red paint faded and peeling. The door of the loft was open, banging in the wind, and ancient hay stuck out. An old wagon with a broken wheel was upturned beside the barn, and stray chickens pecked at the brown grass in front of it.

I delivered the broth and bread and talked for a few minutes with the farm wife in her kitchen. Strands of onion and garlic hung on the walls, and a brown and orange striped cat slept peacefully in a wicker chair in front of the fireplace. The sick child was asleep on a pallet in the corner, her thin cheeks flushed. Her mother cast worried glances at the child as she talked with me. She was peeling potatoes, dropping the peels in an old wooden bucket. Norman Wade had sent the doctor to see the child, she told me, and he had assured her that the flu would go away soon enough. He had left some medicine, but she didn't trust it. She had prepared her own mixture of herbs and spices. I stayed only a short while, too preoccupied to pay much attention to her words.

The clouds were grouping together in great dark shapes as I left and thunder rumbled in the distance. There was a faint greenish glow in the sky, and the clouds cast dark moving shadows over the field as I hurried away from the farmhouse. I had only gone a few yards when the first large drops of rain touched my cheeks. I ran towards the deserted barn. I saw a horse galloping across the field, both horse and rider silhouetted against the horizon. It started to pour and my dress was soon soaked. The horse stopped in front of the barn, and the man leaped down to throw open the doors. He led the horse inside, then he came towards me. He took my arm and led me across the field, hurrying me to the barn. I stumbled once and he threw out a strong arm to support me. He led me inside the barn, and we stood just inside the doorway, watching as the rain turned the field into a mass of dark, muddy puddles.

"You should not have come on foot," he said.

"I had no idea it was going to rain," I replied.

"The skies were laden with it. Anyone should have known. I could hardly believe it when I saw you running across the field. First you go barefooted on the beach, then you run about in the rain. Are you deliberately courting pneumonia?"

"Perhaps I am," I said irritably.

"That wouldn't surprise me," he replied smoothly, grinning.

His clothes were soaked. The pants clung to his legs like a second skin, and the thin white material of his shirt was plastered against his chest. His hair was wet, clinging to his head in glistening black waves. There was a look of amusement in his blue eyes as he looked down at me, his hands on his hips. I knew I must look wretched with the wet yellow dress glued to my body, my hair falling in damp ringlets about my face. Norman Wade seemed to find the sight of me delightful, for he threw back his head and laughed merrily.

I flushed, consumed with anger.

"You're not so smart," I snapped. "You were caught in the rain, too!"

"Yes. It seems we're trapped here together until it stops."

"I'd as soon be out in it," I retorted.

"You find this so unpleasant?"

"Hardly desirable," I replied haughtily.

"Well—you're stuck with me. You're not going to leave here until the rain is over. Then I'll carry you back to Falconridge on the back of my horse."

The horse stomped his hoof on the earth floor behind us. There was a huge pile of damp hay in one corner, a pile of potato sacks beside it. Norman Wade spread the sacks over the hay, arranging them neatly. Old harnesses hung on the wall and from the rafters. Farm tools encrusted with rust were scattered about. The chickens had come inside when it started raining and they roosted on the rafters now, clucking unpleasantly. I could smell the hay and manure and rotting leather. Rain swept in through the opened door, and I stepped back. Only a little light entered the barn, but I could see Norman Wade sitting on the hay, watching me with an amused smile on his lips.

"This may last for a long time," he said. "You may as well join me."

I stood beside the horse, stroking the smooth jaw. He nuzzled the palm of my hand, making a pleased sound. He was a magnificent beast, his sleek black coat glistening with water. I looked over at Norman Wade. He patted the sacks beside him, indicating for me to sit there. I held my chin high, ignoring him.

"Are you afraid I will molest you?" he asked, chuckling.

"Of course not!"

"The circumstances are ideal for that," he added.

"I'll bet you wish I was a full-blown country lass," I said, "all ready to succumb to your—your persuasion. Or perhaps you wish I was Arabella. That would suit you fine, wouldn't it?"

"Arabella still rankles, does she?"

"What do you mean?"

"You know very well what I mean."

"I find you insufferable, Mr. Wade. I don't trust you. Particularly since. . ." I hesitated, not quite daring to go further.

"Since what?"

"Since you've become Master of Falconridge. It's what you've always wanted, isn't it. Now you have it, and you will soon have my aunt's money as well. Everything has worked out very nicely."

Norman Wade got to his feet slowly. There was a dark look in his eyes. He stood there by the hay, looking at me, and he came towards me, moving slowly. I gnawed my lower lip, trying to stare him down. He took both my wrists in his hands and held them tightly. When he spoke his lips were inches from mine.

"Do you want to explain yourself?" he asked. His voice seemed calm, but I could sense the strong undercurrent of anger. His eyes stared steadily into mine. I tried to pull my wrists away, but he held them in a tight grip.

"Let me go," I whispered.

"What is it you accuse me of?"

"I—I don't know."

He released me and stepped back. I rubbed my wrists, not looking up at him. I leaned against the horse's flank, looking out at the wavering sheets of greenish rain that turned the field to brown mud. My heart was pounding, but I knew I had to defy this man.

"Tell me," he said quietly.

"I can't," I replied. "I can't explain it. Something is wrong. Something has been wrong ever since I came to Falconridge. There are so many little things that—don't fit."

"Tell me about them," he said.

I threw all caution to the wind. I told Norman Wade everything I had seen or imagined that did not seem to fit into the smooth, silent routine of Falconridge. I knew that it was unwise. It might even be dangerous, but I had to speak to someone. I had to give voice to all those doubts and suspicions that had plagued me for so long. His eyes were calm, his face impassive. When I told him about the incident in the kitchen this morning, he seemed to grow tense. He narrowed his eyes, and a deep frown creased his brow.

"What do you think is wrong?" he asked when I had finished.

"I wish I knew. Something out of the ordinary...."

"You think Charles Lloyd was murdered?"

He asked the question calmly, but the words came like a splash of cold water, chilling me. I looked at the man who had spoken it. He examined me with blue eyes that were icy. There was a long moment during which there was no sound but the falling rain. I was afraid, but I knew I had to face up to him.

"How do you think it happened?" he asked.

"The boat. Someone could have fooled with the boat. It was dark that night. He could have taken it out without being aware of whatever was wrong with it—a loose plank on the floorboard, perhaps, or a small hole that would let the water in."

"That sounds highly unlikely," Norman Wade replied casually.

"Someone could have been waiting in the boathouse. When he got into the boat, they could have struck him unconscious, smashed a hole in the boat and pushed it out into the water. The force of the storm would have carried it out far."

"You have a vivid imagination," he said.

"Is it—imagination?" I asked, my voice trembling.

"You think I killed him?"

"You weren't there when Lavinia came. You could have done it."

"And how was I to know he was going out like that?"

"I don't know."

"I could have heard the commotion. I could have come in. I could have been standing in the hall, listening without being seen. Then I could have gone to the boathouse and waited...." He paused, a curious smile playing on his lips.

"Yes," I said, staring at him defiantly.

"But why?" he asked.

"You had everything to gain," I said, "Falconridge, the money. You must have known about the unusual policy, and you must have known you could get it from Helena easily enough. You never got along with my uncle. You argued constantly. You said he was ruining Falconridge. You said you could not stand by and see him do that."

"And so you think I killed him," he said flatly.

"Did you?"

The question hung in the air. Norman Wade did

not answer. He did not look at me. His eyes were reflective, and he seemed to be turning something over in his mind. That same curious smile was on his lips. He was so close that I could see the little black hairs curling on the nape of his neck. Outside the rain began to slacken until it was no more than a thin green mist through which I could see the distant field of golden brown grain beyond its grayed wooden fence. The chickens began to grow restless, fluffing their feathers and cackling. One hopped down from the rafter and scratched about in the hay.

Norman Wade looked up at me. His face was grim.

"You could be right," he said, speaking slowly. "Yes, you could be right. You have thought it out very carefully. Of course there are a few major points you have overlooked, but you have built up a rather compact case against me. The motive, the means—they're both there. If a murder was committed, it's quite conceivable that I did it. You have been very astute, but if what you believe is true— you realize your own position, don't you?"

"I am not afraid," I said. My voice quivered.

"One does not confront a murderer with the facts of his crime in an isolated spot," he said. "One keeps silent, waiting for the right opportunity to expose him. One does not expose himself to danger as you have done—repeatedly. You're a fool, Lauren. I never quite realized just how much a fool until now."

I backed away a little. He noticed and smiled.

"What do you intend to do?" I asked.

The smile broadened. It was a harsh smile, frightening. "I am not going to strangle you," he said. "There's no need to look so alarmed. You are going to leave Falconridge. I am sending you to London. I know some people there who will look after you until I can make more permanent arrangements. A special coach will bring the money to Falconridge tomorrow. When it returns, you will be on it."

"And if I refuse?"

"You won't," he said simply.

"Helena...."

"I will deal with Helena. I should send her away with you. I may. She hates to travel, but, as you know, I can be very persuasive. Now I am going to take you back to Falconridge. You will go to your room, and you will remain there until it is time for you to come down for the evening meal. By that time I will have more definite instructions. Do you have any more questions?"

"What do you hope to prove by all this?" I asked.

"I don't hope to prove anything," he replied. "I just want to get you safely out of the way. You don't realize how lucky you are."

I did not reply. Norman Wade took me back to Falconridge. I rode behind him on the horse, my arms around his waist. The field was muddy, and the horse's hooves splattered in the puddles. Drops of water clung to the grain, and the sky was like a bolt of wet gray silk. Neither of us said a word. Norman Wade had shown his hand, and I knew that words were of no value now. Now was the time for action. I did not have any idea what I would do, but I knew that I did not intend to leave Falconridge, and I did not intend to let him get away with his treachery.

XV

HE LEFT ME at the door of my room. I was surprised that he did not lock it behind me. I could hear him going down the hall to his room. Outside the sky was gray, darkening, deep purple stains on the horizon. I sat down on the bed, my hands in my lap, staring out the window and trying to form some plan in my mind. I could not let him get away with what he had done. I must do something, but I did not know what it would be. He had every intention of sending me away tomorrow, and I knew I was not going. I could not leave him here with Helena.

I could go to Helena. I could tell her all I knew and guessed. She would listen intently. She would smile. She would pat my hand and tell me I was imagining things. She would suggest I take some of her laudanum and get more sleep. Norman Wade was her nephew, and she admired him. She would not believe him capable of doing what I knew in my heart he had done. If I told her I thought he was using her in order to get his hands on the money she would receive tomorrow she would tell me that what Norman desired to do with it was her desire, too. No, I could not go to Helena for help. It was my place to protect her, not to involve her in this affair any more than she was already innocently involved.

If only I had some proof, I thought. All the little things added up to one major crime, but it was all speculation on my part. I had not a shred of evidence on my side. My uncle had been killed when *The Falcon* capsized in the water. It had been an accident, pure and simple. Even Mr. Stephens had been satisfied on that score, and he had been representing a firm that had a great deal of money at stake. If only I had something definite to go on, something I could present to the authorities that would not be mere assumption on my part.

I suddenly thought about Lucy. She had something to tell me. Whatever it was had seemed imperative to the child. She had been on the verge of telling me this morning, but the presence of Martha Victor had restrained her. She was going to tell me tonight. Whatever Lucy knew, whatever it was she wanted to tell me, had been powerful enough to give her a severe shock. Perhaps she knew about the murder. Perhaps she had proof of it. Naturally she would be hesitant about talking about it, particularly after she had been accused of lying so many times, but it must have been preying on her mind all this time until she could no longer keep it to herself.

Tonight I would know, and perhaps Lucy's revelation, combined with my own speculations, would be enough to convince the authorities that Norman Wade was a murderer.

How would I let them know? I thought about that. Time was important. I had only a few hours. He would see to it that I was on the coach that would be returning to London tomorrow. I must slip out tonight. I would slip out of the house after everyone had gone to bed. Then I would take one of the horses and ride to the village. I would find the sheriff and bring him back to Falconridge with me. Norman Wade was not going to get away with his crime, not if I could help it.

I wondered why he had not killed me as well. He had the opportunity twice, in the boathouse and in the barn. It would have been easy to do, and he could have arranged it to look like an accident as he had done before. Why had he spared me? Why was he sending me away to London where I might still talk and cause trouble for him? Was he afraid? Did he think he might not be so successful with his second murder? They said that once a man has killed he has no hesitation about killing again, yet Norman Wade was content merely to get me "out of the way." I wondered about that.

Did he think my loyalty to Helena would prevent me from causing a scandal that would be painful for her? Perhaps, but I thought there was another reason why he had spared my life, and I lay back on the bed, looking up at the ceiling and thinking about that reason. It was foolish, of course, and incredibly schoolgirlish, but I couldn't help but remember the look in his eyes on occasion when he was looking at me, thinking I did not notice. He probably looked that way at all the young women—Arabella, for example, and the country lasses—yet still there had been something in the dark blue depths that I had instinctively recognized.

I sat up, frowning, not pleased with the emotions that had come over me so suddenly. I would not permit myself to think about that. I had to be cool. I had to be calm. I had to be strong if I were going to defeat Norman Wade. I could not think about the look in his eyes, and I could not dwell on that first day in the clearing when he had taken me for a peasant lass and had kissed me so casually and yet so passionately there among the poppies. I must forget all that. I must remember that he was a murderer and not think about the way he looked with his clothes all wet and his glossy black hair plastered in damp waves about his handsomely shaped head.

The sky was almost all purple now, misty, with dark red plumes of light on the horizon. From my window I could see the trees, all black silhouettes. Night was almost here. The light was quickly vanishing. I would have to go down to dinner. I would have to face Norman Wade again and it was going to be a task that would demand all my strength. I must look my best, and I must be calm and gracious and act as though nothing were wrong. He must not have the least suspicion of what I was planning to do. I must be prepared to chatter with Helena and tell her about my day. He would be watching me carefully. I must not make any little slip.

I glanced at the clock and wondered why Lucy hadn't come up. She usually came about this time to help me dress and to arrange my hair. I had repeatedly insisted that it was not necessary, but she loved to do it. It made her feel like a proper lady's maid, she claimed. Perhaps she would be here in a few minutes, I thought, sitting down in front of the mirror to brush my hair.

My face looked drawn. There were tiny hollows under each cheek bone, and soft brown shadows etched over my eyelids. I could not look haggard.

Helena would comment on it. I took out the pot of rouge and smoothed a little over each cheek, rubbing it in to make the color seem natural. I brushed my hair until the glossy auburn waves shone with rich copper highlights, pulling it away from my face and tying it with a ribbon in back, letting the heavy waves cascade down my shoulders. I laid out my dress, still wondering about Lucy, a little concerned now.

The dress was one of the finest Lavinia had made, white and lilac striped satin with tiny purple velvet bows, worn over several underskirts of stiff lilac crinoline that rustled when I walked. I put it on and admired the effect in the mirror. I put on the ruby pendant that Clarissa had given me so long ago. The drop of red added just the right amount of color.

The clock ticked on. The noise seemed terribly loud. Lucy still had not come. What was keeping her? She was always here by this time. Had Martha Victor prevented her from coming? She had heard Lucy's hurried words to me when we were standing by the stairs this morning, and she knew Lucy intended to tell me something very important tonight. It would be like her to invent some extra task to keep the child too busy to come up to my room before dinner. Anyway, I would see her tonight before I went to bed, and she would tell me her secret then.

I suddenly remembered something that made my pulses leap. My knees felt weak, and I had to cling to the bed poster to support myself. Martha Victor was not the only one who knew that Lucy was going to tell me something vitally important. Norman Wade knew, too. I had told him about it in the barn. I had chatted on, blithely telling him about the incident in the kitchen and in the hall afterwards, not once thinking about the child and the possible danger to her. So that was why Lucy hadn't come! Norman Wade had stopped her. He had probably locked her in her room, forbidding her to speak to me before I left tomorrow.

There were just a few minutes before it would be time for me to make my appearance in the dining room. I hurried on downstairs, being very quiet as I came around the curve of the staircase that led to the main hallway. Instead of turning towards the dining room, I went the other way through the narrow halls that led to the region of the house where the servants stayed. I found Lucy's little room tucked away under the old staircase and opened the door.

I saw the narrow little cot, the tight walls covered with fading yellow wallpaper, the tiny window through which so little light came. Lucy was not there. One of her dresses was laid neatly over a wooden chair, and a hair ribbon I had given her had dropped beside the cot. A bunch of wildflowers was withering in a chipped vase, and on the wall a picture of an old castle hung crookedly. It was a pathetic room, so tiny and so stuffy, smelling as it did of grease and dust. I could imagine the child lying away on the lumpy cot, her mind bothered with the knowledge of a terrible crime.

Cook was in the middle of dinner preparations, her face flushed, her temper flaring when I hurried into the kitchen to inquire about Lucy. Two of the maids scurried out, dishing up food, jumping when she gave her orders. A frown of anger crossed her face when I asked if she had seen Lucy. "That lazy child," she said. "I sent her out to the woodshed to fetch some wood over an hour ago, 'n she ain't come back yet. Probably daydreamin' somewhere, and my stove about to burn itself out for lack of fuel...." I did not remain to hear the rest of her complaint. The woodshed was on the other side of the carriage house, and I hurried through the hallways towards the courtyard.

Something drove me; something hurried me on. I ran down the hall, my heels clattering loudly. I did not care if anyone heard me now. My only concern was Lucy. She had been gone an hour, a full hour, and it should have taken her five minutes, ten at the most, to fetch the wood. I was out of breath as I neared the foyer that led out to the courtyard. I had to stop. I leaned against the wall. My breath came in short gasps. My wrists felt weak, limp.

Then I heard the pistol shot. It was a loud explosion of noise that made my heart leap. Leaning against the wall, I closed my eyes. It was a while before I could summon enough strength to go on down the hall and out to the courtyard. The last rays of light were fading on the horizon, and the courtyard was dim, already shrouded in the thin evening mists. I saw the frail little body huddled by the shrubberies, and I saw the dark red stains. I saw Hugo, his body still twitching in its final agony. I saw the broken leash dangling from the post where it had been fastened. I saw Norman Wade standing over the dog, the pistol in his hand still smoking. He looked up at me with solemn eyes.

"The dog attacked her. She's dead. I had to shoot him. Now do you see why you must leave this place as soon as possible?"

*   *   *

Whatever he had given me was beginning to wear off. My head felt heavy, and it seemed almost impossible to lift my eyelids. The room was flooded with misty silver moonlight, and I could hear the sound of the sea. At first, I thought it was someone beside me, breathing deeply, but as the drug began to wear off I realized it was the waves, washing over the sand and making the noise that was a constant background at Falconridge. I sat up in bed, pressing my fingertips against my temples. My head began to clear, and as that blissful state of semi-consciousness wore off, the horror of reality began to take its place.

He had carried me up here to my room. He had laid me on the bed and left for a few minutes to fetch some medicine. I had been too weak to protest, and I drank the stuff willingly enough. He had stood over me as the fog began to envelop my brain, and I remembered him saying that they had come and taken Lucy away to the church. Helena had gone to her room and sought refuge in her laudanum. It would not wear off. She would still be asleep.

Norman Wade had talked as I grew drowsier and drowsier. He told me he had been in the carriage house, looking for some papers, and he had heard her screams. She had evidently been taunting the dog, and he had broken his leash and gone for her. It had been over very quickly. He had pulled the dog away and taken out the pistol. Once, as he talked, I tried to sit up, but his hands on my shoulders pushed me back down on the pillows. I wanted to tell him that Lucy was terrified of the animal and wouldn't have gone near it. She would never have taunted it. Norman Wade talked, and soon the blessed sedative did its work, and I passed into the soothing arms of oblivion. How long ago had that been, one hour? Two? Five? I was awake now, fully dressed, my head aching miserably from the medicine.

I kept remembering something my uncle had said: "Hugo won't kill unless he's told to do so." Those words kept repeating themselves in my head. He wouldn't kill unless he was told to do so, and he had been told to kill tonight. The man was a fiend. He was a monster. I had to stop him. I had to leave Falconridge now, no matter how drowsy I felt, no matter how weary and heartsick I was. I had to get help tonight. Tomorrow would be too late.

I sat on the edge of the bed, tears pouring down my cheeks as I thought about the pathetic child who had so desperately wanted attention and love, who had such a vivid imagination and so glib a tongue that when she wanted to tell the truth no one would listen to her. I thought of that long, pale blonde hair and that thin little face with the enormous blue eyes. She would not go unavenged. I would see to that.

The door to my room was locked. He had not trusted me a second time. It was a strong oak door, as were all those in the house. There was no way I could get it open without a key. The key, I thought. I kneeled down and peered through the keyhole. I could see no light. It was dark in the hall, and there would be no light anyway, but there was a chance he had left it in the lock. I went to the desk and took out a piece of stationery. I slid it under the door and took a hairpin from my hair. I held my breath as I edged the hairpin into the keyhole, going very slowly so that the key would edge out and not fall away from the paper. I could not feel anything, and for a moment I felt it was all hopeless. Then I felt a budge and there was a little clink as the key fell. I closed my eyes, whispering a silent prayer that it had fallen on the paper. I pulled the paper back into the room, slowly, slowly, and almost gave a little cry of joy as I saw the brass key riding under the edge of the door.

I unlocked the door and opened it cautiously. I did not dare light a lamp. He might see that. For all I knew he was still up. I would have to move under a cover of darkness.

I closed the door to my room behind me and stood for a moment with my hand still on the doorknob. I hesitated, still weak from the drug. The hall was dark, a long black tunnel infested with grayish shadows, and it did not seem possible that I could force myself to walk down it without a light. The air about me was inhabited with my own fear, and I felt my fingers tremble as they held the cold brass doorknob. I had to do it. For Lucy, I told myself. I was not bold. I was not brave. I was merely determined. I braced myself and started down the hall, staying close to the wall, moving very slowly.

I knocked against a small table I had forgotten was there. A vase rocked noisily, and my fingers flew out in the darkness to steady it. I held my breath, certain that the noise had awakened everyone. There was no noise of investigation, no opening doors and lighted lamps. The sound must have been magnified by my own sense of caution. I walked on down the hall, groping my way slowly in the darkness.

When I came to the staircase that led downstairs, I paused. There was a light burning in the hall. I could see just a faint glow from it from where I stood. If there was a light, it meant someone was up. I could not go down here. I could not risk detection. If Norman Wade were downstairs, he would try and stop me from leaving the house. If it were someone else, they would ask questions which I was in no condition to answer. I would have to go down another staircase.

I thought about the closed wing. On down the hall was the staircase that led down into it, and at the end of the wing there was the staircase that led on down to the level where the servants stayed, coming down just over Lucy's little room. There was an exit from the servants' quarters that led out into the backyard. I could go through the closed wing, down the staircase and get outside without anyone seeing me. I shuddered at the thought of entering that musty, closed part of the house with its cobwebs and mildew and sheeted furniture, but it was the only way open to me.

I walked on down the hall, trying to ignore all the noises that were so much a part of Falconridge. The windows rattled, and branches of the trees beat against them like fists pounding on the glass. The old floorboards creaked, no matter how cautiously I walked, and there was a scurrying sound like something moving behind the wainscoting. The stiff crinoline of my underskirts rustled loudly with a noise like whispers, and the faint echoes of my own movements reverberated down the hall, giving me the sensation of being followed.

It was hard to believe that this was real. It was like a vivid nightmare that must surely end when I awoke in my own bed to see the sun coming into my room. The musty odors, the damp walls, the sounds all around me must surely be part of that nightmare. My head was reeling, and I had to stop and lean against the wall to keep from fainting. I stood motionless in the darkness, a darkness that seemed alive, closing in on me, and it took all my will power not to scream.

Norman Wade was a murderer. He was in this house. He was planning to send me away. He was going to steal Helena's money, and he would succeed in all this unless I forced myself to go on. There could be no turning back now. I could rest later. Later I could sleep and sleep and try to forget all this, but now I must go on. I must get out of the house, and I must get to the village somehow. Somehow I must get help before it was too late.

I started down the staircase that led into the closed wing. How well I remembered that first time I had come down it, my first night at Falconridge. I had been frightened by the billowing sheets that covered the furniture, and Martha Victor had terrified me when I saw her standing there in the shadows. I remembered how the old stairs had creaked. They creaked now. The wood of the banister was rotten, and it gave as I ran my hand over it. I was afraid to lean on it. The wood would surely shatter and I would be hurled to the floor below. It seemed hours before I reached the landing.

There was moonlight here on the first floor. The draperies had been removed from the windows, and the light came pouring through. The windows were like squares of silver. The light drifted through them in misty rays that floated with millions of tiny particles of dust. Not a breath of air stirred. The great room was a nest of blue-black shadows that stroked the walls like gigantic black hands. The white sheets covering the furniture stood out against the shadows. I could see strands of cobweb. The smell was almost unbearable, composed of dust and mildew and ancient wax and decay. If Falconridge was a living thing, this part of it was dead, an arm that had withered and rotted away.

I paused only a moment, surveying the room, then hurried across the floor. The carpets had been rolled up, and my heels clattered loudly on the bare floor, but the noise did not bother me now. No one would be anywhere about in this part of the house, certainly not near enough to hear any noise I might make.

I went through one room, then another, each clammy, closed up, the furniture covered with old sheets. The hardest part was behind me. I would soon find the staircase that led down to the servants' quarters, and I would be almost free. Once outside, nothing would stop me. I came to a closed door. I tried to open it. This wing was a series of rooms that led one into another in a straight line, and unless I could get the door open I would be defeated. I shoved against it with all my might, my hand twisting the doorknob. The door was locked. It would not budge. How strange, I thought. Why should this door be locked when all the others were open, held back with doorstops. It was odd.

I froze. Someone was behind the door. I could hear footsteps moving towards it from the other side. I stepped back. There was a little line of yellow showing beneath the door. Someone had a lamp. I heard the key turning in the lock. The door opened slowly. The hinges creaked loudly. Charles Lloyd stood there, one eyebrow arched inquisitively. He wore the black brocade dressing robe with quilted blue satin lapels that I remembered so well. His heavy blond hair was disarrayed, and his face was a little rumpled from sleep.

I did not scream. I was suddenly very calm. Things tumbled together in my mind. Little particles that had been jumbled before fell into place now, and everything was clear. This explained the missing food. Martha Victor must have been bringing it to him every day. And here was Lucy's "ghost." She had seen him. She had known that he was in the house. She had died because of this knowledge. Only three people could command Hugo: Norman Wade, Charles Lloyd and Andrew Graystone. Andrew Graystone was dead.

"Well, my dear," he said. "It seems you never learn. How many times did I warn you about prowling around? And now you have gotten into quite a predicament, yes, quite a predicament indeed."

"I can see now why you didn't want me prowling about. I might have disturbed you and Lavinia during one of your trysts."

"You know about that?"

"I guessed it. Did Lavinia wear a black cloak when she came to Falconridge?"

"You're quite right. She did. If she was covered with black, it would be harder to see her as she came in and out."

"And that's why you didn't fire Andrew Graystone. That's why you let him get away with such disastrous mismanagement. He knew about your affair with his wife, and as long as he kept his job he would say nothing about it."

"Right again. A thoroughly detestable man. I was not sorry when I killed him."

"You killed him the day of the ball," I said. "You carried his body to the boathouse and put it in *The Falcon*. The scene when Lavinia came running in during the storm was carefully rehearsed."

"She is a superb actress," he remarked.

"I should have known before," I said. "I should have guessed that day in Devon when she was so uneasy about meeting me. You had been together in London, hadn't you. She took an earlier train than we did, got off at Devon and then 'accidentally' met us there. She was nervous, afraid I would notice something. She had no sister in Devon. That was all part of the plan."

"You are a remarkably intelligent young lady," my uncle said. He smiled, his lips merely turning up at the corners. His eyes were burning darkly, and a muscle in his cheek twitched. "Unfortunately so, I am afraid. Too bad you couldn't have made this little nocturnal visit one night later. By then I would have had the money and been on my way to Liverpool."

"So that was part of the plan, too," I said.

"Of course it was. I was a fairly wealthy man, but my wealth was in real estate and property holdings. There was no way to get ready money for the elopement. At my age one does not run away with a beautiful woman without enough money to insure her faithfulness."

"So you thought of this scheme," I said.

"Yes. Really very clever, don't you think? The insurance policy was an unusual one, and Stephens did not want to issue it. He was in a quandary over the matter until he met you in the restaurant. I suppose he felt any man who had such an attractive niece was planning to live a long, long time."

"You weren't planning to live very long, were you?"

"Just long enough to be decent about the matter. I had planned to wait yet another month or so, but Graystone was getting difficult. He was going to explode the whole thing, so I had to do it rather sooner. Graystone and I were about the same size, had the same color hair. Wearing my clothes and the Falcon ring he would be taken for me without any question, particularly after he had been in the water for a while and knocked about a bit. I made sure of that before I pushed the boat off. No one would have recognized him if the body had been recovered the day after the accident."

"Having him run off with the rent money was a brilliant idea," I said. "I suppose that money paid Lavinia's fare to Liverpool."

"With a little left over for emergencies," he added.

"And you forged the letter," I told him. "I saw a scratch pad in the library. You had practiced the signature on it. When I saw you in the village, you had just given the letter to the sailor and paid him to mail it from America for you. You had been planning to murder Andrew Graystone all along."

"My dear, he was marked for death the moment I laid eyes on Lavinia."

"And Lucy...." I said, my voice trembling for the first time.

"Unfortunate," he said. "I really hated to do that. Just as I will hate to arrange your accident."

"You won't get away with it," I whispered.

"My dear, I have gotten away with everything so far. You don't believe I am going to let a prying little schoolgirl ruin things now, do you."

"Norman Wade knows," I said.

"He suspects. He knows nothing. I think he knew about the affair with Lavinia. He saw us together once. He never mentioned anything. He wanted to protect Helena. He may have been suspicious about the accident, but he was too elated about inheriting Falconridge to do anything about it. He is welcome to the place. After tomorrow, after I've taken the money from the safe and left, I will never see it again. There is only one problem, and that, my dear, is you."

He took my arm and pulled me into the room. I did not struggle. I was fascinated by the man, almost hypnotized. He had discussed all of his intrigue and crime in a casual, off hand manner, the way other men might have discussed the weather. He was amoral. He had no feelings. Killing Andrew Graystone and Lucy had meant nothing to him, just as killing me would mean nothing. He closed the door behind him and released me. I looked around the room he had been living in all these weeks. The bed had been neatly made with fresh sheets, rumpled now, and the furniture was newly polished. A window was open, a fresh breeze coming through it. A tray holding the remnants of his dinner was beside the bed. Martha had been very faithful in her service to him.

"Poor woman," he said, as though reading my thoughts. "She thinks I am going to take her with me. She will be so disappointed."

"Martha has known all along, hasn't she."

"She knew everything, from the first."

Charles Lloyd creased his brow in a deep frown, his eyes focused inward hazily, examining some mental image.

"Now what shall it be?" he said, holding his head to one side and speaking to himself as though confronting a minor problem. "It has to look like an accident, of course. I could throttle you here and now, but that would mean a great deal of work later, arranging things. Let me see. . . ." he paused, looking up at me as though I might have an answer for him. "Ah, yes—I begin to see now. You were terribly grieved over the death of your devoted little maid. Your poor brain couldn't take it. You left your room in the middle of the night—you've made that part quite simple for me—and ran outside to the cliff. . . ."

He smiled now, the frown going away. His problem had been solved. I watched him, still fascinated by his hypnotic power. I knew it would be useless to scream. My head was still groggy from the drug, and all this had the same nightmare quality that I had noticed before. It could not be happening. It was not real. I wasn't afraid, not yet. Charles Lloyd drew the belt tighter about his robe and came towards me, smiling with satisfaction at his solution to the problem.

"We will go outside now," he said casually. "It will do you no good to scream and struggle. That would only make it more difficult, I can assure you."

"You—can't—do this. . . ." I whispered.

"Oh, but I can, my dear."

Charles Lloyd took my arm and led me out of the room, opening the door that was directly opposite the one we had come in. We went through two more rooms, both shrouded in white and smelling of dust, and then we came to the staircase that led down to the servants' quarters. His fingers held my elbow firmly, and I moved as one in a trance might move. We went down the staircase slowly. Little by little the effects of the drug were wearing off. My head cleared, and awareness of danger began to sharpen my perceptions. I grew tense, rigid. Charles Lloyd noticed it. He merely took a firmer hold on my elbow and shoved me forward.

We reached the landing beside Lucy's room. A light was burning in a nearby room, and the faint yellow glow melted into the darkness. The area was shadowy. I could see the outlines and edges of furniture. The hall was cold, chilly zephyrs of air stirring all around us. Someone had left a window open. The cold air did more than anything else to drive away the last vestiges of the drug. My head was clear, my brain was alert, and every nerve was alive to danger.

I had to get away from him, but how? He could overpower me so easily. I stood no chance of eluding him in these dark halls. It would be foolish to try and break away now. Outside there would be moonlight and there would be no dark corners and stairs to hinder my escape. It would be easy to outrun him, if only I could break loose. I must not let him sense my anxiety. I must continue trance-like and obedient until we are free of the confining walls of Falconridge.

There were footsteps in the hall. Charles Lloyd stepped quickly into a darkened doorway, pulling me after him. His large hand covered my mouth, his free arm wrapped around my waist and holding me tightly against him. The footsteps halted nearby. Charles Lloyd pressed my head against his shoulder, the fingers over my mouth almost smothering me. The footsteps receded, disappeared. Charles Lloyd relaxed, loosening his grip. A servant had probably come to check a window or get a glass of water.

He led me down the hall, past Lucy's room and around a corner. The door was in a darkened alcove. The moonlight made the glass panes into blocks of silver. Charles Lloyd unlocked the door and thrust it open. A great gust of wind swept past us, stirring down the hall with vigorous energy. I heard a great crash behind us. The wind had knocked a vase off of one of the hall tables. The noise would surely awaken someone, I thought. Charles Lloyd pushed me outside and pulled the door shut behind him. His arm was still wrapped loosely about my waist. He was breathing a little heavily, not so relaxed as before. The noise had unnerved him, destroying the earlier diabolical calm.

The lawns were bathed in silver, sloping down to the edge of the cliff. The trees and shrubberies were stark black against the silver, casting long blue black shadows that slid over the ground like velvet. Above, the sky was pale gray, filled with ponderous black clouds that spilled moonlight over their sides. It was icy cold, the air crisp and chilled. Crickets were rasping under the flat stones of the terrace and the wind whistled through the leaves of the trees. The sound of the sea was loud, demanding. The waters crashed over the rocks violently, the noise dominating all others.

"You've done very well," Charles Lloyd said, his voice that of a parent complimenting an obedient child. "Just keep it up, and it will all be over very quickly, very neatly. You know you have to die. Don't make it difficult."

He pushed me forward, forcing me down towards the slope. There were almost a hundred and fifty yards before we would reach the treacherous precipice. I let him move me towards it. As we left the area of the house, he relaxed again, breathing easier. Success was almost at hand now, and he was no longer tense. He made a little noise deep in his throat, a growl of satisfaction. I tensed myself, then suddenly fell limp against him. He thought I had swooned. He was taken by surprise. He loosened his hold, stepping back a little. I broke loose, my feet flying of their own volition.

Charles Lloyd gave a cry of frustration. I ran blindly, my heart pounding. I could hear him behind me. I ran faster and faster, and it seemed my lungs would burst. I stumbled, falling forward. I got to my feet, panting. The noise of the waves on the rocks were deafening now. I realized with horror that I was yards from the edge. I had run directly towards the cliff. I turned, poised to run back, and he threw his arms around me.

I struggled violently. Charles Lloyd gripped my arms and held me fast. I realized that it was hopeless. My back was to the cliff and he was forcing me backwards, nearer and nearer the edge. I kicked out at him, catching him with a powerful blow on the shin. He gasped, releasing me. The suddenness of the release caused me to stumble back. I fell to the ground, only a few feet away from the edge.

Charles Lloyd drew himself up. The skirt of his robe beat against his trousers. The satin lapels gleamed in the moonlight. His hair blew wildly about his head, and I stared up in horrified fascination at his face. It was heavily lined, grim, the lips turned down. His heavy eyelids were lowered, hooding the dark eyes. He looked down at me huddled there at his feet. He swelled his chest, sighing deeply. His fists were balled up tightly, and he seemed to be trying to control his anger. He moistened his lips with the tip of his tongue and stepped back a little so that he could see me better.

"That was very foolish," he said, his voice level. "I wanted it to be pleasant. You have made it very unpleasant. I expected better from you, my dear. Now I suppose you will scream and thrash about. Go ahead. No one can hear you."

I was too terrified to speak. My head was whirling, and I fought to maintain consciousness. My whole body was weak, limp, and I could not move. It seemed that black wings were closing in on my brain, shutting out everything but the sound of the pounding waves below. I tried to sit up, but I couldn't. I wanted to scream, but no sound came from my parched throat. The black wings fluttered, pressing in on my brain. I gnawed my lower lip and fought them.

Charles Lloyd heaved his shoulders and took a deep breath. He came forward, kneeling down to take my shoulders. I heard the explosion and saw the incredible orange streak flash across the darkness like a minute bolt of lightning. Charles Lloyd straightened up, his face stamped with an expression of sheer agony. He staggered forward, his hands clutching his chest. His foot slipped on the edge of the precipice, and for a moment he stood balanced in mid-air. He threw out both his arms as though to embrace the space, and then he fell. The waves crashed and thundered below, claiming their victim.

Norman Wade helped me to my feet. Tiny plumes of smoke curled from the barrel of his pistol. He wrapped one arm around me, supporting me against him. I closed my eyes, giving way now to the fluttering wings. I was aware of nothing but the thundering noise of the sea and the marvelous strength of the arm that held me so securely against the man who had saved my life.

XVI

I STOOD AT the edge of the cliff, looking down at the waters. They were calm today, washing gently over the sand and leaving a lacy residue of foam. Far out, the light blue water turned darker, richer blue, until it merged into a thin purple line on the horizon where the sea seemed to touch the luminous pearl gray sky. Sunlight sparkled on the waves, and a sea gull spiraled in the sky, its wings almost silver in the light. A gentle breeze blew wisps of hair about my temples, and the salty tang in the air was bracing. Three weeks had passed, and this was the first time I had been able to summon enough courage to come here. I wanted to stare at the sea, to put aside forever any terror it might hold for me. I sighed softly as I watched the waves lap the sands.

It was all over now. That night of terror would live forever in my memory, but it seemed years ago. I thought about my foolishness. If I had not left my room, none of it would have happened, and yet if I had not done so Charles Lloyd would probably have been successful in his devious plan. Norman Wade had been pacing up and down in the library that night. He had heard the crash in the hall, and he had run up to my room. When he found it empty, he had seized his pistol and run outside, arriving just in time to see Charles Lloyd standing over me at the edge of the cliff, where I stood now.

Norman had been suspicious all along, but he had been unable to put the pieces together. Of course he had known about the affair with Lavinia, and when both Charles Lloyd and Andrew Graystone had disappeared his suspicions grew stronger. It was not until I told him about the missing food in the pantry that he suspected the truth. When he had found Lucy's body in the courtyard he had known that Charles Lloyd was alive and in the house somewhere. That was why he had locked me in my room. He wanted me to be safe until he could get me away from Falconridge and away from danger.

How unfair I had been to him. It had amused him to know that I was convinced he was a murderer. It did not amuse me. I was ashamed. I had convicted him in my own mind. He had been cool yet cordial during these past three weeks, too busy to pay much heed to me. I tried to suppress my feelings toward him. I did not want him to know how I felt. I did not want him to laugh at me and call me an infatuated schoolgirl.

I thought about Lavinia. Those sad, tragic eyes must be filled with regret now. She had been apprehended in Liverpool where she was waiting for my uncle to come for her. When they told her about his death, she had burst into tears, they reported. She would have a long time to cry now, I thought. She would spend many, many years in prison. I was sorry for her. It seemed her life had been marked for tragedy from the very first.

The strangest thing of all was the disappearance

of Martha Victor. When Charles Lloyd's body was brought into the house, she stood over it for a long time, studying the lines of the face she had loved so well. Then she left the room, moving as quietly as ever. She left the house. No one had seen her go. She literally disappeared. The authorities had not found her yet, and I doubted if they ever would. Without her master to look after, I imagined the old woman would live her remaining years with a heavily laden, embittered heart.

My uncle had been buried quietly, privately, without a proper funeral. That had already taken place, and so far as the citizens of the community were concerned, the body in that lonely cemetery was the body of Charles Lloyd. The gold had been returned to London on the same coach it came in along with a long letter to Mr. Stephens. Everything had been taken care of. The nightmare was over, and Falconridge itself was a different place. It seemed as though a dark pall had been lifted. It was old and damp and drafty, but it no longer had that ominous aura. I was beginning to see why Helena and her nephew loved the place so much, and I hoped that I, too, could grow to love it in time.

I turned around to look at the house, my back to the sea. The sun sparkled on the huge gray stones and the dark green roof. The towers and turrets rose tall to touch the sky, and the two wings sprawled out over the lawns. To one side I could see the gardens, in gorgeous bloom now. I saw Helena, looking very tiny, moving among the pink and yellow roses, the three dogs bounding behind her. She wore a blue dress and a floppy white sun hat. She stooped down to touch a blossom. Helena was a happy woman now, as happy as it was possible for one who has had so much tragedy in her life to be. Her days were full and exciting, as they would always be for one so vital.

Norman Wade was strolling down the lawn towards me. He must have just come back from the fields, for he was wearing the tall brown boots and tight, faded beige pants and white linen shirt that were his customary clothes for work. He carried a thin leather riding crop, slapping it against the side of his boot as he walked. His raven black hair blew in the breeze, and the gathered sleeves of his shirt billowed a little. I knew that he had been out inspecting the fields this morning. He had come in early. I wondered what he wanted with me.

I turned back to the sea, not wanting him to see the expression on my face. I was afraid it would betray me. In a moment I could feel him standing behind me. I said nothing, ignoring him.

"Thinking?" he asked.

"Yes."

"About what?"

"Many things."

"About me?"

"Perhaps."

He turned me around so that he could look into my eyes. His own were sparkling with devilish merriment as they had been that first day I had met him in the clearing. He was grinning. The grin irritated me. He must always make fun of me. He must always be the merry rake, teasing. He must always treat me like a schoolgirl.

"Now," he said. "What were you thinking about?"

"As a matter of fact," I snapped, "I was thinking

about a letter. I have to write to Clarissa and tell her I will be coming to visit soon. She will be with her parents in the country, and I am quite anxious to get away from this place."

"Why is that?" he asked.

"I think you know!"

"You're angry." He clicked his tongue. "Such spirit! It will take a lot of breaking, a lot of curbing. Thoroughbreds always do. I think I can manage."

"Do you really?"

"I'm positive," he said decisively.

"Well, don't be so certain you have the job," I told him.

"I think I do," he said, still grinning.

"You've been ignoring me for three weeks."

"I know. I've been busy. I've arranged a loan from a firm in London. I'll be able to make all those improvements now. I've been out inspecting the fields. The harvest is going to be great this year. There's every sign that it will be the best in years. Falconridge is going to be just as I've planned."

"That's why you've ignored me?"

"I wanted to wait until I had something to offer."

"I see," I replied crisply.

"Where are you going?"

"I'm going to write that letter."

"What are you going to say?"

"I'm going to tell Clarissa that I probably won't see her for a long time."

Norman Wade burst into laughter. The rich, melodious sound followed me as I hurried up the sloping green lawn to Falconridge.

Don't Miss these Ace Romance Bestsellers!

___ #75157 **SAVAGE SURRENDER** $1.95
The million-copy bestseller by Natasha Peters, author of Dangerous Obsession.

___ #29802 **GOLD MOUNTAIN** $1.95

___ #88965 **WILD VALLEY** $1.95
Two vivid and exciting novels by Phoenix Island author, Charlotte Paul.

___ #80040 **TENDER TORMENT** $1.95
A sweeping romantic saga in the Dangerous Obsession tradition.

Available wherever paperbacks are sold or use this coupon

ace books,
Book Mailing Service, P.O. Box 690, Rockville Centre, N.Y. 11570

Please send me titles checked above.

I enclose $ . . . . Add 35c handling fee per copy.

Name . . . .

Address . . . .

City. . . . . State. . . . . Zip. . . . . . .